Philip K. Dick

VINTAGE **PKD**

Philip K. Dick was born in Chicago in 1928 and lived
most of his life in California. He briefly attended the
University of California, but dropped out before completing any classes. In 1952 he began writing professionally, going on to write thirty-six novels, including
Martian Time-Slip, *A Scanner Darkly*, and *Ubik*, and five
short-story collections. He won the 1963 Hugo Award
for best novel for *The Man in the High Castle* and the
1975 John W. Campbell Memorial Award for best novel
of the year for *Flow My Tears, the Policeman Said*. Philip K.
Dick died in 1982.

NOVELS BY PHILIP K. DICK

VINTAGE PKD

Philip K. Dick

VINTAGE BOOKS
A Division of Random House, Inc.
New York

A VINTAGE ORIGINAL, JUNE 2006

The pieces in this collection were originally published as follows:

Selection from *The Man in the High Castle*, copyright © 1962 by Philip K. Dick
Selection from *The Three Stigmata of Palmer Eldritch*, copyright © 1964 by Philip K. Dick
Selection from *Ubik*, copyright © 1969 by Philip K. Dick
Selection from *A Scanner Darkly*, copyright © 1977 by Philip K. Dick
Selection from *VALIS*, copyright © 1981 by Philip K. Dick
"The Lucky Dog Pet Store," copyright © 1979 by Philip K. Dick (*Foundation*, a
British journal)
"The Days of Perky Pat," "A Little Something for Us Tempunauts," and "I Hope I Shall
Arrive Soon" from *Selected Stories of Philip K. Dick*, copyright © 2002 by the Estate
of Philip K. Dick
"The Zebra Papers" from Volume 5 of *The Selected Letters of Philip K. Dick (1977–1979)*,
copyright © 1992 by the Estate of Philip K. Dick

Library of Congress Cataloging-in-Publication Data
Dick, Philip K.
[Selections. 2006]
Vintage PKD / Philip K. Dick.
p. cm.
"A Vintage original"—T.p. verso.
I. Title: Vintage PKD. II. Title.
PS3554.I3A6 2006
813'.54—dc22
2005058486

Vintage ISBN-10: 1-4000-9607-3
Vintage ISBN-13: 978-1-4000-9607-7

Book design by Jo Anne Metsch

www.vintagebooks.com

Printed in the United States of America
10 9 8 7 6 5 4 3 2

CONTENTS

VINTAGE PKD

Chapter One

from THE MAN IN THE HIGH CASTLE

For a week Mr. R. Childan had been anxiously watching the mail. But the valuable shipment from the Rocky Mountain States had not arrived. As he opened up his store on Friday morning and saw only letters on the floor by the mail slot he thought, I'm going to have an angry customer.

Pouring himself a cup of instant tea from the five-cent wall dispenser he got a broom and began to sweep; soon he had the front of American Artistic Handcrafts Inc. ready for the day, all spick and span with the cash register full of change, a fresh vase of marigolds, and the radio playing background music. Outdoors along the sidewalk businessmen hurried toward their offices along Montgomery Street. Far off, a cable car passed; Childan halted to watch it with pleasure. Women in their long colorful silk dresses . . . he watched them, too. Then the phone rang. He turned to answer it.

"Yes," a familiar voice said to his answer. Childan's heart sank. "This is Mr. Tagomi. Did my Civil War recruiting poster arrive yet, sir? Please recall; you promised it sometime last week." The fussy, brisk voice, barely polite, barely keeping the code. "Did I not give you a deposit, sir, Mr. Childan, with that stipulation? This is to be a gift, you see. I explained that. A client."

"Extensive inquiries," Childan began, "which I've had made at my own expense, Mr. Tagomi, sir, regarding the promised parcel, which you realize originates outside of this region and is therefore—"

But Tagomi broke in, "Then it has not arrived."

"No, Mr. Tagomi, sir."

An icy pause.

"I can wait no furthermore," Tagomi said.

"No sir." Childan gazed morosely through the store window at the warm bright day and the San Francisco office buildings.

"A substitute, then. Your recommendation, Mr. Childan?" Tagomi deliberately mispronounced the name; insult within the code that made Childan's ears burn. Place pulled, the dreadful mortification of their situation. Robert Childan's aspirations and fears and torments rose up and exposed themselves, swamped him, stopping his tongue. He stammered, his hand sticky on the phone. The air of his store smelled of marigolds; the music played on, but he felt as if he were falling into some distant sea.

"Well . . ." he managed to mutter. "Butter churn. Ice-cream maker circa 1900." His mind refused to think. Just when you forgot about it; just when you fool yourself. He was thirty-eight years old, and he could remember the prewar days, the other times. Franklin D. Roosevelt and the World's Fair; the former better world. "Could I bring various desirable items out to your business location?" he mumbled.

An appointment was made for two o'clock. Have to shut store, he knew as he hung up the phone. No choice. Have to keep goodwill of such customers; business depends on them.

Standing shakily, he became aware that someone—a couple had entered the store. Young man and girl, both handsome, well-dressed. Ideal. He calmed himself and moved professionally, easily, in their direction, smiling. They were bending to scrutinize a counter display, had picked up a lovely ashtray. Married, he guessed. Live out in City of the Winding Mists, the new exclusive apartments on Skyline overlooking Belmont.

"Hello," he said, and felt better. They smiled at him without any superiority, only kindness. His displays—which really were the best of their kind on the Coast—had awed them a little; he saw that and was grateful. They understood.

"Really excellent pieces, sir," the young man said.

Childan bowed spontaneously.

Their eyes, warm not only with human bond but with the shared enjoyment of the art objects he sold, their mutual tastes and satisfactions, remained fixed on him; they were thanking him for having things like these for them to see, pick up and examine, handle perhaps without even buying. Yes, he thought, they know what sort of store they are in; this is not tourist trash, not redwood plaques reading *Muir Woods, Marin County, PSA*, or funny signs or girly rings or postcards or views of the Bridge. The girl's eyes especially, large, dark. How easily, Childan thought, I could fall in love with a girl like this. How tragic my life, then; as if it weren't bad enough already. The stylish black hair, lacquered nails, pierced ears for the long dangling brass handmade earrings.

"Your earrings," he murmured. "Purchased here, perhaps?"

"No," she said. "At home."

Childan nodded. No contemporary American art; only the past could be represented here, in a store such as his. "You are here for long?" he asked. "To our San Francisco?"

"I'm stationed here indefinitely," the man said. "With Standard of Living for Unfortunate Areas Planning Commission of Inquiry." Pride showed on his face. Not the military. Not one of the gum-chewing boorish draftees with their greedy peasant faces, wandering up Market Street, gaping at the bawdy shows, the sex movies, the shooting galleries, the cheap nightclubs with photos of middle-aged blondes holding their nipples between their wrinkled fingers and leering . . . the honkytonk jazz slums that made up most of the flat part of San Francisco, rickety tin and board shacks that had sprung up from the ruins even before the last bomb fell. No—this man was of the elite. Cultured, educated, even more so than Mr. Tagomi, who was after all a high official with the ranking Trade Mission on the Pacific Coast. Tagomi was an old man. His attitudes had formed in the War Cabinet days.

"Had you wished American traditional ethnic art objects as a gift?" Childan asked. "Or to decorate perhaps a new apartment for your stay here?" If the latter . . . his heart picked up.

"An accurate guess," the girl said. "We are starting to decorate. A bit undecided. Do you think you could inform us?"

"I could arrange to arrive at your apartment, yes," Childan said. "Bringing several hand cases, I can suggest in context, at your leisure. This, of course, is our specialty." He dropped his eyes so as to conceal his hope. There might be thousands of dollars involved. "I am getting in a New England table, maple, all wood-pegged, no nails. Immense beauty and worth. And a mirror from the time of the 1812 War. And also the aboriginal art: a group of vegetable-dyed goat-hair rugs."

"I myself," the man said, "prefer the art of the cities."

"Yes," Childan said eagerly. "Listen, sir. I have a mural from WPA post-office period, original, done on board, four sections, depicting Horace Greeley. Priceless collector's item."

"Ah," the man said, his dark eyes flashing.

"And a Victrola cabinet of 1920 made into a liquor cabinet."

"Ah."

"And, sir, listen: *framed signed picture of Jean Harlow.*"

The man goggled at him.

"Shall we make arrangements?" Childan said, seizing this correct psychological instant. From his inner coat pocket he brought his pen, notebook. "I shall take your name and address, sir and lady."

Afterward, as the couple strolled from his store, Childan stood, hands behind his back, watching the street. Joy. If all business days were like this . . . but it was more than business, the success of his store. It was a chance to meet a young Japanese couple socially, on a basis of acceptance of him as a man rather than him as a *yank* or, at best, a tradesman who sold art objects. Yes, these new young people, of the rising generation, who did not remember the days before the war or even the war itself—they were the hope of the world. Place difference did not have the significance for them.

It will end, Childan thought. Someday. The very idea of place. Not governed and governing, but people.

And yet he trembled with fear, imagining himself knocking at their door. He examined his notes. The Kasouras. Being admitted, no doubt offered tea. Would he do the right thing? Know the proper act and utterance at each moment? Or would he disgrace himself, like an animal, by some dismal faux pas?

The girl's name was Betty. Such understanding in her face, he thought. The gentle, sympathetic eyes. Surely, even in the short time in the store, she had glimpsed his hopes and defeats.

His hopes—he felt suddenly dizzy. What aspirations bordering on the insane if not the suicidal did he have? But it was known, relations between Japanese and *yanks*, although generally it was between a Japanese man and *yank* woman. This . . . he quailed at the idea. And she was married. He whipped his mind away from the pageant of his involuntary thoughts and began busily opening the morning's mail.

His hands, he discovered, were still shaking. And then he recalled his two o'clock appointment with Mr. Tagomi; at that, his hands ceased shaking and his nervousness became determination. I've got to come up with something acceptable, he said to himself. Where? How? What? A phone call. Sources. Business ability. Scrape up a fully restored 1929 Ford including fabric top (black). Grand slam to keep patronage forever. Crated original mint trimotor airmail plane discovered in barn in Alabama, etc. Produce mummified head of Mr. B. Bill, including flowing white hair; sensational American artifact. Make my reputation in top connoisseur circles throughout Pacific, not excluding Home Islands.

To inspire himself, he lit up a marijuana cigarette, excellent Land-O-Smiles brand.

In his room on Hayes Street, Frank Frink lay in bed wondering how to get up. Sun glared past the blind onto the heap of clothes that had fallen to the floor. His glasses, too. Would he step on them? Try to get to bathroom by other route, he thought. Crawl or roll. His head ached but he did not feel sad. Never look back, he decided. Time? The clock on the dresser. Eleven-thirty! Good grief. But still he lay.

I'm fired, he thought.

Yesterday he had done wrong at the factory. Spouted the wrong kind of talk to Mr. Wyndam-Matson, who had a dished-in face with Socrates-type nose, diamond ring, gold fly zipper. In other words, a power. A throne. Frink's thoughts wandered groggily.

Yes, he thought, and now they'll blacklist me; my skill is no use—I have no trade. Fifteen years' experience. Gone.

And now he would have to appear at the Laborers' Justification

Commission for a revision of his work category. Since he had never been able to make out Wyndam-Matson's relationship to the *pinocs*—the puppet white government at Sacramento—he could not fathom his ex-employer's power to sway the real authorities, the Japanese. The LJC was *pinoc* run. He would be facing four or five middle-aged plump white faces, on the order of Wyndam-Matson's. If he failed to get justification there, he would make his way to one of the Import-Export Trade Missions which operated out of Tokyo, and which had offices throughout California, Oregon, Washington, and the parts of Nevada included in the Pacific States of America. But if he failed successfully to plead there . . .

Plans roamed his mind as he lay in bed gazing up at the ancient light fixture in the ceiling. He could for instance slip across into the Rocky Mountain States. But it was loosely banded to the PSA, and might extradite him. What about the South? His body recoiled. Ugh. Not that. As a white man he would have plenty of place, in fact more than he had here in the PSA. But . . . he did not want that kind of place.

And, worse, the South had a cat's cradle of ties, economic, ideological, and god knew what, with the Reich. And Frank Frink was a Jew.

His original name was Frank Fink. He had been born on the East Coast, in New York, and in 1941 he had been drafted into the Army of the United States of America, right after the collapse of Russia. After the Japs had taken Hawaii he had been sent to the West Coast. When the war ended, there he was, on the Japanese side of the settlement line. And here he was today, fifteen years later.

In 1947, on Capitulation Day, he had more or less gone berserk. Hating the Japs as he did, he had vowed revenge; he had buried his Service weapons ten feet underground, in a basement, well-wrapped and oiled, for the day he and his buddies arose. However, time was the great healer, a fact he had not taken into account. When he thought of the idea now, the great blood bath, the purging of the *pinocs* and their masters, he felt as if he were reviewing one of those stained yearbooks from his high school days, coming upon an account of his boyhood aspirations. Frank "Goldfish" Fink is going to be a paleontologist and vows to marry Norma Prout. Norma Prout was the class *schones Mädchen*, and he really had vowed to marry her. That was all so goddam long ago, like listening to Fred Allen or seeing a W. C. Fields movie. Since 1947 he had probably seen or talked to six hundred thousand Japanese, and the desire to do violence to any or all of them had simply never materialized, after the first few months. It just was not relevant any more.

But wait. There was one, a Mr. Omuro, who had bought control of a great area of rental property in downtown San Francisco, and who for a time had been Frank's landlord. There was a bad apple, he thought. A shark who had never made repairs, had partitioned rooms smaller and smaller, raised rents . . . Omuro had gouged the poor, especially the nearly destitute jobless ex-servicemen during the depression years of the early fifties. However, it had been one of the Japanese trade missions which had cut off Omuro's head for his profiteering. And nowadays such a violation of the harsh, rigid, but just Japanese civil law was unheard of. It was a credit to the incorruptibility of the Jap occupation officials, especially those who had come in after the War Cabinet had fallen.

Recalling the rugged, stoic honesty of the Trade Missions, Frink felt reassured. Even Wyndam-Matson would be waved off like a noisy fly. W-M Corporation owner or not. At least, so he hoped. I guess I really have faith in this Co-Prosperity Pacific Alliance stuff, he said to himself. Strange. Looking back to the early days . . . it had seemed such an obvious fake, then. Empty propaganda. But now . . .

He rose from the bed and unsteadily made his way to the bathroom. While he washed and shaved, he listened to the midday news on the radio.

"Let us not deride this effort," the radio was saying as he momentarily shut off the hot water.

No, we won't, Frink thought bitterly. He knew which particular effort the radio had in mind. Yet, there was after all something humorous about it, the picture of stolid, grumpy Germans walking around on Mars, on the red sand where no humans had ever stepped before. Lathering his jowls, Frank began a chanting satire to himself. *Gott, Herr Kreisleiter. Ist dies vielleicht der Ort wo man das*

Konzentrationslager bilden kann? Das Wetter ist so schon. Heiss, aber doch schon . . .

The radio said: "Co-Prosperity Civilization must pause and consider whether in our quest to provide a balanced equity of mutual duties and responsibilities coupled with remunerations . . ." Typical jargon from the ruling hierarchy, Frink noted. ". . . we have not failed to perceive the future arena in which the affairs of man will be acted out, be they Nordic, Japanese, Negroid . . ." On and on it went.

As he dressed, he mulled with pleasure his satire. *The weather is schon, so schon. But there is nothing to breathe . . .*

However, it was a fact; the Pacific had done nothing toward colonization of the planets. It was involved—bogged down, rather—in South America. While the Germans were busy bustling enormous robot construction systems across space, the Japs were still burning off the jungles in the interior of Brazil, erecting eight-floor clay apartment houses for ex-headhunters. By the time the Japs got their first spaceship off the ground the Germans would have the entire solar system sewed up tight. Back in the quaint old history-book days, the Germans had missed out while the rest of Europe put the final touches on their colonial empires. However, Frink reflected, they were not going to be last this time; they had learned.

And then he thought about Africa, and the Nazi experiment there. And his blood stopped in his veins, hesitated, at last went on.

That huge empty ruin.

The radio said: ". . . we must consider with pride however our emphasis on the fundamental physical needs of peoples of all place, their subspiritual aspirations which must be . . ."

Frank shut the radio off. Then, calmer, he turned it back on.

Christ on the crapper, he thought. Africa. For the ghosts of dead tribes. Wiped out to make a land of—what? Who knew? Maybe even the master architects in Berlin did not know. Bunch of automatons, building and toiling away. Building? Grinding down. Ogres out of a paleontology exhibit, at their task of making a cup from an enemy's skull, the whole family industriously scooping out the contents—the raw brains—first, to eat. Then useful utensils of men's leg bones. Thrifty, to think not only of eating the people you did not like, but eating them out of their own skull. The first technicians! Prehistoric man in a sterile white lab coat in some Berlin university lab, experimenting with uses to which other people's skull, skin, ears, fat could be put to. Ja, Herr Doktor. A new use for the big toe; see, one can adapt the joint for a quick-acting cigarette lighter mechanism. Now, if only Herr Krupp can produce it in quantity . . .

It horrified him, this thought: the ancient gigantic cannibal near-man flourishing now, ruling the world once more. We spent a million years escaping him, Frink thought, and now he's back. And not merely as the adversary . . . but as the master.

". . . we can deplore," the radio, the voice of the little yellow-bellies from Tokyo was saying. God, Frink thought; and we called them monkeys, these civilized bandy-legged shrimps who would no more set up gas ovens than they would melt their wives into sealing wax. ". . . and we have deplored often in the past the dreadful waste of humans in this fanatical striving which sets the broader mass of men wholly outside the legal community." They, the Japs, were so strong on law. ". . . To quote a Western saint familiar to all: 'What profit it a man if he gain the whole world but in this enterprise lose his soul?'" The radio paused. Frink, tying his tie, also paused. It was the morning ablution.

I have to make my pact with them here, he realized. Blacklisted or not; it'd be death for me if I left Japanese-controlled land and showed up in the South or in Europe—anywhere in the Reich.

I'll have to come to terms with old Wyndam-Matson.

Seated on his bed, a cup of lukewarm tea beside him, Frink got down his copy of the *I Ching*. From their leather tube he took the forty-nine yarrow stalks. He considered, until he had his thoughts properly controlled and his questions worked out.

Aloud he said, "How should I approach Wyndam-Matson in order to come to decent terms with him?" He wrote the question down on the tablet, then began whipping the yarrow stalks from hand to hand until he had the first line, the beginning. An eight. Half the sixty-four hexagrams eliminated already. He divided the stalks and obtained the second line. Soon, being so expert, he had all six lines; the hexagram lay before him, and he did not need to identify it by the chart. He could recognize it as Hexagram Fifteen. Ch'ien. Modesty. Ah. The low will be raised up, the high brought down, powerful families humbled; he did not have to refer to the text—he knew it by heart. A good omen. The oracle was giving him favorable council.

And yet he was a bit disappointed. There was something fatuous about Hexagram Fifteen. Too goody-goody. *Naturally* he should be modest. Perhaps there was an idea in it, however. After all, he had no power over old W-M. He could not compel him to take him back. All he could do was adopt the point of view of Hexagram Fifteen; this was that sort of moment, when one had to petition, to hope, to await with faith. Heaven in its time would raise him up to his old job or perhaps even to something better.

He had no lines to read, no nines or sixes; it was static. So he was through. It did not move into a second hexagram.

A new question, then. Setting himself, he said aloud, "Will I ever see Juliana again?"

That was his wife. Or rather his ex-wife. Juliana had divorced him a year ago, and he had not seen her in months; in fact he did not even know where she lived. Evidently she had left San Francisco. Perhaps even the PSA. Either their mutual friends had not heard from her or they were not telling him.

Busily he maneuvered the yarrow stalks, his eyes fixed on the tallies. How many times had he asked about Juliana, one question or another? Here came the hexagram, brought forth by the passive chance workings of the vegetable stalks. Random, and yet rooted in the moment in which he lived, in which his life was bound up with all other lives and particles in the universe. The necessary hexagram picturing in its pattern of broken and unbroken lines the *situation*. He, Juliana, the factory on Gough Street, the Trade Missions that ruled, the exploration of the planets, the billion chemical heaps in Africa that were now not even corpses, the aspirations of the thousands around him in the shanty warrens of San Francisco, the mad creatures in Berlin with their calm faces and manic plans—all connected in this moment of casting the yarrow stalks to select the exact wisdom appropriate in a book begun in the thirtieth century B.C. A book created by the sages of China over a period of five thousand years, winnowed, perfected, that superb cosmology—and science—codified before Europe had even learned to do long division.

The hexagram. His heart dropped. Forty-four. Kou. Coming to Meet. Its sobering judgment. *The maiden is powerful. One should not marry such a maiden.* Again he had gotten it in connection with Juliana.

Oy vey, he thought, settling back. So she was wrong for me; I know that. I didn't ask that. Why does the oracle have to remind me? A bad fate for me, to have met her and been in love—be in love—with her.

Juliana—the best-looking woman he had ever married. Soot-black eyebrows and hair; trace amounts of Spanish blood distributed as pure color, even to her lips. Her rubbery, soundless walk; she had worn saddle shoes left over from high school. In fact all her clothes had a dilapidated quality and the definite suggestions of being old and often washed. He and she had been so broke so long that despite her looks she had had to wear a cotton sweater, cloth zippered jacket, brown tweed skirt and bobby socks, and she hated him and it because it made her look, she had said, like a woman who played tennis or (even worse) collected mushrooms in the woods.

But above and beyond everything else, he had originally been drawn by her screwball expression; for no reason, Juliana greeted strangers with a portentous, nudnik, Mona Lisa smile that hung them up between responses, whether to say hello or not. And she was so attractive that more often than not they did say hello, whereupon Juliana glided by. At first he had thought it was just plain bad eyesight, but finally he had decided that it revealed a deep-dyed otherwise concealed stupidity at her core. And so finally her borderline flicker of greeting to strangers had annoyed him, as had her plantlike, silent, I'm-on-a-mysterious-errand way of coming and going. But even then, toward the end, when they had been fighting so much, he still never saw her as anything but a direct, literal invention of God's, dropped into his life for reasons he would never know. And on that account—a sort of religious intuition or faith about her—he could not get over having lost her.

She seemed so close right now . . . as if he still had her. That spirit, still busy in his life, padding through his room in search of— whatever it was Juliana sought. And in his mind whenever he took up the volumes of the oracle.

Seated on his bed, surrounded by lonely disorder, preparing to go out and begin his day, Frank Frink wondered who else in the vast complicated city of San Francisco was at this same moment consulting the oracle. And were they all getting as gloomy advice as he? Was the tenor of the Moment as adverse for them as it was for him?

Chapter Two

from THE MAN IN THE HIGH CASTLE

M r. Nobusuke Tagomi sat consulting the divine Fifth Book of Confucian wisdom, the Taoist oracle called for centuries the *I Ching* or *Book of Changes*. At noon that day, he had begun to become apprehensive about his appointment with Mr. Childan, which would occur in two more hours.

His suite of offices on the twentieth floor of the Nippon Times Building on Taylor Street overlooked the Bay. Through the glass wall he could watch ships entering, passing beneath the Golden Gate Bridge. At this moment a freighter could be seen beyond Alcatraz, but Mr. Tagomi did not care. Going to the wall he unfastened the cord and lowered the bamboo blinds over the view. The large central office became darker; he did not have to squint against the glare. Now he could think more clearly.

It was not within his power, he decided, to please his client. No matter what Mr. Childan came up with: the client would not be impressed. Let us face that, he had said to himself. But we can keep him from becoming displeased, at least.

We can refrain from insulting him by a moldy gift.

The client would soon reach San Francisco airport by avenue of the high-place new German rocket, the Messerschmitt 9-E. Mr. Tagomi had never ridden on such a ship; when he met Mr. Baynes he would have to take care to appear blasé, no matter how large the rocket turned out to be. Now to practice. He stood in front of the mirror on the office wall, creating a face of composure, mildly bored, inspecting his own cold features for any giveaway. Yes, they are very noisy, Mr. Baynes, sir. One cannot read. But then the flight from Stockholm to San Francisco is only forty-five minutes. Perhaps then a word about German mechanical failures? I suppose you heard the radio. That crash over Madagascar. I must say, there is something to be said for the old piston planes.

Essential to avoid politics. For he did not know Mr. Baynes' views on leading issues of the day. Yet they might arise. Mr. Baynes, being Swedish, would be a neutral. Yet he had chosen Lufthansa rather than SAS. A cautious ploy . . . Mr. Baynes, sir, they say Herr Bormann is quite ill. That a new Reichs Chancellor will be chosen by the Partei this autumn. Rumor only? So much secrecy, alas, between Pacific and Reich.

In the folder on his desk, clipping from *New York Times* of a recent speech by Mr. Baynes. Mr. Tagomi now studied it critically, bending due to slight failure of correction by his contact lenses. The speech had to do with need of exploring once more—ninety-eighth time?—for sources of water on the moon. "We may still solve this heartbreaking dilemma," Mr. Baynes was quoted. "Our nearest neighbor, and so far the most unrewarding except for military purposes." *Sic!* Mr. Tagomi thought, using high-place Latin word. Clue to Mr. Baynes. Looks askance at merely military. Mr. Tagomi made a mental note.

Touching the intercom button Mr. Tagomi said, "Miss Ephreikian, I would like you to bring in your tape recorder, please."

The outer office door slid to one side and Miss Ephreikian, today pleasantly adorned with blue flowers in her hair, appeared.

"Bit of lilac," Mr. Tagomi observed. Once, he had professionally flower-raised back home on Hokkaido.

Miss Ephreikian, a tall, brown-haired Armenian girl, bowed.

"Ready with Zip-Track Speed Master?" Mr. Tagomi asked.

"Yes, Mr. Tagomi." Miss Ephreikian seated herself, the portable battery-operated tape recorder ready.

Mr. Tagomi began, "I inquired of the oracle, 'Will the meeting between myself and Mr. Childan be profitable?' and obtained to my dismay the ominous hexagram The Preponderance of the Great. The ridgepole is sagging. Too much weight in the middle; all unbalanced. Clearly away from the Tao." The tape recorder whirred.

Pausing, Mr. Tagomi reflected.

Miss Ephreikian watched him expectantly. The whirring ceased.

"Have Mr. Ramsey come in for a moment, please," Mr. Tagomi said.

"Yes, Mr. Tagomi." Rising, she put down the tape recorder; her heels tapped as she departed from the office.

With a large folder of bills-of-lading under his arm, Mr. Ramsey appeared. Young, smiling, he advanced, wearing the natty U.S. Midwest Plains string tie, checkered shirt and tight beltless blue jeans considered so high-place among the style-conscious of the day. "Howdy, Mr. Tagomi," he said. "Right nice day, sir."

Mr. Tagomi bowed.

At that, Mr. Ramsey stiffened abruptly and also bowed.

"I've been consulting the oracle," Mr. Tagomi said, as Miss Ephreikian reseated herself with her tape recorder. "You understand that Mr. Baynes, who as you know is arriving shortly in person, holds to the Nordic ideology regarding so-called Oriental culture. I could make the effort to dazzle him into a better comprehension with authentic works of Chinese scroll art or ceramics of our Tokugawa Period . . . but it is not our job to convert."

"I see," Mr. Ramsey said; his Caucasian face twisted with painful concentration.

"Therefore we will cater to his prejudice and graft a priceless American artifact to him instead."

"Yes."

"You, sir, are of American ancestry. Although you have gone to the trouble of darkening your skin color." He scrutinized Mr. Ramsey.

"A tan achieved by a sun lamp," Mr. Ramsey murmured. "For merely acquiring vitamin D." But his expression of humiliation gave him away. "I assure you that I retain authentic roots with—" Mr. Ramsey stumbled over the words. "I have not cut off all ties with—native ethnic patterns."

Mr. Tagomi said to Miss Ephreikian: "Resume, please." Once more the tape recorder whirred. "In consulting the oracle and obtaining Hexagram Ta Kuo, Twenty-eight, I further received the unfavorable line Nine in the fifth place. It reads:

A withered poplar puts forth flowers.
An older woman takes a husband.
No blame. No praise.

"This clearly indicates that Mr. Childan will have nothing of worth to offer us at two." Mr. Tagomi paused. "Let us be candid. I cannot rely on my own judgment regarding American art objects. That is why a—" He lingered over his choice of terms. "Why you, Mr. Ramsey, who are shall I say *native born*, are required. Obviously we must do the best we can."

Mr. Ramsey had no answer. But, despite his efforts to conceal, his features showed hurt, anger, a frustrated and mute reaction.

"Now," Mr. Tagomi said. "I have further consulted the oracle. For purposes of policy, I cannot divulge to you, Mr. Ramsey, the question." In other words, his tone meant, you and your *pinoc* kind are not entitled to share the important matters which we deal in. "It is sufficient to say, however, that I received a most provocative response. It has caused me to ponder at length."

Both Mr. Ramsey and Miss Ephreikian watched him intently.

"It deals with Mr. Baynes," Mr. Tagomi said.

They nodded.

"My question regarding Mr. Baynes produced through the occult workings of the Tao the Hexagram Sheng, Forty-six. A good judgment. Add lines Six at the beginning and Nine in the second place." His question had been, Will I be able to deal with Mr. Baynes successfully? And the Nine in the second place had assured him that he would. It read:

If one is sincere,
It furthers one to bring even a small offering.
No blame.

Obviously, Mr. Baynes would be satisfied by whatever gift the ranking Trade Mission grafted to him through the good offices of Mr. Tagomi. But Mr. Tagomi, in asking the question, had had a deeper query in the back of his mind, one of which he was barely conscious. As so often, the oracle had perceived that more fundamental query and, while answering the other, had taken it upon itself to answer the subliminal one, too.

"As we know," Mr. Tagomi said, "Mr. Baynes is bringing us detailed account of new injection molds developed in Sweden. Were we successfully to sign agreement with his firm, we could no doubt replace many present metals, quite scarce, with plastics."

For years, the Pacific had been trying to get basic assistance in the synthetics field from the Reich. However, the big German chemical cartels, I. G. Farben in particular, had harbored their patents; had, in fact, created a world monopoly in plastics, especially in the development of the polyesters. By this means, Reich trade had kept an edge over Pacific trade, and in technology the Reich was at least ten years ahead. The interplanetary rockets leaving Festung Europa consisted mainly of heat-resistant plastics, very light in weight, so hard that they survived even major meteor impact. The Pacific had nothing of this sort; natural fibers such as wood were still used, and of course the ubiquitous pot metals. Mr. Tagomi cringed as he thought about it; he had seen at trade fairs some of the advanced German work, including an all-synthetic automobile, the D.S.S.—Der Schnelle Spuk—which sold, in PSA currency, for about six hundred dollars.

But his underlying question, one which he could never reveal to the *pinocs* flitting about Trade Mission offices, had to do with an aspect of Mr. Baynes suggested by the original coded cable from Tokyo. First of all, coded material was infrequent, and dealt usually with matters of security, not with trade deals. And the cipher was the metaphor type, utilizing poetic allusion, which had been adopted to baffle the Reich monitors—who could crack any literal code, no matter how elaborate. So clearly it was the Reich whom the Tokyo authorities had in mind, not quasi-disloyal cliques in the Home Islands. The key phrase, "Skim milk in his diet," referred to *Pinafore*, to the eerie song that expounded the doctrine, ". . . Things are seldom what they seem—Skim milk masquerades as cream." And the *I Ching*, when Mr. Tagomi had consulted it, had fortified his insight. Its commentary:

Here a strong man is presupposed. It is true he does not fit in
with his environment, inasmuch as he is too brusque and pays
too little attention to form. But as he is upright in character, he
meets with response . . .

The insight was, simply, that Mr. Baynes was not what he seemed;
that his actual purpose in coming to San Francisco was not to sign
a deal for injection molds. That, in fact, Mr. Baynes was a spy.

But for the life of him, Mr. Tagomi could not figure out what
sort of spy, for whom or for what.

At one-forty that afternoon, Robert Childan with enormous reluctance locked the front door of American Artistic Handcrafts Inc.
He lugged his heavy cases to the curb, hailed a pedecab, and told
the *chink* to take him to the Nippon Times Building.

The *chink*, gaunt-faced, hunched over and perspiring, gasped a
place-conscious acknowledgment and began loading Mr. Childan's
bags aboard. Then, having assisted Mr. Childan himself into the
carpet-lined seat, the *chink* clicked on the meter, mounted his own
seat and pedaled off along Montgomery Street, among the cars and
buses.

The entire day had been spent finding the item for Mr. Tagomi,
and Childan's bitterness and anxiety almost overwhelmed him as he
watched the buildings pass. And yet—triumph. The separate skill,
apart from the rest of him: he had found the right thing, and Mr.
Tagomi would be mollified and his client, whoever he was, would
be overjoyed. I always give satisfaction, Childan thought. To my
customers.

He had been able to procure, miraculously, an almost mint copy
of Volume One, Number One of *Tip Top Comics*. Dating from the
thirties, it was a choice piece of Americana; one of the first funny
books, a prize collectors searched for constantly. Of course, he had
other items with him, to show first. He would lead up gradually to
the funny book, which lay well protected in a leather case packed
in tissue paper at the center of the largest bag.

The radio of the pedecab blared out popular tunes, competing with the radios of other cabs, cars and buses. Childan did not hear; he was used to it. Nor did he take notice of the enormous neon signs with their permanent ads obliterating the front of virtually every large building. After all, he had his own sign; at night it blazed on and off in company with all the others of the city. What other way did one advertise? One had to be realistic.

In fact, the uproar of radios, traffic noises, the signs and people lulled him. They blotted out his inner worries. And it was pleasurable to be peddled along by another human being, to feel the straining muscles of the *chink* transmitted in the form of regular vibrations; a sort of relaxing machine, Childan reflected. To be pulled instead of having to pull. And—to have, if even for a moment, higher place.

Guiltily, he woke himself. Too much to plan; no time for a midday doze. Was he absolutely properly dressed to enter the Nippon Times Building? Possibly he would faint in the high-speed elevator. But he had motion-illness tablets with him, a German compound. The various modes of address . . . he knew them. Whom to treat politely, whom rudely. Be brusque with the doorman, elevator operator, receptionist, guide, any janitorial person. Bow to any Japanese, of course, even if it obliged him to bow hundreds of times. But the *pinocs*. Nebulous area. Bow, but look straight through them as if they did not exist. Did that cover every situation then? What about a visiting foreigner? Germans often could be seen at the Trade Missions, as well as neutrals.

And then, too, he might see a slave.

German or South ships docked at the port of San Francisco all the time, and blacks occasionally were allowed off for short intervals. Always in groups of fewer than three. And they could not be out after nightfall; even under Pacific law, they had to obey the curfew. But also slaves unloaded at the docks, and these lived perpetually ashore, in shacks under the wharves, above the waterline. None would be in the Trade Mission offices, but if any unloading were taking place—for instance, should he carry his own bags to Mr. Tagomi's office? Surely not. A slave would have to be found, even if he had to stand waiting an hour. Even if he missed his appointment. It was out of the question to let a slave see him carrying something; he had to be quite careful of that. A mistake of that kind would cost him dearly; he would never have place of any sort again, among those who saw.

In a way, Childan thought, I would almost enjoy carrying my own bags into the Nippon Times Building in broad daylight. What a grand gesture. It is not actually illegal; I would not go to jail. And I would show my real feelings, the side of a man which never comes out in public life. But . . .

I could do it, he thought, if there weren't those damn black slaves lurking around; I could endure those above me seeing it, their scorn—after all, they scorn me and humiliate me every day. But to have those beneath see me, to feel their contempt. Like this *chink* peddling away ahead of me. If I hadn't taken a pedecab, if he had seen me trying to *walk* to a business appointment . . .

One had to blame the Germans for the situation. Tendency to bite off more than they could chew. After all, they had barely managed to win the war, and at once they had gone off to conquer the solar system, while at home they had passed edicts which . . . well, at least the idea was good. And after all, they had been successful with the Jews and Gypsies and Bible Students. And the Slavs had been rolled back two thousand years' worth, to their heartland in Asia. Out of Europe entirely, to everyone's relief. Back to riding yaks and hunting with bow and arrow. And those great glossy magazines printed in Munich and circulated around to all the libraries and newsstands . . . one could see the full-page color pictures for oneself: the blue-eyed, blond-haired Aryan settlers who now industriously tilled, culled, plowed, and so forth in the vast grain bowl of the world, the Ukraine. Those fellows certainly looked happy. And their farms and cottages were clean. You didn't see pictures of drunken dull-witted Poles any more, slouched on sagging porches or hawking a few sickly turnips at the village market. All a thing of the past, like rutted dirt roads that once turned to slop in the rainy season, bogging down the carts.

But Africa. They had simply let their enthusiasm get the better of them there, and you had to admire that, although more thoughtful advice would have cautioned them to perhaps let it wait a bit until, for instance, Project Farmland had been completed. Now *there* the Nazis had shown genius; the artist in them had truly emerged. The Mediterranean Sea bottled up, drained, made into tillable farmland, through the use of atomic power—what daring! How the sniggerers had been set back on their heels, for instance certain scoffing merchants along Montgomery Street. And as a matter of fact, Africa had almost been successful . . . but in a project of that sort, *almost* was an ominous word to begin to hear. Rosenberg's well-known powerful pamphlet issued in 1958; the word had first shown up, then. *As to the Final Solution of the African Problem, we have almost achieved our objectives. Unfortunately, however—*

Still, it had taken two hundred years to dispose of the American aborigines, and Germany had almost done it in Africa in fifteen years. So no criticism was legitimately in order. Childan had, in fact, argued it out recently while having lunch with certain of those other merchants. They expected miracles, evidently, as if the Nazis could remold the world by magic. No, it was science and technology and that fabulous talent for hard work; the Germans never stopped applying themselves. And when they did a task, they did it *right*.

And anyhow, the flights to Mars had distracted world attention from the difficulty in Africa. So it all came back to what he had told his fellow store owners; what the Nazis have which we lack is— nobility. Admire them for their love of work or their efficiency . . . but it's the dream that stirs one. Space flights first to the moon, then to Mars; if that isn't the oldest yearning of mankind, our finest hope for glory. Now, the Japanese on the other hand. I know them pretty well; I do business with them, after all, day in and day out. They are—let's face it—Orientals. Yellow people. We whites have to bow to them because they hold the power. But we watch Germany; we see what can be done where whites have conquered, and it's quite different.

"We approach the Nippon Times Building, sir," the *chink* said, his chest heaving from the exertion of the hill climbing. He slowed, now.

To himself, Childan tried to picture Mr. Tagomi's client. Clearly the man was unusually important; Mr. Tagomi's tone on the telephone, his immense agitation, had communicated the fact. Image

of one of Childan's own very important clients, or rather, customers, swam up into his mind, a man who had done a good deal
to create for Childan a reputation among the high-placed personages residing in the Bay Area.

Four years ago, Childan had not been the dealer in the rare and
desirable which he was now; he had operated a small rather dimly
lighted secondhand bookshop on Geary. His neighboring stores
sold used furniture, or hardware, or did laundry. It was not a nice
neighborhood. At night strong-arm robberies and sometimes rape
took place on the sidewalk, despite the efforts of the San Francisco
Police Department and even the Kempeitai, the Japanese higher-
ups. All store windows had iron gratings fitted over them once the
business day had ended, this to prevent forcible entry. Yet, into this
district of the city had come an elderly Japanese ex-Army man, a
Major Ito Humo. Tall, slender, white-haired, walking and standing
stiffly, Major Humo had given Childan his first inkling of what
might be done with his line of merchandise.

"I am a collector," Major Humo had explained. He had spent an
entire afternoon searching among the heaps of old magazines in
the store. In his mild voice he had explained something which
Childan could not quite grasp at the time: to many wealthy, cultured Japanese, the historic objects of American popular civilization were of equal interest alongside the more formal antiques.
Why this was so, the major himself did not know; he was particularly addicted to the collecting of old magazines dealing with U.S.
brass buttons, as well as the buttons themselves. It was on the order
of coin or stamp collecting; no rational explanation could ever be
given. And high prices were being paid by wealthy collectors.

"I will give you an example," the major had said. "Do you know
what is meant by 'Horrors of War' cards?" He had eyed Childan
with avidity.

Searching his memory, Childan had at last recalled. The cards
had been dispensed, during his childhood, with bubble gum. A
cent apiece. There had been a series of them, each card depicting a
different horror.

"A dear friend of mine," the major had gone on, "collects 'Horrors of War.' He lacks but one, now. The *Sinking of the Panay*. He has offered a substantial sum of money for that particular card."

"Flip cards," Childan had said suddenly.

"Sir?"

"We flipped them. There was a head and a tail side on each card." He had been about eight years old. "Each of us had a pack of flip cards. We stood, two of us, facing each other. Each of us dropped a card so that it flipped in the air. The boy whose card landed with the head side up, the side with the picture, won both cards." How enjoyable to recall those good days, those early happy days of his childhood.

Considering, Major Humo had said, "I have heard my friend discuss his 'Horrors of War' cards, and he has never mentioned this. *It is my opinion that he does not know how these cards actually were put to use.*"

Eventually, the major's friend had shown up at the store to hear Childan's historically firsthand account. That man, also a retired officer of the Imperial Army, had been fascinated.

"Bottle caps!" Childan had exclaimed without warning.

The Japanese had blinked uncomprehendingly.

"We used to collect the tops of milk bottles. As kids. The round tops that gave the name of the dairy. There must have been thousands of dairies in the United States. Each one printed a special top."

The officer's eyes glinted with the instinct. "Do you possess any of your sometime collection, sir?"

Naturally, Childan did not. But . . . probably it was still possible to obtain the ancient, long-forgotten tops from the days before the war when milk had come in glass bottles rather than throwaway pasteboard cartons.

And so, by stages, he had gotten into the business. Others had opened similar places, taking advantage of the ever-growing Japanese craze for Americana . . . but Childan had always kept his edge.

"Your fare," the *chink* was saying, bringing him out of his meditation, "is a dollar, sir." He had unloaded the bags and was waiting.

Absentmindedly, Childan paid him. Yes, it was quite likely that the client of Mr. Tagomi resembled Major Humo; at least, Childan

26 PHILIP K. DICK

thought tartly, from my point of view. He had dealt with so many
Japanese . . . but he still had difficulty telling them apart. There
were the short squat ones, built like wrestlers. Then the druggist-
like ones. The tree-shrub-flower-gardener ones . . . he had his cat-
egories. And the young ones, who were to him not like Japanese at
all. Mr. Tagomi's client would probably be portly, a businessman,
smoking a Philippine cigar.

And then, standing before the Nippon Times Building, with his
bags on the sidewalk beside him, Childan suddenly thought with a
chill: Suppose his client isn't Japanese! Everything in the bags had
been selected with them in mind, their tastes—

But the man had to be Japanese. A Civil War recruiting poster
had been Mr. Tagomi's original order; surely only a Japanese would
care about such debris. Typical of their mania for the trivial, their
legalistic fascination with documents, proclamations, ads. He remembered one who had devoted his leisure time to collecting newspaper ads of American patent medicines of the 1900s.

There were other problems to face. Immediate problems. Through
the high doors of the Nippon Times Building men and women
hurried, all of them well-dressed; their voices reached Childan's
ears, and he started into motion. A glance upward at the towering
edifice, the highest building in San Francisco. Wall of offices, windows, the fabulous design of the Japanese architects—and the surrounding gardens of dwarf evergreens, rocks, the karesansui
landscape, sand imitating a dried-up stream winding past roots,
among simple, irregular flat stones . . .

He saw a black who had carried baggage, now free. At once
Childan called, "Porter!"

The black trotted toward him, smiling.

"To the twentieth floor," Childan said in his harshest voice.
"Suite B. At once." He indicated the bags and then strode on
toward the doors of the building. Naturally he did not look back.

A moment later he found himself being crowded into one of
the express elevators; mostly Japanese around him, their clean faces
shining slightly in the brilliant light of the elevator. Then the nau-
seating upward thrust of the elevator, the rapid click of floors passing; he shut his eyes, planted his feet firmly, prayed for the flight to

end. The black, of course, had taken the bags up on a service elevator. It would not have been within the realm of reason to permit him here. In fact—Childan opened his eyes and looked momentarily—he was one of the few whites in the elevator.

When the elevator let him off on the twentieth floor, Childan was already bowing mentally, preparing himself for the encounter in Mr. Tagomi's offices.

THE DAYS OF PERKY PAT

At ten in the morning a terrific horn, familiar to him, hooted Sam Regan out of his sleep, and he cursed the careboy upstairs; he knew the racket was deliberate. The careboy, circling, wanted to be certain that flukers—and not merely wild animals—got the care parcels that were to be dropped.

We'll get them, we'll get them, Sam Regan said to himself as he zipped his dust-proof overalls, put his feet into boots, and then grumpily sauntered as slowly as possible toward the ramp. Several other flukers joined him, all showing similar irritation.

"He's early today," Tod Morrison complained. "And I'll bet it's all staples, sugar and flour and lard—nothing interesting like say candy."

"We ought to be grateful," Norman Schein said.

"Grateful!" Tod halted to stare at him. "GRATEFUL?"

"Yes," Schein said. "What do you think we'd be eating without them: If they hadn't seen the clouds ten years ago."

"Well," Tod said sullenly, "I just don't like them to come *early*; I actually don't exactly mind their coming, as such."

As he put his shoulders against the lid at the top of the ramp, Schein said genially, "That's mighty tolerant of you, Tod boy. I'm sure the careboys would be pleased to hear your sentiments."

Of the three of them, Sam Regan was the last to reach the surface; he did not like the upstairs at all, and he did not care who knew it. And anyhow, no one could compel him to leave the safety of the Pinole Fluke-pit; it was entirely his business, and he noted now that a number of his fellow flukers had elected to remain below in their quarters, confident that those who did answer the horn would bring them back something.

"It's bright," Tod murmured, blinking in the sun.

The care ship sparkled close overhead, set against the gray sky as if hanging from an uneasy thread. Good pilot, this drop, Tod decided. He, or rather *it*, just lazily handles it, in no hurry. Tod waved at the care ship, and once more the huge horn burst out its din, making him clap his hands to his ears. Hey, a joke's a joke, he said to himself. And then the horn ceased; the careboy had relented.

"Wave to him to drop," Norm Schein said to Tod. "You've got the wigwag."

"Sure," Tod said, and began laboriously flapping the red flag, which the Martian creatures had long ago provided, back and forth, back and forth.

A projectile slid from the underpart of the ship, tossed out stabilizers, spiraled toward the ground.

"Sheoot," Sam Regan said with disgust. "It is staples; they don't have the parachute." He turned away, not interested.

How miserable the upstairs looked today, he thought as he surveyed the scene surrounding him. There, to the right, the uncompleted house which someone—not far from their pit—had begun to build out of lumber salvaged from Vallejo, ten miles to the north. Animals or radiation dust had gotten the builder, and so his work remained where it was; it would never be put to use. And, Sam Regan saw, an unusually heavy precipitate had formed since last he had been up here, Thursday morning or perhaps Friday; he had lost exact track. The darn dust, he thought. Just rocks, pieces of rubble, and the dust. World's becoming a dusty object with no one to whisk it off regularly. How about you? he asked silently of the Martian careboy flying in slow circles overhead. Isn't your technology limitless? Can't you appear some morning with a dust rag a million miles in surface area and restore our planet to pristine newness?

Or rather, he thought, to pristine *oldness*, the way it was in the "ol-days," as the children call it. We'd like that. While you're looking for something to give to us in the way of further aid, try that.

The careboy circled once more, searching for signs of writing in the dust: a message from the flukers below. I'll write that, Sam thought. BRING DUST RAG, RESTORE OUR CIVILIZATION. Okay, careboy?

All at once the care ship shot off, no doubt on its way back home to its base on Luna or perhaps all the way to Mars.

From the open fluke-pit hole, up which the three of them had come, a further head poked, a woman. Jean Regan, Sam's wife, appeared, shielded by a bonnet against the gray, blinding sun, frowning and saying, "Anything important? Anything *new*?"

"'Fraid not," Sam said. The care parcel projectile had landed and he walked toward it, scuffing his boots in the dust. The hull of the projectile had cracked open from the impact and he could see the canisters already. It looked to be five thousand pounds of salt—might as well leave it up here so the animals wouldn't starve, he decided. He felt despondent.

How peculiarly anxious the careboys were. Concerned all the time that the mainstays of existence be ferried from their own planet to Earth. They must think we eat all day long, Sam thought. My God . . . the pit was filled to capacity with stored foods. But of course it had been one of the smallest public shelters in Northern California.

"Hey," Schein said, stooping down by the projectile and peering into the crack opened along its side. "I believe I see something we can use." He found a rusted metal pole—once it had helped reinforce the concrete side of an ol-days public building—and poked at the projectile, stirring its release mechanism into action. The mechanism, triggered off, popped the rear half of the projectile open . . . and there lay the contents.

"Looks like radios in that box," Tod said. "Transistor radios." Thoughtfully stroking his short black beard he said, "Maybe we can use them for something new in our layouts."

"Mine's already got a radio," Schein pointed out.

"Well, build an electronic self-directing lawn mower with the parts," Tod said. "You don't have that, do you?" He knew the Scheins' Perky Pat layout fairly well; the two couples, he and his wife with Schein and his, had played together a good deal, being almost evenly matched.

Sam Regan said, "Dibs on the radios, because I can use them." His layout lacked the automatic garage-door opener that both Schein and Tod had; he was considerably behind them.

"Let's get to work," Schein agreed. "We'll leave the staples here and just cart back the radios. If anybody wants the staples, let them come here and get them. Before the do-cats do."

Nodding, the other two men fell to the job of carting the useful contents of the projectile to the entrance of their fluke-pit ramp. For use in their precious, elaborate Perky Pat layouts.

Seated cross-legged with his whetstone, Timothy Schein, ten years old and aware of his many responsibilities, sharpened his knife, slowly and expertly. Meanwhile, disturbing him, his mother and father noisily quarreled with Mr. and Mrs. Morrison, on the far side of the partition. They were playing Perky Pat again. As usual.

How many times today they have to play that dumb game? Timothy asked himself. Forever, I guess. He could see nothing in it, but his parents played on anyhow. And they weren't the only ones; he knew from what other kids said, even from other fluke-pits, that their parents, too, played Perky Pat most of the day, and sometimes even on into the night.

His mother said loudly, "Perky Pat's going to the grocery store and it's got one of those electric eyes that opens the door. Look." A pause. "See, it opened for her, and now she's inside."

"She pushes a cart," Timothy's dad added, in support.

"No, she doesn't," Mrs. Morrison contradicted. "That's wrong. She gives her list to the grocer and he fills it."

"That's only in little neighborhood stores," his mother explained. "And this is a supermarket, you can tell because of the electric eye door."

"I'm sure all grocery stores had electric eye doors," Mrs. Morrison said stubbornly, and her husband chimed in with his agreement. Now the voices rose in anger; another squabble had broken out. As usual.

Aw, cung to them, Timothy said to himself, using the strongest word which he and his friends knew. What's a supermarket anyhow? He tested the blade of his knife—he had made it himself, originally, out of a heavy metal pan—and then hopped to his feet. A moment later he had sprinted silently down the hall and was rapping his special rap on the door of the Chamberlains' quarters.

Fred, also ten years old, answered. "Hi. Ready to go? I see you got that ol' knife of yours sharpened; what do you think we'll catch?"

"Not a do-cat," Timothy said. "A lot better than that; I'm tired of eating do-cat. Too peppery."

"Your parents playing Perky Pat?"

"Yeah."

Fred said, "My mom and dad have been gone for a long time, off playing with the Benteleys." He glanced sideways at Timothy, and in an instant they had shared their mute disappointment regarding their parents. Gosh, and maybe the darn game was all over the world, by now; that would not have surprised either of them.

"How come your parents play it?" Timothy asked.

"Same reason yours do," Fred said.

Hesitating, Timothy said, "Well, why? I don't know why they do; I'm asking you, can't you say?"

"It's because—" Fred broke off. "Ask them. Come on; let's get upstairs and start hunting." His eyes shone. "Let's see what we can catch and kill today."

Shortly, they had ascended the ramp, popped open the lid, and were crouching amidst the dust and rocks, searching the horizon. Timothy's heart pounded; this moment always overwhelmed him, the first instant of reaching the upstairs. The thrilling initial sight of the expanse. Because it was never the same. The dust, heavier today, had a darker gray color to it than before; it seemed denser, more mysterious.

Here and there, covered by many layers of dust, lay parcels dropped from past relief ships—dropped and left to deteriorate. Never to be claimed. And, Timothy saw, an additional new projectile which had arrived that morning. Most of its cargo could be seen within; the grown-ups had not had any use for the majority of the contents, today.

"Look," Fred said softly.

Two do-cats—mutant dogs or cats; no one knew for sure— could be seen, lightly sniffing at the projectile. Attracted by the unclaimed contents.

"We don't want them," Timothy said.

"That one's sure nice and fat," Fred said longingly. But it was Timothy who had the knife; all he himself had was a string with a metal bolt on the end, a bull-roarer that could kill a bird or a small animal at a distance—but useless against a do-cat, which generally weighed fifteen to twenty pounds and sometimes more.

High up in the sky a dot moved at immense speed, and Timothy knew that it was a care ship heading for another fluke-pit, bringing supplies to it. Sure are busy, he thought to himself. Those careboys always coming and going; they never stop, because if they did, the grown-ups would die. Wouldn't that be too bad? he thought ironically. Sure be sad.

Fred said, "Wave to it and maybe it'll drop something." He grinned at Timothy, and then they both broke out laughing.

"Sure," Timothy said. "Let's see; what do I want?" Again the two of them laughed at the idea of them wanting something. The two boys had the entire upstairs, as far as the eye could see . . . they had even more than the careboys had, and that was plenty, more than plenty.

"Do you think they know," Fred said, "that our parents play Perky Pat with furniture made out of what they drop? I bet they don't know about Perky Pat; they never have seen a Perky Pat doll, and if they did they'd be really mad."

"You're right," Timothy said. "They'd be so sore they'd probably stop dropping stuff." He glanced at Fred, catching his eye.

"Aw no," Fred said. "We shouldn't tell them; your dad would beat you again if you did that, and probably me, too."

Even so, it was an interesting idea. He could imagine first the surprise and then the anger of the careboys; it would be fun to see that, see the reaction of the eight-legged Martian creatures who had so much charity inside their warty bodies, the cephalopodic univalve mollusk-like organisms who had voluntarily taken it upon themselves to supply succor to the waning remnants of the human race . . . this was how they got paid back for their charity, this utterly wasteful, stupid purpose to which their goods were being put. This stupid Perky Pat game that all the adults played.

And anyhow it would be very hard to tell them; there was almost no communication between humans and careboys. They were too different. Acts, deeds, could be done, conveying something . . . but not mere words, not mere *signs*. And anyhow—

A great brown rabbit bounded by to the right, past the half-completed house. Timothy whipped out his knife. "Oh boy!" he said aloud in excitement. "Let's go!" He set off across the rubbly ground, Fred a little behind him. Gradually they gained on the rabbit; swift running came easy to the two boys: they had done much practicing.

"Throw the knife!" Fred panted, and Timothy, skidding to a halt, raised his right arm, paused to take aim, and then hurled the sharpened, weighted knife. His most valuable, self-made possession.

It cleaved the rabbit straight through its vitals. The rabbit tumbled, slid, raising a cloud of dust.

"I bet we can get a dollar for that!" Fred exclaimed, leaping up and down. "The hide alone—I bet we can get fifty cents just for the darn hide!"

Together, they hurried toward the dead rabbit, wanting to get there before a red-tailed hawk or a day-owl swooped on it from the gray sky above.

Bending, Norman Schein picked up his Perky Pat doll and said sullenly, "I'm quitting; I don't want to play anymore."

Distressed, his wife protested, "But we've got Perky Pat all the way downtown in her new Ford hardtop convertible and parked and a dime in the meter and she's shopped and now she's in the analyst's office reading *Fortune*—we're way ahead of the Morrisons! Why do you want to quit, Norm?"

"We just don't agree," Norman grumbled. "You say analysts

charged twenty dollars an hour and I distinctly remember them charging only ten; nobody could charge twenty. So you're penalizing our side, and for what? The Morrisons agree it was only ten. Don't you?" he said to Mr. and Mrs. Morrison, who squatted on the far side of the layout which combined both couples' Perky Pat sets.

Helen Morrison said to her husband, "You went to the analyst more than I did; are you sure he charged only ten?"

"Well, I went mostly to group therapy," Tod said. "At the Berkeley State Mental Hygiene Clinic, and they charged according to your ability to pay. And Perky Pat is at a *private* psychoanalyst."

"We'll have to ask someone else," Helen said to Norman Schein. "I guess all we can do now this minute is suspend the game." He found himself being glared at by her, too, now, because by his insistence on the one point he had put an end to their game for the whole afternoon.

"Shall we leave it all set up?" Fran Schein said. "We might as well; maybe we can finish tonight after dinner."

Norman Schein gazed down at their combined layout, the swanky shops, the well-lit streets with the parked new-model cars, all of them shiny, the split-level house itself, where Perky Pat lived and where she entertained Leonard, her boyfriend. It was the *house* that he perpetually yearned for; the house was the real focus of the layout—of all the Perky Pat layouts, however much they might otherwise differ.

Perky Pat's wardrobe, for instance, there in the closet of the house, the big bedroom closet. Her capri pants, her white cotton short-shorts, her two-piece polka-dot swimsuit, her fuzzy sweaters ... and there, in her bedroom, her hi-fi set, her collection of long-playing records ...

It had been this way, once, really been like this in the ol-days. Norm Schein could remember his own l-p record collection, and he had once had clothes almost as swanky as Perky Pat's boyfriend Leonard, cashmere jackets and tweed suits and Italian sportshirts and shoes made in England. He hadn't owned a Jaguar XKE sports car, like Leonard did, but he had owned a fine-looking old 1963 Mercedes-Benz, which he had used to drive to work.

We lived then, Norm Schein said to himself, *like Perky Pat and Leonard do now.* This is how it actually was.

To his wife he said, pointing to the clock radio which Perky Pat kept beside her bed, "Remember our G.E. clock radio? How it used to wake us up in the morning with classical music from that FM station, KSFR? The 'Wolf-gangers,' the program was called. From six A.M. to nine every morning."

"Yes," Fran said, nodding soberly. "And you used to get up before me; I knew I should have gotten up and fixed bacon and hot coffee for you, but it was so much fun just indulging myself, not stirring for half an hour longer, until the kids woke up."

"Woke up, hell; they were awake before we were," Norm said. "Don't you remember? They were in the back watching 'The Three Stooges' on TV until eight. Then I got up and fixed hot cereal for them, and then I went on to my job at Ampex down at Redwood City."

"Oh yes," Fran said. "The TV." Their Perky Pat did not have a TV set; they had lost it to the Regans in a game a week ago, and Norm had not yet been able to fashion another one realistic-looking enough to substitute. So, in a game, they pretended now that "the TV repairman had come for it." That was how they explained their Perky Pat not having something she really would have had.

Norm thought, Playing this game . . . it's like being back there, back in the world before the war. That's why we play it, I suppose. He felt shame, but only fleetingly; the shame, almost at once, was replaced by the desire to play a little longer.

"Let's not quit," he said sullenly. "I'll agree the psychoanalyst would have charged Perky Pat twenty dollars. Okay?"

"Okay," both the Morrisons said together, and they settled back down once more to resume the game.

Tod Morrison had picked up their Perky Pat; he held it, stroking its blond hair—theirs was blond, whereas the Scheins' was a brunette—and fiddling with the snaps of its skirt.

"Whatever are you doing?" his wife inquired.

"Nice skirt she has," Tod said. "You did a good job sewing it."

Norm said, "Ever know a girl, back in the ol-days, that looked like Perky Pat?"

"No," Tod Morrison said somberly. "Wish I had, though. I *saw* girls like Perky Pat, especially when I was living in Los Angeles during the Korean War. But I just could never manage to know them personally. And of course there were really terrific girl singers, like Peggy Lee and Julie London . . . they looked a lot like Perky Pat."

"Play," Fran said vigorously. And Norm, whose turn it was, picked up the spinner and spun.

"Eleven," he said. "That gets my Leonard out of the sports car repair garage and on his way to the racetrack." He moved the Leonard doll ahead.

Thoughtfully, Tod Morrison said, "You know, I was out the other day hauling in perishables which the careboys had dropped . . . Bill Ferner was there, and he told me something interesting. He met a fluker from a fluke-pit down where Oakland used to be. And at that fluke-pit you know what they play? Not Perky Pat. They never have heard of Perky Pat."

"Well, what do they play, then?" Helen asked.

"They have another doll entirely." Frowning, Tod continued, "Bill says the Oakland fluker called it a Connie Companion doll. Ever hear of that?"

"A 'Connie Companion' doll," Fran said thoughtfully. "How strange. I wonder what she's like. Does she have a boyfriend?"

"Oh sure," Tod said. "His name is Paul. Connie and Paul. You know, we ought to hike down there to that Oakland Fluke-pit one of these days and see what Connie and Paul look like and how they live. Maybe we could learn a few things to add to our own layouts."

Norm said, "Maybe we could play them."

Puzzled, Fran said, "Could a Perky Pat play a Connie Companion? Is that possible? I wonder what would happen?"

There was no answer from any of the others. Because none of them knew.

As they skinned the rabbit, Fred said to Timothy, "Where did the name 'fluker' come from? It's sure an ugly word; why do they use it?"

"A fluker is a person who lived through the hydrogen war," Timothy explained. "You know, by a fluke. A fluke of fate? See? Because almost everyone was killed; there used to be thousands of people."

"But what's a 'fluke' then? When you say a 'fluke of fate—'"

"A fluke is when fate has decided to spare you," Timothy said, and that was all he had to say on the subject. That was all he knew.

Fred said thoughtfully, "But you and I, we're not flukers because we weren't alive when the war broke out. We were born after."

"Right," Timothy said.

"So anybody who calls me a fluker," Fred said, "is going to get hit in the eye with my bull-roarer."

"And 'careboy,'" Timothy said, "that's a made-up word, too. It's from when stuff was dumped from jet planes and ships to people in a disaster area. They are called 'care parcels' because they came from people who cared."

"I know that," Fred said. "I didn't ask that."

"Well, I told you anyhow," Timothy said.

The two boys continued skinning the rabbit.

Jean Regan said to her husband, "Have you heard about the Connie Companion doll?" She glanced down the long rough-board table to make sure none of the other families was listening. "Sam," she said, "I heard it from Helen Morrison; she heard it from Tod and he heard it from Bill Ferner, I think. So it's probably true."

"What's true?" Sam said.

"That in the Oakland Fluke-pit they don't have Perky Pat; they have Connie Companion . . . and it occurred to me that maybe some of this—you know, this sort of emptiness, this boredom we feel now and then—maybe if we saw the Connie Companion doll and how she lives, maybe we could add enough to our own layout to—" She paused, reflecting. "To make it more complete."

"I don't care for the name," Sam Regan said. "Connie Companion; it sounds cheap." He spooned up some of the plain, utilitarian grain-mash which the careboys had been dropping, of late. And, as he ate a mouthful, he thought, I'll bet Connie Companion doesn't eat slop like this; I'll bet she eats cheeseburgers with all the trimmings, at a high-type drive-in.

"Could we make a trek down there?" Jean asked.

"To Oakland Fluke-pit?" Sam stared at her. "It's *fifteen miles*, all the way on the other side of the Berkeley Fluke-pit!"

"But this is important," Jean said stubbornly. "And Bill says that a fluker from Oakland came all the way up here, in search of electronic parts or something . . . so if he can do it, we can. We've got the dust suits they dropped us. I know we could do it."

Little Timothy Schein, sitting with his family, had overheard her; now he spoke up. "Mrs. Regan, Fred Chamberlain and I, we could trek down that far, if you pay us. What do you say?" He nudged Fred, who sat beside him. "Couldn't we? For maybe five dollars."

Fred, his face serious, turned to Mrs. Regan and said, "We could get you a Connie Companion doll. For five dollars for *each* of us."

"Good grief," Jean Regan said, outraged. And dropped the subject.

But later, after dinner, she brought it up again when she and Sam were alone in their quarters.

"Sam, I've got to see it," she burst out. Sam, in a galvanized tub, was taking his weekly bath, so he had to listen to her. "Now that we know it exists we have to play against someone in the Oakland Fluke-pit; at least we can do that. Can't we? Please." She paced back and forth in the small room, her hands clasped tensely. "Connie Companion may have a Standard Station and an airport terminal with jet landing strip and color TV and a French restaurant where they serve escargot, like the one you and I went to when we were first married . . . I just have to see her layout."

"I don't know," Sam said hesitantly. "There's something about Connie Companion doll that—makes me uneasy."

"What could it possibly be?"

"I don't know."

Jean said bitterly, "It's because you know her layout is so much better than ours and she's so much more than Perky Pat."

"Maybe that's it," Sam murmured.

"If you don't go, if you don't try to make contact with them down at the Oakland Fluke-pit, someone else will—someone with more ambition will get ahead of you. Like Norman Schein. He's not afraid the way you are."

Sam said nothing; he continued with his bath. But his hands shook.

A careboy had recently dropped complicated pieces of machinery which were, evidently, a form of mechanical computer. For several weeks the computers—if that was what they were—had sat about the pit in their cartons, unused, but now Norman Schein was finding something to do with one. At the moment he was busy adapting some of its gears, the smallest ones, to form a garbage disposal unit for his Perky Pat's kitchen.

Using the tiny special tools—designed and built by inhabitants of the fluke-pit—which were necessary in fashioning environmental items for Perky Pat, he was busy at his hobby bench. Thoroughly engrossed in what he was doing, he all at once realized that Fran was standing directly behind him, watching.

"I get nervous when I'm watched," Norm said, holding a tiny gear with a pair of tweezers.

"Listen," Fran said, "I've thought of something. Does this suggest anything to you?" She placed before him one of the transistor radios which had been dropped the day before.

"It suggests that garage-door opener already thought of," Norm said irritably. He continued with his work, expertly fitting the miniature pieces together in the sink drain of Pat's kitchen; such delicate work demanded maximum concentration.

Fran said, "It suggests that there must be radio *transmitters* on Earth somewhere, or the careboys wouldn't have dropped these."

"So?" Norm said, uninterested.

"Maybe our Mayor has one," Fran said. "Maybe there's one right here in our own pit, and we could use it to call the Oakland Fluke-pit. Representatives from there could meet us halfway . . . say at the

Berkeley Fluke-pit. And we could play there. So we wouldn't have that long fifteen-mile trip."

Norman hesitated in his work; he set the tweezers down and said slowly, "I think possibly you're right." But if their Mayor Hooker Glebe had a radio transmitter, would he let them use it? And if he did—

"We can try," Fran urged. "It wouldn't hurt to try."

"Okay," Norm said, rising from his hobby bench.

The short, sly-faced man in Army uniform, the Mayor of the Pinole Fluke-pit, listened in silence as Norm Schein spoke. Then he smiled a wise, cunning smile. "Sure, I have a radio transmitter. Had it all the time. Fifty-watt output. But why would you want to get in touch with the Oakland Fluke-pit?"

Guardedly, Norm said, "That's my business."

Hooker Glebe said thoughtfully, "I'll let you use it for fifteen dollars."

It was a nasty shock, and Norm recoiled. Good Lord; all the money he and his wife had—they needed every bill of it for use in playing Perky Pat. Money was the tender in the game; there was no other criterion by which one could tell if he had won or lost. "That's too much," he said aloud.

"Well, say ten," the Mayor said, shrugging.

In the end they settled for six dollars and a fifty-cent piece.

"I'll make the radio contact for you," Hooker Glebe said. "Because you don't know how. It will take time." He began turning a crank at the side of the generator of the transmitter. "I'll notify you when I've made contact with them. But give me the money now." He held out his hand for it, and, with great reluctance, Norm paid him.

It was not until late that evening that Hooker managed to establish contact with Oakland. Pleased with himself, beaming in self-satisfaction, he appeared at the Scheins' quarters, during their dinner hour. "All set," he announced. "Say, you know there are actually *nine* fluke-pits in Oakland? I didn't know that. Which you want? I've got one with the radio code of Red Vanilla." He chuckled.

"They're tough and suspicious down there; it was hard to get any of them to answer."

Leaving his evening meal, Norman hurried to the Mayor's quarters, Hooker puffing along after him.

The transmitter, sure enough, was on, and static wheezed from the speaker of its monitoring unit. Awkwardly, Norm seated himself at the microphone. "Do I just talk?" he asked Hooker Glebe.

"Just say, This is Pinole Fluke-pit calling. Repeat that a couple of times and then when they acknowledge, you say what you want to say." The Mayor fiddled with controls of the transmitter, fussing in an important fashion.

"This is Pinole Fluke-pit," Norm said loudly into the microphone.

Almost at once a clear voice from the monitor said, "This is Red Vanilla Three answering." The voice was cold and harsh; it struck him forcefully as distinctly alien. Hooker was right.

"Do you have Connie Companion down there where you are?"

"Yes we do," the Oakland fluker answered.

"Well, I challenge you," Norman said, feeling the veins in his throat pulse with the tension of what he was saying. "We're Perky Pat in this area; we'll play Perky Pat against your Connie Companion. Where can we meet?"

"Perky Pat," the Oakland fluker echoed. "Yeah, I know about her. What would the stakes be, in your mind?"

"Up here we play for paper money mostly," Norman said, feeling that his response was somehow lame.

"We've got lots of paper money," the Oakland fluker said cuttingly. "That wouldn't interest any of us. What else?"

"I don't know." He felt hampered, talking to someone he could not see; he was not used to that. People should, he thought, be face-to-face, then you can see the other person's expression. This was not natural. "Let's meet halfway," he said, "and discuss it. Maybe we could meet at the Berkeley Fluke-pit; how about that?"

The Oakland fluker said, "That's too far. You mean lug our Connie Companion layout all that way? It's too heavy and something might happen to it."

"No, just to discuss rules and stakes," Norman said.

Dubiously, the Oakland fluker said, "Well, I guess we could do that. But you better understand—we take Connie Companion doll pretty damn seriously; you better be prepared to talk terms."

"We will," Norm assured him.

All this time Mayor Hooker Glebe had been cranking the handle of the generator; perspiring, his face bloated with exertion, he motioned angrily for Norm to conclude his palaver.

"At the Berkeley Fluke-pit," Norm finished. "In three days. And send your best player, the one who has the biggest and most authentic layout. Our Perky Pat layouts are works of art, you understand."

The Oakland fluker said, "We'll believe that when we see them. After all, we've got carpenters and electricians and plasterers here, building our layouts; I'll bet you're all unskilled."

"Not as much as you think," Norm said hotly, and laid down the microphone. To Hooker Glebe—who had immediately stopped cranking—he said, "We'll beat them. Wait'll they see the garbage disposal unit I'm making for my Perky Pat; did you know there were people back in the ol-days, I mean real alive human beings, who didn't have garbage disposal units?"

"I remember," Hooker said peevishly. "Say, you got a lot of cranking for your money; I think you gypped me, talking so long." He eyed Norm with such hostility that Norm began to feel uneasy. After all, the Mayor of the pit had the authority to evict any fluker he wished; that was their law.

"I'll give you the fire alarm box I just finished the other day," Norm said. "In my layout it goes at the corner of the block where Perky Pat's boyfriend Leonard lives."

"Good enough," Hooker agreed, and his hostility faded. It was replaced, at once, by desire. "Let's see it, Norm. I bet it'll go good in my layout; a fire alarm box is just what I need to complete my first block where I have the mailbox. Thank you."

"You're welcome," Norm sighed, philosophically.

When he returned from the two-day trek to the Berkeley Fluke-pit his face was so grim that his wife knew at once that the parley with the Oakland people had not gone well.

That morning a careboy had dropped cartons of a synthetic tea-like drink; she fixed a cup of it for Norman, waiting to hear what had taken place eight miles to the south.

"We haggled," Norm said, seated wearily on the bed which he and his wife and child all shared. "They don't want money; they don't want goods—naturally not goods, because the darn careboys are dropping regularly down there, too."

"What will they accept, then?"

Norm said, "Perky Pat herself." He was silent, then.

"Oh good Lord," she said, appalled.

"But if we win," Norm pointed out, "we win Connie Companion."

"And the layouts? What about them?"

"We keep our own. It's just Perky Pat herself, not Leonard, not anything else."

"But," she protested, "what'll we *do* if we lose Perky Pat?"

"I can make another one," Norm said. "Given time. There's still a big supply of thermoplastics and artificial hair, here in the pit. And I have plenty of different paints; it would take at least a month, but I could do it. I don't look forward to the job, I admit. But—" His eyes glinted. "Don't look on the dark side; *imagine what it would be like to win Connie Companion doll.* I think we may well win; their delegate seemed smart and, as Hooker said, tough . . . but the one I talked to didn't strike me as being very flukey. You know, on good terms with luck."

And, after all, the element of luck, of chance, entered into each stage of the game through the agency of the spinner.

"It seems wrong," Fran said, "to put up Perky Pat herself. But if you say so—" She managed to smile a little. "I'll go along with it. And if you won Connie Companion—who knows? You might be elected Mayor when Hooker dies. Imagine, to have won somebody else's *doll*—not just the game, the money, but the *doll itself.*"

"I can win," Norm said soberly. "Because I'm very flukey." He could feel it in him, the same flukeyness that had got him through the hydrogen war alive, that had kept him alive ever since. You either have it or you don't, he realized. And I do.

His wife said, "Shouldn't we ask Hooker to call a meeting of everyone in the pit, and send the best player out of our entire group. So as to be the surest of winning."

"Listen," Norm Schein said emphatically. "I'm the best player. I'm going. And so are you; we make a good team, and we don't want to break it up. Anyhow, we'll need at least two people to carry Perky Pat's layout." All in all, he judged, their layout weighed sixty pounds.

His plan seemed to him to be satisfactory. But when he mentioned it to the others living in the Pinole Fluke-pit he found himself facing sharp disagreement. The whole next day was filled with argument.

"You can't lug your layout all that way yourselves," Sam Regan said. "Either take more people with you or carry your layout in a vehicle of some sort. Such as a cart." He scowled at Norm.

"Where'd I get a cart?" Norm demanded.

"Maybe something could be adapted," Sam said. "I'll give you every bit of help I can. Personally, I'd go along but as I told my wife this whole idea worries me." He thumped Norm on the back. "I admire your courage, you and Fran, setting off this way. I wish I had what it takes." He looked unhappy.

In the end, Norm settled on a wheelbarrow. He and Fran would take turns pushing it. That way neither of them would have to carry any load above and beyond their food and water, and of course knives by which to protect them from the do-cats.

As they were carefully placing the elements of their layout in the wheelbarrow, Norm Schein's boy Timothy came sidling up to them. "Take me along, Dad," he pleaded. "For fifty cents I'll go as guide and scout, and also I'll help you catch food along the way."

"We'll manage fine," Norm said. "You stay here in the fluke-pit; you'll be safer here." It annoyed him, the idea of his son tagging along on an important venture such as this. It was almost—sacrilegious.

"Kiss us goodbye," Fran said to Timothy, smiling at him briefly; then her attention returned to the layout within the wheelbarrow. "I hope it doesn't tip over," she said fearfully to Norm.

"Not a chance," Norm said. "If we're careful." He felt confident.

A few moments later they began wheeling the wheelbarrow up the ramp to the lid at the top, to upstairs. Their journey to the Berkeley Fluke-pit had begun.

A mile outside the Berkeley Fluke-pit he and Fran began to stumble over empty drop-canisters and some only partly empty: remains of past care parcels such as littered the surface near their own pit. Norm Schein breathed a sigh of relief; the journey had not been so bad after all, except that his hands had become blistered from gripping the metal handles of the wheelbarrow, and Fran had turned her ankle so that now she walked with a painful limp. But it had taken them less time than he had anticipated, and his mood was one of buoyancy.

Ahead, a figure appeared, crouching low in the ash. A boy. Norm waved at him and called, "Hey, sonny—we're from the Pinole pit; we're supposed to meet a party from Oakland here . . . do you remember me?"

The boy, without answering, turned and scampered off.

"Nothing to be afraid of," Norm said to his wife. "He's going to tell their Mayor. A nice old fellow named Ben Fennimore."

Soon several adults appeared, approaching warily.

With relief, Norm set the legs of the wheelbarrow down into the ash, letting go and wiping his face with his handkerchief. "Has the Oakland team arrived yet?" he called.

"Not yet," a tall, elderly man with a white armband and ornate cap answered. "It's you, Schein, isn't it?" he said, peering. This was Ben Fennimore. "Back already with your layout." Now the Berkeley flukers had begun crowding around the wheelbarrow, inspecting the Scheins' layout. Their faces showed admiration.

"They have Perky Pat here," Norm explained to his wife. "But—" He lowered his voice. "Their layouts are only basic. Just a house, wardrobe, and car . . . they've built almost nothing. No imagination."

One Berkeley fluker, a woman, said wonderingly to Fran, "And you made each of the pieces of furniture yourselves?" Marveling, she turned to the man beside her. "See what they've accomplished, Ed?"

"Yes," the man answered, nodding. "Say," he said to Fran and Norm, "can we see it all set up? You're going to set it up in our pit, aren't you?"

"We are indeed," Norm said.

The Berkeley flukers helped push the wheelbarrow the last mile. And before long they were descending the ramp, to the pit below the surface.

"It's a big pit," Norm said knowingly to Fran. "Must be two thousand people here. This is where the University of California was."

"I see," Fran said, a little timid at entering a strange pit; it was the first time in years—since the war, in fact—that she had seen any strangers. And so many at once. It was almost too much for her; Norm felt her shrink back, pressing against him in fright.

When they reached the first level and were starting to unload the wheelbarrow, Ben Fennimore came up to them and said softly, "I think the Oakland people have been spotted; we just got a report of activity upstairs. So be prepared." He added, "We're rooting for you, of course, because you're Perky Pat, the same as us."

"Have you ever seen Connie Companion doll?" Fran asked him.

"No ma'am," Fennimore answered courteously. "But naturally we've heard about it, being neighbors to Oakland and all. I'll tell you one thing . . . we hear that Connie Companion doll is a bit older than Perky Pat. You know—more, um, *mature*." He explained, "I just wanted to prepare you."

Norm and Fran glanced at each other. "Thanks," Norm said slowly. "Yes, we should be as much prepared as possible. How about Paul?"

"Oh, he's not much," Fennimore said. "Connie runs things; I don't even think Paul has a real apartment of his own. But you better wait until the Oakland flukers get here; I don't want to mislead you—my knowledge is all hearsay, you understand."

Another Berkeley fluker, standing nearby, spoke up. "I saw Connie once, and she's much more grown up than Perky Pat."

"How old do you figure Perky Pat is?" Norm asked him.

"Oh, I'd say seventeen or eighteen," Norm was told.

"And Connie?" He waited tensely.

"Oh, she might be twenty-five, even."

From the ramp behind them they heard noises. More Berkeley flukers appeared, and, after them, two men carrying between them a platform on which, spread out, Norm saw a great, spectacular layout.

This was the Oakland team, and they weren't a couple, a man and wife; they were both men, and they were hard-faced with stern, remote eyes. They jerked their heads briefly at him and Fran, acknowledging their presence. And then, with enormous care, they set down the platform on which their layout rested.

Behind them came a third Oakland fluker carrying a metal box, much like a lunch pail. Norm, watching, knew instinctively that in the box lay Connie Companion doll. The Oakland fluker produced a key and began unlocking the box.

"We're ready to begin playing any time," the taller of the Oakland men said. "As we agreed in our discussion, we'll use a numbered spinner instead of dice. Less chance of cheating that way."

"Agreed," Norm said. Hesitantly he held out his hand. "I'm Norman Schein and this is my wife and play-partner Fran."

The Oakland man, evidently the leader, said, "I'm Walter R. Wynn. This is my partner here, Charley Dowd, and the man with the box, that's Peter Foster. He isn't going to play; he just guards our layout." Wynn glanced about, at the Berkeley flukers, as if saying, I know you're all partial to Perky Pat, in here. But we don't care; we're not scared.

Fran said, "We're ready to play, Mr. Wynn." Her voice was low but controlled.

"What about money?" Fennimore asked.

"I think both teams have plenty of money," Wynn said. He laid out several thousand dollars in greenbacks, and now Norm did the same. "The money of course is not a factor in this, except as a means of conducting the game."

Norm nodded; he understood perfectly. Only the dolls themselves mattered. And now, for the first time, he saw Connie Companion doll.

She was being placed in her bedroom by Mr. Foster who evidently was in charge of her. And the sight of her took his breath away. Yes, she was older. A grown woman, not a girl at all . . . the difference between her and Perky Pat was acute. And so life-like. Carved, not poured; she obviously had been whittled out of wood and then painted—she was not a thermoplastic. And her hair. It appeared to be genuine hair.

He was deeply impressed.

"What do you think of her?" Walter Wynn asked, with a faint grin.

"Very—impressive," Norm conceded.

Now the Oaklanders were studying Perky Pat. "Poured thermoplastic," one of them said. "Artificial hair. Nice clothes, though; all stitched by hand, you can see that. Interesting; what we heard was correct. Perky Pat isn't a grown-up, she's just a teenager."

Now the male companion to Connie appeared; he was set down in the bedroom beside Connie.

"Wait a minute," Norm said. "You're putting Paul or whatever his name is, in her bedroom with her? Doesn't he have his own apartment?"

Wynn said, "They're married."

"Married!" Norman and Fran stared at him, dumbfounded.

"Why sure," Wynn said. "So naturally they live together. Your dolls, they're not, are they?"

"N-no," Fran said. "Leonard is Perky Pat's boyfriend . . ." Her voice trailed off. "Norm," she said, clutching his arm, "I don't believe him; I think he's just saying they're married to get the advantage. Because if they both start out from the same room—"

Norm said aloud, "You fellows, look here. It's not fair, calling them married."

Wynn said, "We're not 'calling' them married; they are married. Their names are Connie and Paul Lathrope, of 24 Arden Place, Piedmont. They've been married for a year, most players will tell you." He sounded calm.

Maybe, Norm thought, it's true. He was truly shaken.

"Look at them together," Frank said, kneeling down to examine the Oaklanders' layout. "In the same bedroom, in the same house. Why, Norm; do you see? There's just the one bed. A big double bed." Wild-eyed, she appealed to him. "How can Perky Pat and Leonard play against them?" Her voice shook. "It's not morally *right*."

"This is another type of layout entirely," Norm said to Walter Wynn. "This, that you have. Utterly different from what we're used to, as you can see." He pointed to his own layout. "I insist that in this game Connie and Paul *not* live together and *not* be considered married."

"But they are," Foster spoke up. "It's a fact. Look—their clothes are in the same closet." He showed them the closet. "And in the same bureau drawers." He showed them that, too. "And look in the bathroom. Two toothbrushes. His and hers, in the same rack. So you can see we're not making it up."

There was silence.

Then Fran said in a choked voice, "And if they're married—you mean they've been—intimate?"

Wynn raised an eyebrow, then nodded. "Sure, since they're married. Is there anything wrong with that?"

"Perky Pat and Leonard have never—" Fran began, and then ceased.

"Naturally not," Wynn agreed. "Because they're only going together. We understand that."

Fran said, "We just can't play. We can't." She caught hold of her husband's arm. "Let's go back to Pinole pit—please, Norman."

"Wait," Wynn said, at once. "If you don't play, you're conceding; you have to give up Perky Pat."

The three Oaklanders all nodded. And, Norm saw, many of the Berkeley flukers were nodding, too, including Ben Fennimore.

"They're right," Norm said heavily to his wife. "We'd have to give her up. We better play, dear."

"Yes," Fran said, in a dead, flat voice. "We'll play." She bent down and listlessly spun the needle of the spinner. It stopped at six.

Smiling, Walter Wynn knelt down and spun. He obtained a four.

The game had begun.

———

Crouching behind the strewn, decayed contents of a care parcel that had been dropped long ago, Timothy Schein saw coming across the surface of ash his mother and father, pushing the wheelbarrow ahead of them. They looked tired and worn.

"Hi," Timothy yelled, leaping out at them in joy at seeing them again; he had missed them very much.

"Hi, son," his father murmured, nodding. He let go of the handles of the wheelbarrow, then halted and wiped his face with his handkerchief.

Now Fred Chamberlain raced up, panting. "Hi, Mr. Schein, hi; Mrs. Schein. Hey, did you win? Did you beat the Oakland flukers? I bet you did, didn't you?" He looked from one of them to the other and then back.

In a low voice Fran said, "Yes, Freddy. We won."

Norm said, "Look in the wheelbarrow."

The two boys looked. And, there among Perky Pat's furnishings, lay another doll. Larger, fuller-figured, much older than Pat . . . they stared at her and she stared up sightlessly at the gray sky overhead. So this is Connie Companion doll, Timothy said to himself. Gee.

"We were lucky," Norm said. Now several people had emerged from the pit and were gathering around them, listening. Jean and Sam Regan, Tod Morrison and his wife Helen, and now their Mayor, Hooker Glebe himself, waddling up excited and nervous, his face flushed, gasping for breath from the labor—unusual for him—of ascending the ramp.

Fran said, "We got a cancellation-of-debts card, just when we were most behind. We owed fifty thousand, and it made us even with the Oakland flukers. And then, after that, we got an advance-ten-squares card, and that put us right on the jackpot square, at least in our layout. We had a very bitter squabble, because the Oaklanders showed us that on their layout it was a tax lien slapped on real-estate-holdings square, but we had spun an odd number so that put us back on our own board." She sighed. "I'm glad to be back. It was hard, Hooker; it was a tough game."

Hooker Glebe wheezed, "Let's all get a look at the Connie Companion doll, folks." To Fran and Norm he said, "Can I lift her up and show them?"

"Sure," Norm said, nodding.

Hooker picked up Connie Companion doll. "She sure is realistic," he said, scrutinizing her. "Clothes aren't as nice as ours generally are; they look machine-made."

"They are," Norm agreed. "But she's carved, not poured."

"Yes, so I see." Hooker turned the doll about, inspecting her from all angles. "A nice job. She's—um, more filled out than Perky Pat. What's this outfit she has on? Tweed suit of some sort."

"A business suit," Fran said. "We won that with her; they had agreed on that in advance."

"You see, she has a job," Norm explained. "She's a psychology consultant for a business firm doing marketing research. In consumer preferences. A high-paying position . . . she earns twenty thousand a year, I believe Wynn said."

"Golly," Hooker said. "And Pat's just going to college; she's still in school." He looked troubled. "Well, I guess they were bound to be ahead of us in some ways. What matters is that you won." His jovial smile returned. "Perky Pat came out ahead." He held the Connie Companion doll up high, where everyone could see her. "Look what Norm and Fran came back with, folks!"

Norm said, "Be careful with her, Hooker." His voice was firm.

"Eh?" Hooker said, pausing. "Why, Norm?"

"Because," Norm said, "she's going to have a baby."

There was a sudden chill silence. The ash around them stirred faintly; that was the only sound.

"How do you know?"

"They told us. The Oaklanders told us. And we won that, too—after a bitter argument that Fennimore had to settle." Reaching into the wheelbarrow he brought out a little leather pouch; from it he carefully took a carved pink newborn baby. "We won this too because Fennimore agreed that from a technical standpoint it's literally part of Connie Companion doll at this point."

Hooker stared a long, long time.

"She's married," Fran explained. "To Paul. They're not just going together. She's three months pregnant, Mr. Wynn said. He didn't tell us until after we won; he didn't want to, then, but they felt they had to. I think they were right; it wouldn't have done not to say."

Norm said, "And in addition there's actually an embryo outfit—"

"Yes," Fran said. "You have to open Connie up, of course, to see—"

"No," Jean Regan said. "Please, no."

Hooker said, "No, Mrs. Schein, don't." He backed away.

Fran said, "It shocked us of course at first, but—"

"You see," Norm put in, "it's logical; you have to follow the logic. Why, eventually Perky Pat—"

"No," Hooker said violently. He bent down, picked up a rock from the ash at his feet. "No," he said, and raised his arm. "You stop, you two. Don't say any more."

Now the Regans, too, had picked up rocks. No one spoke.

Fran said, at last, "Norm, we've got to get out of here."

"You're right," Tod Morrison told them. His wife nodded in grim agreement.

"You two go back to Oakland," Hooker told Norman and Fran Schein. "You don't live here anymore. You're different than you were. You—changed."

"Yes," Sam Regan said slowly, half to himself. "I was right; there was something to fear." To Norm Schein he said, "How difficult a trip is it to Oakland?"

"We just went to Berkeley," Norm said. "To the Berkeley Fluke-pit." He seemed baffled and stunned by what was happening. "My God," he said, "we can't turn around and push this wheelbarrow back all the way to Berkeley again—we're worn out, we need rest!"

Sam Regan said, "What if somebody else pushed?" He walked up to the Scheins, then, and stood with them. "I'll push the darn thing. You lead the way, Schein." He looked toward his own wife, but Jean did not stir. And she did not put down her handful of rocks.

Timothy Schein plucked at his father's arm. "Can I come this time, Dad? Please let me come."

"Okay," Norm said, half to himself. Now he drew himself together. "So we're not wanted here." He turned to Fran. "Let's go.

Sam's going to push the wheelbarrow; I think we can make it back there before nightfall. If not, we can sleep out in the open; Timothy'll help protect us against the do-cats."

Fran said, "I guess we have no choice." Her face was pale.

"And take this," Hooker said. He held out the tiny carved baby. Fran Schein accepted it and put it tenderly back in its leather pouch. Norm laid Connie Companion back down in the wheelbarrow, where she had been. They were ready to start back.

"It'll happen up here eventually," Norm said, to the group of people, to the Pinole flukers. "Oakland is just more advanced; that's all."

"Go on," Hooker Glebe said. "Get started."

Nodding, Norm started to pick up the handles of the wheelbarrow, but Sam Regan moved him aside and took them himself. "Let's go," he said.

The three adults, with Timothy Schein going ahead of them with his knife ready—in case a do-cat attacked—started into motion, in the direction of Oakland and the south. No one spoke. There was nothing to say.

"It's a shame this had to happen," Norm said at last, when they had gone almost a mile and there was no further sign of the Pinole flukers behind them.

"Maybe not," Sam Regan said. "Maybe it's for the good." He did not seem downcast. And after all, he had lost his wife; he had given up more than anyone else, and yet—he had survived.

"Glad you feel that way," Norm said somberly.

They continued on, each with his own thoughts.

After a while, Timothy said to his father, "All these big fluke-pits to the south . . . there's lots more things to do there, isn't there? I mean, you don't just sit around playing that game." He certainly hoped not.

His father said, "That's true, I guess."

Overhead, a care ship whistled at great velocity and then was gone again almost at once; Timothy watched it go but he was not really interested in it, because there was so much more to look forward to, on the ground and below the ground, ahead of them to the south.

His father murmured, "Those Oaklanders; their game, their particular doll, it taught them something. Connie had to grow and it forced them all to grow along with her. Our flukers never learned about that, not from Perky Pat. I wonder if they ever will. She'd have to grow up the way Connie did. Connie must have been like Perky Pat, once. A long time ago."

Not interested in what his father was saying—who really cared about dolls and games with dolls?—Timothy scampered ahead, peering to see what lay before them, the opportunities and possibilities, for him and for his mother and dad, for Mr. Regan also.

"I can't wait," he yelled back at his father, and Norm Schein managed a faint, fatigued smile in answer.

Chapter One

from THE THREE STIGMATA
OF PALMER ELDRITCH

His head unnaturally aching, Barney Mayerson woke to find himself in an unfamiliar bedroom in an unfamiliar conapt building. Beside him, the covers up to her bare, smooth shoulders, an unfamiliar girl slept on, breathing lightly through her mouth, her hair a tumble of cottonlike white.

I'll bet I'm late for work, he said to himself, slid from the bed, and tottered to a standing position with eyes shut, keeping himself from being sick. For all he knew he was several hours' drive from his office; perhaps he was not even in the United States. However he *was* on Earth; the gravity that made him sway was familiar and normal.

And there in the next room by the sofa a familiar suitcase, that of his psychiatrist Dr. Smile.

Barefoot, he padded into the living room, and seated himself by the suitcase; he opened it, clicked switches, and turned on Dr. Smile. Meters began to register and the mechanism hummed. "Where am I?" Barney asked it. "And how far am I from New York?" That was the main point. He saw now a clock on the wall of the apt's kitchen; the time was 7:30 A.M. Not late at all.

The mechanism which was the portable extension of Dr. Smile, connected by micro-relay to the computer itself in the basement level of Barney's own conapt building in New York, the Renown 33, tinnily declared, "Ah, Mr. Bayerson."

"Mayerson," Barney corrected, smoothing his hair with fingers that shook. "What do you remember about last night?" Now he saw, with intense physical aversion, half-empty bottles of bourbon and sparkling water, lemons, bitters, and ice cube trays on the sideboard in the kitchen. "Who is this girl?"

Dr. Smile said, "This girl in the bed is Miss Rondinella Fugate. Roni, as she asked you to call her."

It sounded vaguely familiar, and oddly, in some manner, tied up with his job. "Listen," he said to the suitcase, but then in the bedroom the girl began to stir; at once he shut off Dr. Smile and stood up, feeling humble and awkward in only his underpants.

"Are you up?" the girl asked sleepily. She thrashed about, and sat facing him; quite pretty, he decided, with lovely, large eyes. "What time is it and did you put on the coffee pot?"

He tramped into the kitchen and punched the stove into life; it began to heat water for coffee. Meanwhile he heard the shutting of a door; she had gone into the bathroom. Water ran. Roni was taking a shower.

Again in the living room he switched Dr. Smile back on. "What's she got to do with P. P. Layouts?" he asked.

"Miss Fugate is your new assistant; she arrived yesterday from People's China where she worked for P. P. Layouts as their Pre-Fash consultant for that region. However, Miss Fugate, although talented, is highly inexperienced, and Mr. Bulero decided that a short period as your assistant, I would say 'under you,' but that might be misconstrued, considering—"

"Great," Barney said. He entered the bedroom, found his clothes—they had been deposited, no doubt by him, in a heap on the floor—and began with care to dress; he still felt terrible, and it remained an effort not to give up and be violently sick. "That's right," he said to Dr. Smile as he came back to the living room buttoning his shirt. "I remember the memo from Friday about Miss Fugate. She's erratic in her talent. Picked wrong on that U.S. Civil War Picture Window item . . . if you can imagine it, she thought it'd be a smash hit in People's China." He laughed.

The bathroom door opened a crack; he caught a glimpse of Roni, pink and rubbery and clean, drying herself. "Did you call me, dear?"

"No," he said. "I was talking to my doctor."

"Everyone makes errors," Dr. Smile said, a trifle vacuously.

Barney said, "How'd she and I happen to——" He gestured toward the bedroom. "After so short a time."

"Chemistry," Dr. Smile said.

"Come on."

"Well, you're both precogs. You previewed that you'd eventually hit it off, become erotically involved. So you both decided—after a few drinks—that why should you wait? 'Life is short, art is—'" The suitcase ceased speaking, because Roni Fugate had appeared from the bathroom, naked, to pad past it and Barney back once more into the bedroom. She had a narrow, erect body, a truly superb carriage, Barney noted, and small, up-jutting breasts with nipples no larger than matched pink peas. Or rather matched pink pearls, he corrected himself.

Roni Fugate said, "I meant to ask you last night—why are you consulting a psychiatrist? And my lord, you carry it around everywhere with you; not once did you set it down—and you had it turned on right up until——" She raised an eyebrow and glanced at him searchingly.

"At least I did turn it off then," Barney pointed out.

"Do you think I'm pretty?" Rising on her toes she all at once stretched, reached above her head, then, to his amazement, began to do a brisk series of exercises, hopping and leaping, her breasts bobbing.

"I certainly do," he murmured, taken aback.

"I'd weigh a ton," Roni Fugate panted, "if I didn't do these UN Weapons Wing exercises every morning. Go pour the coffee, will you, dear?"

Barney said, "Are you really my new assistant at P. P. Layouts?"

"Yes, of course; you mean you don't remember? But I guess you're like a lot of really topnotch precogs: you see the future so well that you have only a hazy recollection of the past. Exactly what do you recall about last night?" She paused in her exercises, gasping for breath.

"Oh," he said vaguely, "I guess everything."

"Listen. The only reason why you'd be carrying a psychiatrist around with you is that you must have gotten your draft notice. Right?"

After a pause he nodded. *That* he remembered. The familiar elongated blue-green envelope had arrived one week ago; next Wednesday he would be taking his mental at the UN military hospital in the Bronx.

"Has it helped? Has he—" She gestured at the suitcase. "—Made you sick enough?"

Turning to the portable extension of Dr. Smile, Barney said, "Have you?"

The suitcase answered, "Unfortunately you're still quite viable, Mr. Mayerson; you can handle ten Freuds of stress. Sorry. But we still have several days; we've just begun."

Going into the bedroom, Roni Fugate picked up her underwear, and began to step into it. "Just think," she said reflectively. "If you're drafted, Mr. Mayerson, and you're sent to the colonies . . . maybe I'll find myself with your job." She smiled, showing superb, even teeth.

It was a gloomy possibility and his precog ability did not assist him: the outcome hung nicely, at perfect balance on the scales of cause-and-effect to be.

"You can't handle my job," he said. "You couldn't even handle it in People's China and that's a relatively simple situation in terms of factoring out pre-elements." But someday she could; without difficulty he foresaw that. She was young and overflowing with innate talent: all she required to equal him—and he was the best in the trade—was a few years' experience. Now he became fully awake as awareness of his situation filtered back to him. He stood a good chance of being drafted, and even if he was not, Roni Fugate might well snatch his fine, desirable job from him, a job up to which he had worked by slow stages over a thirteen-year period.

A peculiar solution to the grimness of the situation, this going to bed with her; he wondered how he had arrived at it.

Bending over the suitcase, he said in a low voice to Dr. Smile, "I wish you'd tell me why the hell with everything so dire I decided to—"

"I can answer that," Roni Fugate called from the bedroom; she had now put on a somewhat tight pale green sweater and was buttoning it before the mirror of her vanity table. "You informed me last night, after your fifth bourbon and water. You said—" She paused, eyes sparkling. "It's inelegant. What you said was this. 'If you can't lick 'em, join 'em.' Only the verb you used, I regret to say, wasn't 'join.'"

"Hmm," Barney said, and went into the kitchen to pour himself a cup of coffee. Anyhow, he was not far from New York; obviously if Miss Fugate was a fellow employee at P. P. Layouts he was within commute distance of his job. They could ride in together. Charming. He wondered if their employer Leo Bulero would approve of this if he knew. Was there an official company policy about employees sleeping together? There was about almost everything else . . . although how a man who spent all his time at the resort beaches of Antarctica or in German E Therapy clinics could find time to devise dogma on every topic eluded him.

Someday, he said to himself, I'll live like Leo Bulero; instead of being stuck in New York City in 180 degree heat—

Beneath him now a throbbing began; the floor shook. The building's cooling system had come on. Day had begun.

Outside the kitchen window the hot, hostile sun took shape beyond the other conapt buildings visible to him; he shut his eyes against it. Going to be another scorcher, all right, probably up to the twenty Wagner mark. He did not need to be a precog to foresee this.

In the miserably high-number conapt building 492 on the outskirts of Marilyn Monroe, New Jersey, Richard Hnatt ate breakfast indifferently while, with something greater than indifference, he glanced over the morning homeopape's weather-syndrome readings of the previous day.

The key glacier, Ol' Skintop, had retreated 4.62 Grables during the last twenty-four-hour period. And the temperature, at noon in New York, had exceeded the previous day's by 1.46 Wagners. In addition the humidity, as the oceans evaporated, had increased by 16 Selkirks. So things were hotter and wetter; the great procession of nature clanked on, and toward what? Hnatt pushed the 'pape away, and picked up the mail which had been delivered before dawn . . . it had been some time since mailmen had crept out in daylight hours.

The first bill which caught his eye was the apt's cooling pro-rated swindle; he owed Conapt 492 exactly ten and a half skins for the last month—a rise of three-fourths of a skin over April. Some-day, he said to himself, it'll be so hot that *nothing* will keep this place from melting; he recalled the day his l-p record collection had fused together in a lump, back around '04, due to a momentary failure of the building's cooling network. Now he owned iron oxide tapes; they did not melt. And at the same moment every parakeet and Venusian ming bird in the building had dropped dead. And his neighbor's turtle had been boiled dry. Of course this had been during the day and everyone—at least the men—had been at work. The wives, however, had huddled at the lowest subsurface level, thinking (he remembered Emily telling him this) that the fatal moment had at last arrived. And not a century from now but *now*. The Caltech predictions had been wrong . . . only of course they hadn't been; it had just been a broken power-lead from the N.Y. utility people. Robot workmen had quickly shown up and repaired it.

In the living room his wife sat in her blue smock, painstakingly painting an unfired ceramic piece with glaze; her tongue protruded and her eyes glowed . . . the brush moved expertly and he could see already that this was going to be a good one. The sight of Emily at work recalled to him the task that lay before him, today: one which he did not relish.

He said, peevishly, "Maybe we ought to wait before we approach him."

Without looking up, Emily said, "We'll never have a better dis-play to present to him than we have now."

"What if he says no?"

"We'll go on. What did you expect, that we'd give up just because my onetime husband can't foresee—or won't foresee—how successful these new pieces will eventually be in terms of the market?"

Richard Hnatt said, "You know him; I don't. He's not vengeful, is he? He wouldn't carry a grudge?" And anyhow what sort of grudge could Emily's former husband be carrying? No one had done him any harm; if anything it had gone the other way, or so he understood from what Emily had related.

It was strange, hearing about Barney Mayerson all the time and never having met him, never having direct contact with the man. Now that would end, because he had an appointment to see Mayerson at nine this morning in the man's office at P. P. Layouts. Mayerson of course would hold the whip hand; he could take one brief glance at the display of ceramics and decline ad hoc. No, he would say, P. P. Layouts is not interested in a min of this. Believe my precog ability, my Pre-Fash marketing talent and skill. And—out would go Richard Hnatt, the collection of pots under his arm, with absolutely no other place to go.

Looking out the window he saw with aversion that already it had become too hot for human endurance; the footer runnels were abruptly empty as everyone ducked for cover. The time was eight-thirty and he now had to leave; rising, he went to the hall closet to get his pith helmet and his mandatory cooling-unit; by law one had to be strapped to every commuter's back until nightfall.

"Goodbye," he said to his wife, pausing at the front door.

"Goodbye and lots of luck." She had become even more involved in her elaborate glazing and he realized all at once that this showed how vast her tension was; she could not afford to pause even a moment. He opened the door and stepped out into the hall, feeling the cool wind of the portable unit as it chugged from behind him. "Oh," Emily said, as he began to shut the door; now she raised her head, brushing her long brown hair back from her eyes. "Vid me as soon as you're out of Barney's office, as soon as you know one way or another."

"Okay," he said, and shut the door behind him.

Downramp, at the building's bank, he unlocked their safety deposit box and carried it to a privacy room; there he lifted out the display case containing the spread of ceramic ware which he was to show Mayerson.

Shortly, he was aboard a thermosealed interbuilding commute car, on his way to downtown New York City and P. P. Layouts, the great pale synthetic-cement building from which Perky Pat and all the units of her miniature world originated. The doll, he reflected, which had conquered man as man at the same time had conquered the planets of the Sol system. Perky Pat, the obsession of the colonists. What a commentary on colonial life . . . what more did one need to know about those unfortunates who, under the selective service laws of the UN, had been kicked off Earth, required to begin new, alien lives on Mars or Venus or Ganymede or wherever else the UN bureaucrats happened to imagine they could be deposited . . . and after a fashion survive.

And we think we've got it bad here, he said to himself.

The individual in the seat next to him, a middle-aged man wearing the gray pith helmet, sleeveless shirt, and shorts of bright red popular with the businessman class, remarked, "It's going to be another hot one."

"Yes."

"What you got there in that great big carton? A picnic lunch for a hovel of Martian colonists?"

"Ceramics," Hnatt said.

"I'll bet you fire them just by sticking them outdoors at high noon." The businessman chuckled, then picked up his morning 'pape, opened it to the front page. "Ship from outside the Sol system reported crash-landed on Pluto," he said. "Team being sent to find it. You suppose it's *things*? I can't stand those things from other war systems."

"It's more likely one of our own ships reporting back," Hnatt said.

"Ever seen a Proxima thing?"

"Only pics."

"Grisly," the businessman said. "If they find that wrecked ship on Pluto and it is a thing I hope they laser it out of existence; after all we do have a law against them coming into our system."

"Right."

"Can I see your ceramics? I'm in neckties, myself. The Werner simulated-handwrought living tie in a variety of Titanian colors— I have one on, see? The colors are actually a primitive life form that we import and then grow in cultures here on Terra. Just how we induce them to reproduce is our trade secret, you know, like the formula for Coca-Cola."

Hnatt said, "For a similar reason I can't show you these ceramics, much as I'd like to. They're new. I'm taking them to a Pre-Fash precog at P. P. Layouts; if he wants to miniaturize them for the Perky Pat layouts then we're in: it's just a question of flashing the info to the P. P. disc jockey—what's his name?—circling Mars. And so on."

"Werner handwrought ties are part of the Perky Pat layouts," the man informed him. "Her boyfriend Walt has a closetful of them." He beamed. "When P. P. Layouts decided to min our ties—"

"It was Barney Mayerson you talked to?"

"*I* didn't talk to him; it was our regional sales manager. They say Mayerson is difficult. Goes on what seems like impulse and once he's decided it's irreversible."

"Is he ever wrong? Declines items that become fash?"

"Sure. He may be a precog but he's only human. I'll tell you one thing that might help. He's very suspicious of women. His marriage broke up a couple of years ago and he never got over it. See, his wife became pregnant *twice*, and the board of directors of his conapt building, I think it's 33, met and voted to expel him and his wife because they had violated the building code. Well, you know 33; you know how hard it is to get into any of the buildings in that low range. So instead of giving up his apt he elected to divorce his wife and let her move, taking their child. And then later on apparently he decided he made a mistake and he got embittered; he blamed himself, naturally, for making a mistake like that. A natural mistake, though; for God's sake, what wouldn't you and I give to have an apt in 33 or 34? He never remarried; maybe he's a Neo-Christian. But anyhow when you go to try to sell him on your ceramics, be very careful about how you deal with the feminine angle; don't say 'these will appeal to the ladies' or anything like that. Most retail items are purchased—"

"Thanks for the tip," Hnatt said, rising; carrying his case of ceramics he made his way down the aisle to the exit. He sighed. It was going to be tough, possibly even hopeless; he wasn't going to be able to lick the circumstances which long predated his relationship with Emily and her pots, and that was that.

Fortunately he managed to snare a cab; as it carried him through downtown cross-traffic he read his own morning 'pape, in particular the lead story about the ship believed to have returned from Proxima only to crash on Pluto's frozen wastes—an understatement! Already it was conjectured that this might be the well-known interplan industrialist Palmer Eldritch, who had gone to the Prox system a decade ago at the invitation of the Prox Council of humanoid types; they had wanted him to modernize their autofacs along Terran lines. Nothing had been heard from Eldritch since. Now this.

It would probably be better for Terra if this wasn't Eldritch coming back, he decided. Palmer Eldritch was too wild and dazzling a solo pro; he had accomplished miracles in getting autofac production started on the colony planets, but—as always he had gone too far, schemed too much. Consumer goods had piled up in unlikely places where no colonists existed to make use of them. Mountains of debris, they had become, as the weather corroded them bit by bit, inexorably. Snowstorms, if one could believe that such still existed somewhere . . . there were places which were actually cold. Too cold, in actual fact.

"Thy destination, your eminence," the autonomic cab informed him, halting before a large but mostly subsurface structure. P. P. Layouts, with employees handily entering by its many thermal-protected ramps.

He paid the cab, hopped from it, and scuttled across a short open space for a ramp, his case held with both hands; briefly, naked sunlight touched him and he felt—or imagined—himself sizzle. Baked like a toad, dried of all life-juices, he thought as he safely reached the ramp.

Presently he was subsurface, being allowed into Mayerson's office by a receptionist. The rooms, cool and dim, invited him to relax but he did not; he gripped his display case tighter and tensed himself and, although he was not a Neo-Christian, he mumbled a prolix prayer.

"Mr. Mayerson," the receptionist, taller than Hnatt and impressive in her open-bodice dress and resort-style heels, said, speaking

not to Hnatt but to the man seated at the desk. "This is Mr. Hnatt,"
she informed Mayerson. "This is Mr. Mayerson, Mr. Hnatt." Behind
Mayerson stood a girl in a pale green sweater and with absolutely
white hair. The hair was too long and the sweater too tight. "This
is Miss Fugate, Mr. Hnatt. Mr. Mayerson's assistant. Miss Fugate,
this is Mr. Richard Hnatt."

At the desk Barney Mayerson continued to study a document
without acknowledging the entrance of anyone and Richard Hnatt
waited in silence, experiencing a mixed bag of emotions; anger
touched him, lodged in his windpipe and chest, and of course
Angst, and then, above even those, a tendril of growing curiosity.
So this was Emily's former husband, who, if the living necktie
salesman could be believed, still chewed mournfully, bitterly, on
the regret of having abolished the marriage. Mayerson was a rather
heavy-set man, in his late thirties, with unusually—and not particularly fashionable—loose and wavy hair. He looked bored but
there was no sign of hostility about him. But perhaps he had not as
yet—

"Let's see your pots," Mayerson said suddenly.

Laying the display case on the desk Richard Hnatt opened it, got
out the ceramic articles one by one, arranged them, and then
stepped back.

After a pause Barney Mayerson said, "No."

"'No'?" Hnatt said. "No what?"

Mayerson said, "They won't make it." He picked up his document and resumed reading it.

"You mean you decided just like that?" Hnatt said, unable to
believe that it was already done.

"Exactly like that," Mayerson agreed. He had no further interest
in the display of ceramics; as far as he was concerned Hnatt had
already packed up his pots and left.

Miss Fugate said, "Excuse me, Mr. Mayerson."

Glancing at her Barney Mayerson said, "What is it?"

"I'm sorry to say this, Mr. Mayerson," Miss Fugate said; she went
over to the pots, picked one up and held it in her hands, weighing
it, rubbing its glazed surface. "But I get a distinctly different impression than you do. I feel these ceramic pieces will make it."

Hnatt looked from one to the other of them.

"Let me have that." Mayerson pointed to a dark gray vase; at once Hnatt handed it to him. Mayerson held it for a time. "No," he said finally. He was frowning, now. "I still get no impression of this item making it big. In my opinion you're mistaken, Miss Fugate." He set the vase back down. "However," he said to Richard Hnatt, "in view of the disagreement between myself and Miss Fugate—" He scratched his nose thoughtfully. "Leave this display with me for a few days; I'll give it further attention." Obviously, however, he would not.

Reaching, Miss Fugate picked up a small, oddly shaped piece and cradled it against her bosom almost tenderly. "This one in particular. I receive very powerful emanations from it. This one will be the most successful of all."

In a quiet voice Barney Mayerson said, "You're out of your mind, Roni." He seemed really angry, now; his face was violent and dark. "I'll vid you," he said to Richard Hnatt. "When I've made my final decision. I see no reason why I should change my mind, so don't be optimistic. In fact don't bother to leave them." He shot a hard, harsh glance toward his assistant, Miss Fugate.

from UBIK

*Friends, this is clean-up time and we're
discounting all our silent, electric Ubiks by this
much money. Yes, we're throwing away the blue-
book. And remember: every Ubik on our lot has
been used only as directed.*

At three-thirty A.M. on the night of June 5, 1992, the top
telepath in the Sol System fell off the map in the offices of
Runciter Associates in New York City. That started vid-phones
ringing. The Runciter organization had lost track of too many of
Hollis' psis during the last two months; this added disappearance
wouldn't do.

"Mr. Runciter? Sorry to bother you." The technician in charge
of the night shift at the map room coughed nervously as the
massive, sloppy head of Glen Runciter swam up to fill the vid-
screen. "We got this news from one of our inertials. Let me look."
He fiddled with a disarranged stack of tapes from the recorder
which monitored incoming messages. "Our Miss Dorn reported
it; as you may recall she had followed him to Green River, Utah,
where—"

Sleepily, Runciter grated, "Who? I can't keep in mind at all
times which inertials are following what teep or precog." With his
hand he smoothed down his ruffled gray mass of wirelike hair.
"Skip the rest and tell me which of Hollis' people is missing now."

"S. Dole Melipone," the technician said.

"What? Melipone's gone? You kid me."

"I not kid you," the technician assured him. "Edie Dorn and two other inertials followed him to a motel named the Bonds of Erotic Polymorphic Experience, a sixty-unit subsurface structure catering to businessmen and their hookers who don't want to be entertained. Edie and her colleagues didn't think he was active, but just to be on the safe side we had one of our own telepaths, Mr. G. G. Ashwood, go in and read him. Ashwood found a scramble pattern surrounding Melipone's mind, so he couldn't do anything; he therefore went back to Topeka, Kansas, where he's currently scouting a new possibility."

Runciter, more awake now, had lit a cigarette; chin in hand, he sat propped up somberly, smoke drifting across the scanner of his end of the bichannel circuit. "You're sure the teep was Melipone? Nobody seems to know what he looks like; he must use a different physiognomic template every month. What about his field?"

"We asked Joe Chip to go in there and run tests on the magnitude and minitude of the field being generated there at the Bonds of Erotic Polymorphic Experience Motel. Chip says it registered, at its height, 68.2 blr units of telepathic aura, which only Melipone, among all the known telepaths, can produce." The technician finished, "So that's where we stuck Melipone's identflag on the map. And now he—it—is gone."

"Did you look on the floor? Behind the map?"

"It's gone electronically. The man it represents is no longer on Earth or, as far as we can make out, on a colony world either."

Runciter said, "I'll consult my dead wife."

"It's the middle of the night. The moratoriums are closed now."

"Not in Switzerland," Runciter said, with a grimacing smile, as if some repellent midnight fluid had crept up into his aged throat. "Goodeve." Runciter hung up.

As owner of the Beloved Brethren Moratorium, Herbert Schoenheit von Vogelsang, of course, perpetually came to work before his employees. At this moment, with the chilly, echoing building just beginning to stir, a worried-looking clerical individual with nearly opaque glasses and wearing a tabby-fur blazer and pointed yellow shoes waited at the reception counter, a claim-check stub in his hand. Obviously, he had shown up to holiday-greet a relative. Resurrection Day—the holiday on which the half-lifers were publicly honored—lay just around the corner; the rush would soon be beginning.

"Yes, sir," Herbert said to him with an affable smile. "I'll take your stub personally."

"It's an elderly lady," the customer said. "About eighty, very small, and wizened. My grandmother."

"'Twill only be a moment." Herbert made his way back to the cold-pac bins to search out number 3054039-B.

When he located the correct party he scrutinized the lading report attached. It gave only fifteen days of half-life remaining. Not very much, he reflected; automatically he pressed a portable protophason amplifier into the transparent plastic hull of the casket, tuned it, listened at the proper frequency for indication of cephalic activity.

Faintly from the speaker a voice said, ". . . and then Tillie sprained her ankle and we never thought it'd heal; she was so foolish about it, wanting to start walking immediately . . ."

Satisfied, he unplugged the amplifier and located a union man to perform the actual task of carting 3054039-B to the consultation lounge, where the customer would be put in touch with the old lady.

"You checked her out, did you?" the customer asked as he paid the poscreds due.

"Personally," Herbert answered. "Functioning perfectly." He kicked a series of switches, then stepped back. "Happy Resurrection Day, sir."

"Thank you." The customer seated himself facing the casket, which steamed in its envelope of cold-pac; he pressed an earphone against the side of his head and spoke firmly into the microphone. "Flora, dear, can you hear me? I think I can hear you already. Flora?"

When I pass, Herbert Schoenheit von Vogelsang said to himself, I think I'll will my heirs to revive me one day a century. That way I can observe the fate of all mankind. But that meant a rather high maintenance cost to the heirs—and he knew what that meant. Sooner or later they would rebel, have his body taken out of cold-pac and—god forbid—buried.

"Burial is barbaric," Herbert muttered aloud. "Remnant of the primitive origins of our culture."

"Yes, sir," his secretary agreed, at her typewriter.

In the consultation lounge several customers now communed with their half-lifer relations, in rapt quiet, distributed at intervals each with his separate casket. It was a tranquil sight, these faithfuls, coming as they did so regularly to pay homage. They brought messages, news of what took place in the outside world; they cheered the gloomy half-lifers in these intervals of cerebral activity. And—they paid Herbert Schoenheit von Vogelsang. It was a profitable business, operating a moratorium.

"My dad seems a little frail," a young man said, catching Herbert's attention. "I wonder if you could take a moment of your time to check him over. I'd really appreciate it."

"Certainly," Herbert said, accompanying the customer across the lounge to his deceased relative. The lading for this one showed only a few days remaining; that explained the vitiated quality of cerebration. But still . . . he turned up the gain of the protophason amplifier, and the voice from the half-lifer became a trifle stronger in the earphone. He's almost at an end, Herbert thought. It seemed obvious to him that the son did not want to see the lading, did not actually care to know that contact with his dad was diminishing, finally. So Herbert said nothing; he merely walked off, leaving the son to commune. Why tell him that this was probably the last time he would come here? He would find out soon enough in any case.

A truck had now appeared at the loading platform at the rear of the moratorium; two men hopped down from it, wearing familiar pale-blue uniforms. Atlas Interplan Van and Storage, Herbert perceived. Delivering another half-lifer who had just now passed, or here to pick up one which had expired. Leisurely, he started in that direction, to supervise; at that moment, however, his secretary called to him. "Herr Schoenheit von Vogelsang; sorry to break into your meditation, but a customer wishes you to assist in revving up his relative." Her voice took on special coloration as she said, "The customer is Mr. Glen Runciter, all the way here from the North American Confederation."

A tall, elderly man, with large hands and a quick, sprightly stride, came toward him. He wore a varicolored Dacron wash-and-wear suit, knit cummerbund and dip-dyed cheesecloth cravat. His head, massive like a tomcat's, thrust forward as he peered through slightly protruding, round and warm and highly alert eyes. Runciter kept, on his face, a professional expression of greeting, a fast atten-tiveness which fixed on Herbert, then almost at once strayed past him, as if Runciter had already fastened onto future matters. "How is Ella?" Runciter boomed, sounding as if he possessed a voice electronically augmented. "Ready to be cranked up for a talk? She's only twenty; she ought to be in better shape than you or me." He chuckled, but it had an abstract quality; he always smiled and he always chuckled, his voice always boomed, but inside he did not notice anyone, did not care; it was his body which smiled, nodded and shook hands. Nothing touched his mind, which remained remote; aloof, but amiable, he propelled Herbert along with him, sweeping his way in great strides back into the chilled bins where the half-lifers, including his wife, lay.

"You have not been here for some time, Mr. Runciter," Herbert pointed out; he could not recall the data on Mrs. Runciter's lading sheet, how much half-life she retained.

Runciter, his wide, flat hand pressing against Herbert's back to urge him along, said, "This is a moment of importance, von Vogel-sang. We, my associates and myself, are in a line of business that surpasses all rational understanding. I'm not at liberty to make disclosures at this time, but we consider matters at present to be ominous but not however hopeless. Despair is not indicated—not by any means. Where's Ella?" He halted, glanced rapidly about.

"I'll bring her from the bin to the consultation lounge for you," Herbert said; customers should not be here in the bins. "Do you have your numbered claim-check, Mr. Runciter?"

"God, no," Runciter said. "I lost it months ago. But you know who my wife is; you can find her. Ella Runciter, about twenty.

Brown hair and eyes." He looked around him impatiently. "Where did you put the lounge? It used to be located where I could find it."

"Show Mr. Runciter to the consultation lounge," Herbert said to one of his employees, who had come meandering by, curious to see what the world-renowned owner of an anti-psi organization looked like.

Peering into the lounge, Runciter said with aversion, "It's full. I can't talk to Ella in there." He strode after Herbert, who had made for the moratorium's files. "Mr. von Vogelsang," he said, overtaking him and once more dropping his big paw onto the man's shoulder; Herbert felt the weight of the hand, its persuading vigor. "Isn't there a more private sanctum sanctorum for confidential communications? What I have to discuss with Ella my wife is not a matter which we at Runciter Associates are ready at this time to reveal to the world."

Caught up in the urgency of Runciter's voice and presence, Herbert found himself readily mumbling, "I can make Mrs. Runciter available to you in one of our offices, sir." He wondered what had happened, what pressure had forced Runciter out of his bailiwick to make this belated pilgrimage to the Beloved Brethren Moratorium to crank up—as Runciter crudely phrased it—his half-lifer wife. A business crisis of some sort, he theorized. Ads over TV and in the homeopapes by the various anti-psi prudence establishments had shrilly squawked their harangues of late. Defend your privacy, the ads yammered on the hour, from all media. Is a stranger tuning in on you? Are you *really* alone? That for the telepaths . . . and then the queasy worry about precogs. Are your actions being predicted by someone you never met? Someone you would not want to meet or invite into your home? Terminate anxiety; contacting your nearest prudence organization will first tell you if in fact you are the victim of unauthorized intrusions, and then, on your instructions, nullify these intrusions—at moderate cost to you.

"Prudence organizations." He liked the term; it had dignity and it was accurate. He knew this from personal experience; two years ago a telepath had infiltrated his moratorium staff, for reasons which he had never discovered. To monitor confidences between

half-lifers and their visitors, probably; perhaps those of one specific half-lifer—anyhow, a scout from one of the anti-psi organizations had picked up the telepathic field, and he had been notified.
Upon his signing of a work contract an anti-telepath had been dis-
patched, had installed himself on the moratorium premises. The
telepath had not been located but it had been nullified, exactly as
the TV ads promised. And so, eventually, the defeated telepath had
gone away. The moratorium was now psi-free, and, to be sure it
stayed so, the anti-psi prudence organization surveyed his establishment routinely once a month.

"Thanks very much, Mr. Vogelsang," Runciter said, following
Herbert through an outer office in which clerks worked to an
empty inner room that smelled of drab and unnecessary micro-
documents.

Of course, Herbert thought musingly to himself, I took their
word for it that a telepath got in here; they showed me a graph
they had obtained, citing it as proof. Maybe they faked it, made
up the graph in their own labs. And I took their word for it that
the telepath left; he came, he left—and I paid two thousand poscreds. Could the prudence organizations be, in fact, rackets?
Claiming a need for their services when sometimes no need actually exists?

Pondering this he set off in the direction of the files once more.
This time Runciter did not follow him; instead, he thrashed about
noisily, making his big frame comfortable in terms of a meager
chair. Runciter sighed, and it seemed to Herbert, suddenly, that the
massively built old man was tired, despite his customary show of
energy.

I guess when you get into that bracket, Herbert decided, you
have to act in a certain way; you have to appear more than a human
with merely ordinary failings. Probably Runciter's body contained
a dozen artiforgs, artificial organs grafted into place in his physio-
logical apparatus as the genuine, original ones, failed. Medical science, he conjectured, supplies the material groundwork, and out of
the authority of his mind Runciter supplies the remainder. I wonder how old he is, he wondered. Impossible any more to tell by
looks, especially after ninety.

"Miss Beason," he instructed his secretary, "have Mrs. Ella Runciter located and bring me the ident number. She's to be taken to office 2-A." He seated himself across from her, busied himself with a pinch or two of Fribourg & Treyer *Princes* snuff as Miss Beason began the relatively simple job of tracking down Glen Runciter's wife.

from UBIK

The best way to ask for beer is to sing out Ubik.
Made from select hops, choice water, slow-aged
for perfect flavor, Ubik is the nation's number-one
choice in beer. Made only in Cleveland.

Upright in her transparent casket, encased in an effluvium of icy mist, Ella Runciter lay with her eyes shut, her hands lifted permanently toward her impassive face. It had been three years since he had seen Ella, and of course she had not changed. She never would, now, at least not in the outward physical way. But with each resuscitation into active half-life, into a return of cerebral activity, however short, Ella died somewhat. The remaining time left to her pulse-phased out and ebbed.

Knowledge of this underwrote his failure to rev her up more often. He rationalized this way: that it doomed her, that to activate her constituted a sin against her. As to her own stated wishes, before her death and in early half-life encounters—this had become handily nebulous in his mind. Anyway, he would know better, being four times as old as she. What had she wished? To continue to function with him as co-owner of Runciter Associates; something vague on that order. Well, he had granted this wish. Now, for example. And six or seven times in the past. He did consult her at each crisis of the organization. He was doing so at this moment.

Damn this earphone arrangement, he grumbled as he fitted the plastic disc against the side of his head. And this microphone; all impediments to *natural* communication. He felt impatient and uncomfortable as he shifted about on the inadequate chair which Vogelsang or whatever his name was had provided him; he watched her rev back into sentience and wished she would hurry. And then in panic he thought, Maybe she isn't going to make it; maybe she's worn out and they didn't tell me. Or they don't know. Maybe, he thought, I ought to get that Vogelsang creature in here to explain. Maybe something terrible is wrong.

Ella, pretty and light-skinned; her eyes, in the days when they had been open, had been bright and luminous blue. That would not again occur; he could talk to her and hear her answer; he could communicate with her . . . but he would never again see her with eyes opened; nor would her mouth move. She would not smile at his arrival. When he departed she would not cry. Is this worth it? he asked himself. Is this better than the old way, the direct road from full-life to the grave? I still do have her with me, in a sense, he decided. The alternative is nothing.

In the earphone words, slow and uncertain, formed: circular thoughts of no importance, fragments of the mysterious dream which she now dwelt in. How did it feel, he wondered, to be in half-life? He could never fathom it from what Ella had told him; the basis of it, the experience of it, couldn't really be transmitted. Gravity, she had told him, once; it begins not to affect you and you float, more and more. When half-life is over, she had said, I think you float out of the System, out into the stars. But she did not know either; she only wondered and conjectured. She did not, however, seem afraid. Or unhappy. He felt glad of that.

"Hi, Ella," he said clumsily into the microphone.

"Oh," her answer came, in his ear; she seemed startled. And yet of course her face remained stable. Nothing showed; he looked away. "Hello, Glen," she said, with a sort of childish wonder, surprised, taken aback, to find him here. "What—" She hesitated. "How much time has passed?"

"Couple years," he said.

"Tell me what's going on."

"Aw, christ," he said, "everything's going to pieces, the whole organization. That's why I'm here; you wanted to be brought into major policy-planning decisions, and god knows we need that now, a new policy, or anyhow a revamping of our scout structure."

"I was dreaming," Ella said. "I saw a smoky red light, a horrible light. And yet I kept moving toward it. I couldn't stop."

"Yeah," Runciter said, nodding. "The *Bardo Thödol*, the *Tibetan Book of the Dead*, tells about that. You remember reading that; the doctors made you read it when you were—" He hesitated. "Dying," he said then.

"The smoky red light is bad, isn't it?" Ella said.

"Yeah, you want to avoid it." He cleared his throat. "Listen, Ella, we've got problems. You feel up to hearing about it? I mean, I don't want to overtax you or anything; just say if you're too tired or if there's something else you want to hear about or discuss."

"It's so weird. I think I've been dreaming all this time, since you last talked to me. Is it really two years? Do you know, Glen, what I think? I think that other people who are around me—we seem to be progressively growing together. A lot of my dreams aren't about me at all. Sometimes I'm a man and sometimes a little boy; sometimes I'm an old fat woman with varicose veins . . . and I'm in places I've never seen, doing things that make no sense."

"Well, like they say, you're heading for a new womb to be born out of. And that smoky red light—that's a bad womb; you don't want to go that way. That's a humiliating, low sort of womb. You're probably anticipating your next life, or whatever it is." He felt foolish, talking like this; normally he had no theological convictions. But the half-life experience was real and it had made theologians out of all of them. "Hey," he said, changing the subject. "Let me tell you what's happened, what made me come here and bother you. S. Dole Melipone has dropped out of sight."

A moment of silence, and then Ella laughed. "Who or what is an S. Dole Melipone? There can't be any such thing." The laugh, the unique and familiar warmth of it, made his spine tremble; he remembered that about her, even after so many years. He had not heard Ella's laugh in over a decade.

"Maybe you've forgotten," he said.

Ella said, "I haven't forgotten; I wouldn't forget an S. Dole Melipone. Is it like a hobbit?"

"It's Raymond Hollis' top telepath. We've had at least one iner- tial sticking close to him ever since G. G. Ashwood first scouted him, a year and a half ago. We *never* lose Melipone; we can't afford to. Melipone can when necessary generate twice the psi field of any other Hollis employee. And Melipone is only one of a whole string of Hollis people who've disappeared—anyhow, disappeared as far as we're concerned. As far as all prudence organizations in the Society can make out. So I thought, Hell, I'll go ask Ella what's up and what we should do. Like you specified in your will—remember?"

"I remember." But she sounded remote. "Step up your ads on TV. Warn people. Tell them . . ." Her voice trailed off into silence then.

"This bores you," Runciter said gloomily.

"No. I—" She hesitated and he felt her once more drift away. "Are they all telepaths?" she asked after an interval.

"Telepaths and precogs mostly. They're nowhere on Earth; I know that. We've got a dozen inactive inertials with nothing to do because the psis they've been nullifying aren't around, and what worries me even more, a lot more, is that requests for anti-psis have dropped—which you would expect, given the fact that so many psis are missing. But I know they're on one single project; I mean, I believe. Anyhow, I'm sure of it; somebody's hired the bunch of them, but only Hollis knows who it is or where it is. Or what it's all about." He lapsed into brooding silence then. How would Ella be able to help him figure it out? he asked himself. Stuck here in this casket, frozen out of the world—she knew only what he told her. Yet, he had always relied on her sagacity, that particular female form of it, a wisdom not based on knowledge or experience but on something innate. He had not, during the period she had lived, been able to fathom it; he certainly could not do so now that she lay in chilled immobility. Other women he had known since her death—there had been several—had a little of it, trace amounts perhaps. Intimations of a greater potentiality which, in them, never emerged as it had in Ella.

"Tell me," Ella said, "what this Melipone person is like."

"A screwball."

"Working for money? Or out of conviction? I always feel wary about that, when they have that psi mystique, that sense of purpose and cosmic identity. Like that awful Sarapis had; remember him?"

"Sarapis isn't around any more. Hollis allegedly bumped him off because he connived to set up his own outfit in competition with Hollis. One of his precogs tipped Hollis off." He added, "Melipone is much tougher on us than Sarapis was. When he's hot it takes three inertials to balance his field, and there's no profit in that; we collect—or *did* collect—the same fee we get with one inertial. Because the Society has a rate schedule now which we're bound by." He liked the Society less each year; it had become a chronic obsession with him, its uselessness, its cost. Its vainglory. "As near as we can tell, Melipone is a money-psi. Does that make you feel better? Is that less bad?" He waited, but heard no response from her. "Ella," he said. Silence. Nervously he said, "Hey, hello there, Ella; can you hear me? Is something wrong?" Oh, god, he thought. She's gone.

A pause, and then thoughts materialized in his right ear. "My name is Jory." Not Ella's thoughts; a different *élan*, more vital and yet clumsier. Without her deft subtlety.

"Get off the line," Runciter said in panic. "I was talking to my wife Ella; where'd you come from?"

"I am Jory," the thoughts came, "and no one talks to me. I'd like to visit with you awhile, mister, if that's okay with you. What's your name?"

Stammering, Runciter said, "I want my wife, Mrs. Ella Runciter; I paid to talk to her, and that's who I want to talk to, not you."

"I know Mrs. Runciter," the thoughts clanged in his ear, much stronger now. "She talks to me, but it isn't the same as somebody like you talking to me, somebody in the world. Mrs. Runciter is here where we are; it doesn't count because she doesn't know any more than we do. What year is it, mister? Did they send that big ship to Proxima? I'm very interested in that; maybe you can tell me. And if you want, I can tell Mrs. Runciter later on. Okay?"

Runciter popped the plug from his ear, hurriedly set down the earphone and the rest of the gadgetry; he left the stale, dust-saturated office and roamed about among the chilling caskets, row after row, all of them neatly arranged by number. Moratorium employees swam up before him and then vanished as he churned on, searching for the owner.

"Is something the matter, Mr. Runciter?" the von Vogelsang person said, observing him as he floundered about. "Can I assist you?"

"I've got some *thing* coming in over the wire," Runciter panted, halting. "Instead of Ella. Damn you guys and your shoddy business practices; this shouldn't happen, and what does it mean?" He followed after the moratorium owner, who had already started in the direction of office 2-A. "If I ran my business this way—"

"Did the individual identify himself?"

"Yeh, he called himself Jory."

Frowning with obvious worry, von Vogelsang said, "That would be Jory Miller. I believe he's located next to your wife. In the bin."

"But I can see it's Ella!"

"After prolonged proximity," van Vogelsang explained, "there is occasionally a mutual osmosis, a suffusion between the mentalities of half-lifers. Jory Miller's cephalic activity is particularly good; your wife's is not. That makes for an unfortunately one-way passage of protophasons."

"Can you correct it?" Runciter asked hoarsely; he found himself still spent, still panting and shaking. "Get that thing out of my wife's mind and get her back—that's your job!"

Von Vogelsang said, in a stilted voice, "If this condition persists your money will be returned to you."

"Who cares about the money? Snirt the money." They had reached office 2-A now; Runciter unsteadily reseated himself, his heart laboring so that he could hardly speak. "If you don't get this Jory person off the line," he half gasped, half snarled, "I'll sue you; I'll close down this place!"

Facing the casket, von Vogelsang pressed the audio outlet into his ear and spoke briskly into the microphone. "Phase out, Jory; that's a good boy." Glancing at Runciter he said, "Jory passed at fifteen; that's why he has so much vitality. Actually, this has happened

before; Jory has shown up several times where he shouldn't be."
Once more into the microphone he said, "This is very unfair of
you, Jory; Mr. Runciter has come a long way to talk to his wife.
Don't dim her signal, Jory; that's not nice." A pause as he listened
to the earphone. "I know her signal is weak." Again he listened,
solemn and froglike, then removed the earphone and rose to his
feet.

"What'd he say?" Runciter demanded. "Will he get out of there
and let me talk to Ella?"

Von Vogelsang said, "There's nothing Jory can do. Think of two
AM radio transmitters, one close by but limited to only five-hundred
watts of operating power. Then another, far off, but on the same or
nearly the same frequency, and utilizing five-thousand watts. When
night comes—"

"And night," Runciter said, "*has* come." At least for Ella. And
maybe himself as well, if Hollis' missing teeps, parakineticists, precogs, resurrectors and animators couldn't be found. He had not
only lost Ella; he had also lost her advice, Jory having supplanted
her before she could give it.

"When we return her to the bin," von Vogelsang was blabbing,
"we won't install her near Jory again. In fact, if you're agreeable as
to paying the somewhat larger monthly fee, we can place her in a
high-grade isolated chamber with walls coated and reinforced with
Teflon-26 so as to inhibit hetero-psychic infusion—from Jory or
anybody else."

"Isn't it too late?" Runciter said, surfacing momentarily from
the depression into which this happening had dropped him.

"She may return. Once Jory phases out. Plus anyone else who
may have gotten into her because of her weakened state. She's
accessible to almost anyone." Von Vogelsang chewed his lip, palpably pondering. "She may not like being isolated, Mr. Runciter. We
keep the containers—the caskets, as they're called by the lay public—close together for a reason. Wandering through one another's
mind gives those in half-life the only—"

"Put her in solitary right now," Runciter broke in. "Better she
be isolated than not exist at all."

"She exists," von Vogelsang corrected. "She merely can't contact you. There's a difference."

Runciter said, "A metaphysical difference which means nothing to me."

"I will put her in isolation," von Vogelsang said, "but I think you're right; it's too late. Jory has permeated her permanently, to some extent at least. I'm sorry."

Runciter said harshly, "So am I."

A LITTLE SOMETHING FOR
US TEMPUNAUTS

Wearily, Addison Doug plodded up the long path of synthetic redwood rounds, step by step, his head down a little, moving as if he were in actual physical pain. The girl watched him, wanting to help him, hurt within her to see how worn and unhappy he was, but at the same time she rejoiced that he was there at all. On and on, toward her, without glancing up, going by feel . . . like he's done this many times, she thought suddenly. Knows the way too well. Why?

"Addi," she called, and ran toward him. "They said on the TV you were dead. All of you were killed!"

He paused, wiping back his dark hair, which was no longer long; just before the launch they had cropped it. But he had evidently forgotten. "You believe everything you see on TV?" he said, and came on again, haltingly, but smiling now. And reaching up for her.

God, it felt good to hold him, and to have him clutch at her again, with more strength than she had expected. "I was going to find somebody else," she gasped. "To replace you."

"I'll knock your head off if you do," he said. "Anyhow, that isn't possible; nobody could replace me."

"But what about the implosion?" she said. "On reentry; they said—"

"I forgot," Addison said, in the tone he used when he meant, I'm not going to discuss it. The tone had always angered her before, but not now. This time she sensed how awful the memory was. "I'm going to stay at your place a couple of days," he said, as together they moved up the path toward the open front door of the tilted A-frame house. "If that's okay. And Benz and Crayne will be joining me, later on; maybe even as soon as tonight. We've got a lot to talk over and figure out."

"Then all three of you survived." She gazed up into his care-worn face. "Everything they said on TV . . ." She understood, then. Or believed she did. "It was a cover story. For—political purposes, to fool the Russians. Right? I mean, the Soviet Union'll think the launch was a failure because on reentry—"

"No," he said. "A chrononaut will be joining us, most likely. To help figure out what happened. General Toad said one of them is already on his way here; they got clearance already. Because of the gravity of the situation."

"Jesus," the girl said, stricken. "Then who's the cover story for?"

"Let's have something to drink," Addison said. "And then I'll outline it all for you."

"Only thing I've got at the moment is California brandy."

Addison Doug said, "I'd drink anything right now, the way I feel." He dropped to the couch, leaned back, and sighed a ragged, distressed sigh, as the girl hurriedly began fixing both of them a drink.

The FM radio in the car yammered, ". . . grieves at the stricken turn of events precipitating out of an unheralded . . ."

"Official nonsense babble," Crayne said, shutting off the radio. He and Benz were having trouble finding the house, having been there only once before. It struck Crayne that this was a somewhat informal way of convening a conference of this importance, meeting at Addison's chick's pad out here in the boondocks of Ojai. On the other hand, they wouldn't be pestered by the curious. And they probably didn't have much time. But that was hard to say; about that no one knew for sure.

The hills on both sides of the road had once been forests, Crayne observed. Now housing tracts and their melted, irregular, plastic roads marred every rise in sight. "I'll bet this was nice once," he said to Benz, who was driving.

"The Los Padres National Forest is near here," Benz said. "I got lost in there when I was eight. For hours I was sure a rattler would get me. Every stick was a snake."

"The rattler's got you now," Crayne said.

"All of us," Benz said.

"You know," Crayne said, "it's a hell of an experience to be dead."

"Speak for yourself."

"But technically—"

"If you listen to the radio and TV." Benz turned toward him, his big gnome face bleak with admonishing sternness. "We're no more dead than anyone else on the planet. The difference for us is that our death date is in the past, whereas everyone else's is set somewhere at an uncertain time in the future. Actually, some people have it pretty damn well set, like people in cancer wards; they're as certain as we are. More so. For example, how long can we stay here before we go back? We have a margin, a latitude that a terminal cancer victim doesn't have."

Crayne said cheerfully, "The next thing you'll be telling us to cheer us up is that we're in no pain."

"Addi is. I watched him lurch off earlier today. He's got it psychosomatically—made it into a physical complaint. Like God's kneeling on his neck; you know, carrying a much-too-great burden that's unfair, only he won't complain out loud . . . just points now and then at the nail hole in his hand." He grinned.

"Addi has got more to live for than we do."

"Every man has more to live for than any other man. I don't have a cute chick to sleep with, but I'd like to see the semis rolling along Riverside Freeway at sunset a few more times. It's not what you have to live for; it's that you want to live to see it, to be there— that's what is so damn sad."

They rode on in silence.

In the quiet living room of the girl's house the three tempunauts sat around smoking, taking it easy; Addison Doug thought to himself that the girl looked unusually foxy and desirable in her stretched-tight white sweater and micro-skirt and he wished, wistfully, that she looked a little less interesting. He could not really afford to get embroiled in such stuff, at this point. He was too tired.

"Does she know," Benz said, indicating the girl, "what this is all about? I mean, can we talk openly? It won't wipe her out?"

"I haven't explained it to her yet," Addison said.

"You goddam well better," Crayne said.

"What is it?" the girl said, stricken, sitting upright with one hand directly between her breasts. As if clutching at a religious artifact that isn't there, Addison thought.

"We got snuffed on reentry," Benz said. He was, really, the cruelest of the three. Or at least the most blunt. "You see, Miss . . ."

"Hawkins," the girl whispered.

"Glad to meet you, Miss Hawkins." Benz surveyed her in his cold, lazy fashion. "You have a first name?"

"Merry Lou."

"Okay, Merry Lou," Benz said. To the other two men he observed, "Sounds like the name a waitress has stitched on her blouse. Merry Lou's my name and I'll be serving you dinner and breakfast and lunch and dinner and breakfast for the next few days or however long it is before you all give up and go back to your own time; that'll be fifty-three dollars and eight cents, please, not including tip. And I hope y'all never come back, y'hear?" His voice had begun to shake; his cigarette, too. "Sorry, Miss Hawkins," he said then. "We're all screwed up by the implosion at reentry. As soon as we got here in ETA we learned about it. We've known longer than anyone else; we knew as soon as we hit Emergence Time."

"But there's nothing we could do," Crayne said.

"There's nothing anyone can do," Addison said to her, and put his arm around her. It felt like a déjà vu thing but then it hit him. We're in a closed time loop, he thought, we keep going through this again and again, trying to solve the reentry problem, each time imagining it's the first time, the only time . . . and never succeeding. Which attempt is this? Maybe the millionth; we have sat here a million times, raking the same facts over and over again and getting nowhere. He felt bone-weary, thinking that. And he felt a sort of vast philosophical hate toward all other men, who did not have this enigma to deal with. We all go to one place, he thought, as the Bible says. But . . . for the three of us, we have been there already. Are lying there now. So it's wrong to ask us to stand around on the surface of Earth afterward and argue and worry about it and try to figure out what malfunctioned. That should be, rightly, for our heirs to do. We've had enough already.

He did not say this aloud, though—for their sake.

"Maybe you bumped into something," the girl said.

Glancing at the others, Benz said sardonically, "Maybe we 'bumped into something.'"

"The TV commentators kept saying that," Merry Lou said, "about the hazard in reentry of being out of phase spatially and colliding right down to the molecular level with tangent objects, any one of which—" She gestured. "You know. 'No two objects can occupy the same space at the same time.' So everything blew up, for that reason." She glanced around questioningly.

"That is the major risk factor," Crayne acknowledged. "At least theoretically, as Dr. Fein at Planning calculated when they got into the hazard question. But we had a variety of safety locking devices provided that functioned automatically. Reentry couldn't occur unless these assists had stabilized us spatially so we would not overlap. Of course, all those devices, in sequence, might have failed. One after the other. I was watching my feedback metric scopes on launch, and they agreed, every one of them, that we were phased properly at that time. And I heard no warning tones. Saw none, neither." He grimaced. "At least it didn't happen then."

Suddenly Benz said, "Do you realize that our next of kin are now rich? All our Federal and commercial life-insurance payoff. Our 'next of kin'—God forbid, that's us, I guess. We can apply for tens of thousands of dollars, cash on the line. Walk into our brokers' offices and say, 'I'm dead; lay the heavy bread on me.'"

Addison Doug was thinking, The public memorial services. That they have planned, after the autopsies. That long line of black-draped Cads going down Pennsylvania Avenue, with all the government dignitaries and double-domed scientist types—*and we'll be there*. Not once but twice. Once in the oak hand-rubbed brass-fitted flag-draped caskets, but also . . . maybe riding in open limos, waving at the crowds of mourners.

"The ceremonies," he said aloud.

The others stared at him, angrily, not comprehending. And then, one by one, they understood; he saw it on their faces.

"No," Benz grated. "That's—impossible."

Crayne shook his head emphatically. "They'll order us to be there, and we will be. Obeying orders."

"Will we have to *smile*?" Addison said. "To fucking *smile*?"

"No," General Toad said slowly, his great wattled head shivering about on his broomstick neck, the color of his skin dirty and mottled, as if the mass of decorations on his stiff-board collar had started part of him decaying away. "You are not to smile, but on the contrary are to adopt a properly grief-stricken manner. In keeping with the national mood of sorrow at this time."

"That'll be hard to do," Crayne said.

The Russian chrononaut showed no response; his thin beaked face, narrow within his translating earphones, remained strained with concern.

"The nation," General Toad said, "will become aware of your presence among us once more for this brief interval; cameras of all major TV networks will pan up to you without warning, and at the same time, the various commentators have been instructed to tell their audiences something like the following." He got out a piece of typed material, put on his glasses, cleared his throat, and said, "'We seem to be focusing on three figures riding together. Can't quite make them out. Can you?'" General Toad lowered the paper. "At this point they'll interrogate their colleagues extempore. Finally they'll exclaim, 'Why, Roger,' or Walter or Ned, as the case may be, according to the individual network—"

"Or Bill," Crayne said. "In case it's the Bufonidae network, down there in the swamp."

General Toad ignored him. "They will severally exclaim, 'Why Roger I believe we're seeing the three tempunauts themselves!

Does this indeed mean that somehow the difficulty—?' And then the colleague commentator says in his somewhat more somber voice, 'What we're seeing at this time, I think, David,' or Henry or Pete or Ralph, whichever it is, 'consists of mankind's first verified glimpse of what the technical people refer to as Emergence Time Activity or ETA. Contrary to what might seem to be the case at first sight, these are *not*—repeat, not—our three valiant tempunauts as such, as we would ordinarily experience them, but more likely picked up by our cameras as the three of them are temporarily suspended in their voyage to the future, which we initially had reason to hope would take place in a time continuum roughly a hundred years from now . . . but it would seem that they somehow undershot and are here now, at this moment, which of course is, as we know, our present.' "

Addison Doug closed his eyes and thought, Crayne will ask him if he can be panned up on by the TV cameras holding a balloon and eating cotton candy. I think we're all going nuts from this, all of us. And then he wondered, How many times have we gone through this idiotic exchange?

I can't prove it, he thought wearily. But I know it's true. We've sat here, done this minuscule scrabbling, listened to and said all this crap, many times. He shuddered. Each rinky-dink word . . .

"What's the matter?" Benz said acutely.

The Soviet chrononaut spoke up for the first time. "What is the maximum interval of ETA possible to your three-man team? And how large a per cent has been exhausted by now?"

After a pause Crayne said, "They briefed us on that before we came in here today. We've consumed approximately one-half of our maximum total ETA interval."

"However," General Toad rumbled, "we have scheduled the Day of National Mourning to fall within the expected period remaining to them of ETA time. This required us to speed up the autopsy and other forensic findings, but in view of public sentiment, it was felt . . ."

The autopsy, Addison Doug thought, and again he shuddered; this time he could not keep his thoughts within himself and he said, "Why don't we adjourn this nonsense meeting and drop down to pathology and view a few tissue sections enlarged and in color, and maybe we'll brainstorm a couple of vital concepts that'll aid medical science in its quest for explanations? Explanations— that's what we need. Explanations for problems that don't exist yet; we can develop the problems later." He paused. "Who agrees?"

"I'm not looking at my spleen up there on the screen," Benz said. "I'll ride in the parade but I won't participate in my own autopsy."

"You could distribute microscopic purple-stained slices of your own gut to the mourners along the way," Crayne said. "They could provide each of us with a doggy bag; right, General? We can strew tissue sections like confetti. I still think we should smile."

"I have researched all the memoranda about smiling," General Toad said, riffling the pages stacked before him, "and the consensus at policy is that smiling is not in accord with national sentiment. So that issue must be ruled closed. As far as your participating in the autopsical procedures which are now in progress—"

"We're missing out as we sit here," Crayne said to Addison Doug. "I always miss out."

Ignoring him, Addison addressed the Soviet chrononaut. "Officer N. Gauki," he said into his microphone, dangling on his chest, "what in your mind is the greatest terror facing a time traveler? That there will be an implosion due to coincidence on reentry, such as has occurred in our launch? Or did other traumatic obsessions bother you and your comrade during your own brief but highly successful time flight?"

N. Gauki, after a pause, answered, "R. Plenya and I exchanged views at several informal times. I believe I can speak for us both when I respond to your question by emphasizing our perpetual fear that we had inadvertently entered a closed time loop and would never break out."

"You'd repeat it forever?" Addison Doug asked.

"Yes, Mr. A. Doug," the chrononaut said, nodding somberly.

A fear that he had never experienced before overcame Addison Doug. He turned helplessly to Benz and muttered, "Shit." They gazed at each other.

"I really don't believe this is what happened," Benz said to him in a low voice, putting his hand on Doug's shoulder; he gripped hard, the grip of friendship. "We just imploded on reentry, that's all. Take it easy."

"Could we adjourn soon?" Addison Doug said in a hoarse, strangling voice, half rising from his chair. He felt the room and the people in it rushing in at him, suffocating him. Claustrophobia, he realized. Like when I was in grade school, when they flashed a surprise test on our teaching machines, and I saw I couldn't pass it. "Please," he said simply, standing. They were all looking at him, with different expressions. The Russian's face was especially sympathetic, and deeply lined with care. Addison wished—"I want to go home," he said to them all, and felt stupid.

He was drunk. It was late at night, at a bar on Hollywood Boulevard; fortunately, Merry Lou was with him, and he was having a good time. Everyone was telling him so, anyhow. He clung to Merry Lou and said, "The great unity in life, the supreme unity and meaning, is man and woman. Their absolute unity; right?"

"I know," Merry Lou said. "We studied that in class." Tonight, at his request, Merry Lou was a small blonde girl, wearing purple bellbottoms and high heels and an open midriff blouse. Earlier she had had a lapis lazuli in her navel, but during dinner at Ting Ho's it had popped out and been lost. The owner of the restaurant had promised to keep on searching for it, but Merry Lou had been gloomy ever since. It was, she said, symbolic. But of what she did not say. Or anyhow he could not remember; maybe that was it. She had told him what it meant, and he had forgotten.

An elegant young black at a nearby table, with an Afro and striped vest and overstuffed red tie, had been staring at Addison for some time. He obviously wanted to come over to their table but was afraid to; meanwhile, he kept on staring.

"Did you ever get the sensation," Addison said to Merry Lou, "that you knew exactly what was about to happen? What someone was going to say? Word for word? Down to the slightest detail. As if you had already lived through it once before?"

"Everybody gets into that space," Merry Lou said. She sipped a Bloody Mary.

The black rose and walked toward them. He stood by Addison. "I'm sorry to bother you, sir."

Addison said to Merry Lou, "He's going to say, 'Don't I know you from somewhere? Didn't I see you on TV?'"

"That was precisely what I intended to say," the black said.

Addison said, "You undoubtedly saw my picture on page forty-six of the current issue of *Time*, the section on new medical discoveries. I'm the G.P. from a small town in Iowa catapulted to fame by my invention of a widespread, easily available cure for eternal life. Several of the big pharmaceutical houses are already bidding on my vaccine."

"That might have been where I saw your picture," the black said, but he did not appear convinced. Nor did he appear drunk; he eyed Addison Doug intensely. "May I seat myself with you and the lady?"

"Sure," Addison Doug said. He now saw, in the man's hand, the ID of the U.S. security agency that had ridden herd on the project from the start.

"Mr. Doug," the security agent said as he seated himself beside Addison, "you really shouldn't be here shooting off your mouth like this. If I recognized you some other dude might and break out. It's all classified until the Day of Mourning. Technically, you're in violation of a Federal Statute by being here; did you realize that? I should haul you in. But this is a difficult situation; we don't want to do something uncool and make a scene. Where are your two colleagues?"

"At my place," Merry Lou said. She had obviously not seen the ID. "Listen," she said sharply to the agent, "why don't you get lost? My husband here has been through a grueling ordeal, and this is his only chance to unwind."

Addison looked at the man. "I knew what you were going to say before you came over here." Word for word, he thought. I am right, and Benz is wrong, and this will keep happening, this replay.

"Maybe," the security agent said, "I can induce you to go back to Miss Hawkins's place voluntarily. Some info arrived"—he tapped the tiny earphone in his right ear—"just a few minutes ago, to all of us, to deliver to you, marked urgent, if we located you. At the launchsite ruins . . . they've been combing through the rubble, you know?"

"I know," Addison said.

"They think they have their first clue. Something was brought back by one of you. From ETA, over and above what you took, in violation of all your prelaunch training."

"Let me ask you this," Addison Doug said. "Suppose somebody does see me? Suppose somebody does recognize me? So what?"

"The public believes that even though reentry failed, the flight into time, the first American time-travel launch, was successful. Three U.S. tempunauts were thrust a hundred years into the future— roughly twice as far as the Soviet launch of last year. That you only went a *week* will be less of a shock if it's believed that you three chose deliberately to remanifest at this continuum because you wished to attend, in fact felt compelled to attend—"

"We wanted to be in the parade," Addison interrupted. "Twice."

"You were drawn to the dramatic and somber spectacle of your own funeral procession, and will be glimpsed there by the alert camera crews of all major networks. Mr. Doug, really, an awful lot of high-level planning and expense have gone into this to help correct a dreadful situation; trust us, believe me. It'll be easier on the public, and that's vital, if there's ever to be another U.S. time shot. And that is, after all, what we all want."

Addison Doug stared at him. "We want what?"

Uneasily, the security agent said, "To take further trips into time. As you have done. Unfortunately, you yourself cannot ever do so again, because of the tragic implosion and death of the three of you. But other tempunauts—"

"We want what? Is that what we want?" Addison's voice rose; people at nearby tables were watching now. Nervously.

"Certainly," the agent said. "And keep your voice down."

"I don't want that," Addison said. "I want to stop. To stop forever. To just lie in the ground, in the dust, with everyone else. To see no more summers—the *same* summer."

"Seen one, you've seen them all," Merry Lou said hysterically. "I think he's right, Addi; we should get out of here. You've had too many drinks, and it's late, and this news about the—"

Addison broke in, "What was brought back? How much extra mass?"

The security agent said, "Preliminary analysis shows that machinery weighing about one hundred pounds was lugged back into the time-field of the module and picked up along with you. This much mass—" The agent gestured. "That blew up the pad right on the spot. It couldn't begin to compensate for that much more than had occupied its open area at launch time."

"Wow!" Merry Lou said, eyes wide. "Maybe somebody sold one of you a quadraphonic phono for a dollar ninety-eight including fifteen-inch air-suspension speakers and a lifetime supply of Neil Diamond records." She tried to laugh, but failed; her eyes dimmed over. "Addi," she whispered, "I'm sorry. But it's sort of— weird. I mean, it's absurd; you all were briefed, weren't you, about your return weight? You weren't even to add so much as a piece of paper to what you took. I even saw Dr. Fein demonstrating the reasons on TV. And one of you hoisted a hundred pounds of machinery into that field? You must have been trying to self-destruct, to do that!" Tears slid from her eyes; one tear rolled out onto her nose and hung there. He reached reflexively to wipe it away, as if helping a little girl rather than a grown one.

"I'll fly you to the analysis site," the security agent said, standing up. He and Addison helped Merry Lou to her feet; she trembled as she stood a moment, finishing her Bloody Mary. Addison felt acute sorrow for her, but then, almost at once, it passed. He wondered why. One can weary even of that, he conjectured. Of caring for someone. If it goes on too long—on and on. Forever. And, at last, even after that, into something no one before, not God Himself, maybe, had ever had to suffer and in the end, for all His great heart, succumb to.

As they walked through the crowded bar toward the street, Addison Doug said to the security agent, "Which one of us—"

"They know which one," the agent said as he held the door to the street open for Merry Lou. The agent stood, now, behind

Addison, signaling for a gray Federal car to land at the red parking area. Two other security agents, in uniform, hurried toward them.

"Was it me?" Addison Doug asked.

"You better believe it," the security agent said.

The funeral procession moved with aching solemnity down Pennsylvania Avenue, three flag-draped caskets and dozens of black limousines passing between rows of heavily coated, shivering mourners. A low haze hung over the day, gray outlines of buildings faded into the rain-drenched murk of the Washington March day.

Scrutinizing the lead Cadillac through prismatic binoculars, TV's top news and public-events commentator, Henry Cassidy, droned on at his vast unseen audience, ". . . sad recollections of that earlier train among the wheatfields carrying the coffin of Abraham Lincoln back to burial and the nation's capital. And what a sad day this is, and what appropriate weather, with its dour overcast and sprinkles!" In his monitor he saw the zoomar lens pan up on the fourth Cadillac, as it followed those with the caskets of the dead tempunauts.

His engineer tapped him on the arm.

"We appear to be focusing on three unfamiliar figures so far not identified, riding together," Henry Cassidy said into his neck mike, nodding agreement. "So far I'm unable to quite make them out. Are your location and vision any better from where you're placed, Everett?" he inquired of his colleague and pressed the button that notified Everett Branton to replace him on the air.

"Why, Henry," Branton said in a voice of growing excitement, "I believe we're actually eyewitness to the three American tempunauts as they remanifest themselves on their historic journey into the future!"

"Does this signify," Cassidy said, "that somehow they have managed to solve and overcome the—"

"Afraid not, Henry," Branton said in his slow, regretful voice. "What we're eyewitnessing to our complete surprise consists of the Western world's first verified glimpse of what the technical people refer to as Emergence Time Activity."

"Ah, yes, ETA," Cassidy said brightly, reading it off the official script the Federal authorities had handed to him before air time.

"Right, Henry. Contrary to what *might* seem to be the case at first sight, these are not—repeat *not*—our three brave tempunauts as such, as we would ordinarily experience them—"

"I grasp it now, Everett," Cassidy broke in excitedly, since his authorized script read CASS BREAKS IN EXCITEDLY. "Our three tempunauts have momentarily been suspended in their historic voyage to the future, which we believe will span across a time-continuum roughly a century from now . . . It would seem that the overwhelming grief and drama of this unanticipated day of mourning has caused them to—"

"Sorry to interrupt, Henry," Everett Branton said, "but I think, since the procession has momentarily halted on its slow march forward, that we might be able to—"

"No!" Cassidy said, as a note was handed him in a swift scribble, reading: *Do not interview nauts. Urgent. Dis. previous inst.* "I don't think we're going to be able to . . ." he continued, ". . . to speak briefly with tempunauts Benz, Crayne, and Doug, as you had hoped, Everett. As we had all briefly hoped to." He wildly waved the boom-mike back; it had already begun to swing out expectantly toward the stopped Cadillac. Cassidy shook his head violently at the mike technician and his engineer.

Perceiving the boom-mike swinging at them Addison Doug stood up in the back of the open Cadillac. Cassidy groaned. He wants to speak, he realized. Didn't they reinstruct *him*? Why am I the only one they get across to? Other boom-mikes representing other networks plus radio station interviewers on foot now were rushing out to thrust up their microphones into the faces of the three tempunauts, especially Addison Doug's. Doug was already beginning to speak, in response to a question shouted up to him by a reporter. With his boom-mike off, Cassidy couldn't hear the question, nor Doug's answer. With reluctance, he signaled for his own boom-mike to trigger on.

". . . before," Doug was saying loudly.

"In what manner, 'All this has happened before'?" the radio reporter, standing close to the car, was saying.

"I mean," U.S. tempunaut Addison Doug declared, his face red and strained, "that I have stood here in this spot and said again and again, and all of you have viewed this parade and our deaths at reentry endless times, a closed cycle of trapped time which must be broken."

"Are you seeking," another reporter jabbered up at Addison Doug, "for a solution to the reentry implosion disaster which can be applied in retrospect so that when you do return to the past you will be able to correct the malfunction and avoid the tragedy which cost—or for you three, will cost—your lives?"

Tempunaut Benz said, "We are doing that, yes."

"Trying to ascertain the cause of the violent implosion and eliminate the cause before we return," tempunaut Crayne added, nodding. "We have learned already that, for reasons unknown, a mass of nearly one hundred pounds of miscellaneous Volkswagen motor parts, including cylinders, the head . . ."

This is awful, Cassidy thought. "This is amazing!" he said aloud, into his neck mike. "The already tragically deceased U.S. tempunauts, with a determination that could emerge only from the rigorous training and discipline to which they were subjected—and we wondered why at the time but can clearly see why now—have already analyzed the mechanical slip-up responsible, evidently, for their own deaths, and have begun the laborious process of sifting through and eliminating causes of that slip-up so that they can return to their original launch site and reenter without mishap."

"One wonders," Branton mumbled onto the air and into his feedback earphone, "what the consequences of this alteration of the near past will be. If in reentry they do *not* implode and are *not* killed, then they will not—well, it's too complex for me, Henry, these time paradoxes that Dr. Fein at the Time Extrusion Labs in Pasadena has so frequently and eloquently brought to our attention."

Into all the microphones available, of all sorts, tempunaut Addison Doug was saying, more quietly now, "We must not eliminate the cause of reentry implosion. The only way out of this trap is for us to die. Death is the only solution for this. For the three of us."

He was interrupted as the procession of Cadillacs began to move forward.

Shutting off his mike momentarily, Henry Cassidy said to his engineer, "Is he nuts?"

"Only time will tell," his engineer said in a hard-to-hear voice.

"An extraordinary moment in the history of the United States's involvement in time travel," Cassidy said, then, into his now live mike. "Only time will tell—if you will pardon the inadvertent pun—whether tempunaut Doug's cryptic remarks uttered impromptu at this moment of supreme suffering for him, as in a sense to a lesser degree it is for all of us, are the words of a man deranged by grief or an accurate insight into the macabre dilemma that in theoretical terms we knew all along might eventually confront—confront and strike down with its lethal blow—a time-travel launch, either ours or the Russians'."

He segued, then, to a commercial.

"You know," Branton's voice muttered in his ear, not on the air but just to the control room and to him, "if he's right they ought to let the poor bastards die."

"They ought to release them," Cassidy agreed. "My God, the way Doug looked and talked, you'd imagine he'd gone through this for a thousand years and then some! I wouldn't be in his shoes for anything."

"I'll bet you fifty bucks," Branton said, "they have gone through this before. Many times."

"Then we have, too," Cassidy said.

Rain fell now, making all the lined-up mourners shiny. Their faces, their eyes, even their clothes—everything glistened in wet reflections of broken, fractured light, bent and sparkling, as, from gathering gray formless layers above them, the day darkened.

"Are we on the air?" Branton asked.

Who knows? Cassidy thought. He wished the day would end.

The Soviet chrononaut N. Gauki lifted both hands impassionedly and spoke to the Americans across the table from him in a voice of extreme urgency. "It is the opinion of myself and my colleague R. Plenya, who for his pioneering achievements in time travel has been certified a Hero of the Soviet People, and rightly so, that based on our own experience and on theoretical material developed both in your own academic circles and in the Soviet Academy of Sciences of the USSR, we believe that tempunaut A. Doug's fears may be justified. And his deliberate destruction of himself and his teammates at reentry, by hauling a huge mass of auto back with him from ETA, in violation of his orders, should be regarded as the act of a desperate man with no other means of escape. Of course, the decision is up to you. We have only advisory position in this matter."

Addison Doug played with his cigarette lighter on the table and did not look up. His ears hummed, and he wondered what that meant. It had an electronic quality. Maybe we're within the module again, he thought. But he didn't perceive it; he felt the reality of the people around him, the table, the blue plastic lighter between his fingers. No smoking in the module during reentry, he thought. He put the lighter carefully away in his pocket.

"We've developed no concrete evidence whatsoever," General Toad said, "that a closed time loop has been set up. There's only the subjective feelings of fatigue on the part of Mr. Doug. Just his belief that he's done all this repeatedly. As he says, it is very probably psychological in nature." He rooted, piglike, among the papers before him. "I have a report, not disclosed to the media, from four psychiatrists at Yale on his psychological makeup. Although unusually stable, there is a tendency toward cyclothymia on his part, culminating in acute depression. This naturally was taken into account long before the launch, but it was calculated that the joyful qualities of the two others in the team would offset this functionally. Anyhow, that depressive tendency in him is exceptionally high, now." He held the paper out, but no one at the table accepted it. "Isn't it true, Dr. Fein," he said, "that an acutely depressed person experiences time in a peculiar way, that is, circular time, time repeating itself, getting nowhere, around and around? The person gets so psychotic that he refuses to let go of the past. Reruns it in his head constantly."

"But you see," Dr. Fein said, "this subjective sensation of being trapped is perhaps all we would have." This was the research physicist whose basic work had laid the theoretical foundation for the project. "If a closed loop did unfortunately lock into being."

"The general," Addison Doug said, "is using words he doesn't understand."

"I researched the one I was unfamiliar with," General Toad said. "The technical psychiatric terms . . . I know what they mean."

To Addison Doug, Benz said, "Where'd you get all those VW parts, Addi?"

"I don't have them yet," Addison Doug said.

"Probably picked up the first junk he could lay his hands on," Crayne said. "Whatever was available, just before we started back."

"Will start back," Addison Doug corrected.

"Here are my instructions to the three of you," General Toad said. "You are not in any way to attempt to cause damage or implosion or malfunction during reentry, either by lugging back extra mass or by any other method that enters your mind. You are to return as scheduled and in replica of the prior simulations. This especially applies to you, Mr. Doug." The phone by his right arm buzzed. He frowned, picked up the receiver. An interval passed, and then he scowled deeply and set the receiver back down, loudly.

"You've been overruled," Dr. Fein said.

"Yes, I have," General Toad said. "And I must say at this time that I am personally glad because my decision was an unpleasant one."

"Then we can arrange for implosion at reentry," Benz said after a pause.

"The three of you are to make the decision," General Toad said. "Since it involves your lives. It's been entirely left up to you. Whichever way you want it. If you're convinced you're in a closed time loop, and you believe a massive implosion at reentry will abolish it—" He ceased talking, as tempunaut Doug rose to his feet. "Are you going to make another speech, Doug?" he said.

"I just want to thank everyone involved," Addison Doug said. "For letting us decide." He gazed haggard-faced and wearily around at all the individuals seated at the table. "I really appreciate it."

"You know," Benz said slowly, "blowing us up at reentry could add nothing to the chances of abolishing a closed loop. In fact that could do it, Doug."

"Not if it kills us all," Crayne said.

"You agree with Addi?" Benz said.

"Dead is dead," Crayne said. "I've been pondering it. What other way is more likely to get us out of this? Than if we're dead? What possible other way?"

"You may be in no loop," Dr. Fein pointed out.

"But we may be," Crayne said.

Doug, still on his feet, said to Crayne and Benz, "Could we include Merry Lou in our decision-making?"

"Why?" Benz said.

"I can't think too clearly anymore," Doug said. "Merry Lou can help me; I depend on her."

"Sure," Crayne said. Benz, too, nodded.

General Toad examined his wristwatch stoically and said, "Gentlemen, this concludes our discussion."

Soviet chrononaut Gauki removed his headphones and neck mike and hurried toward the three U.S. tempunauts, his hand extended; he was apparently saying something in Russian, but none of them could understand it. They moved away somberly, clustering close.

"In my opinion you're nuts, Addi," Benz said. "But it would appear that I'm the minority now."

"If he *is* right," Crayne said, "if—one chance in a billion—if we are going back again and again forever, that would justify it."

"Could we go see Merry Lou?" Addison Doug said. "Drive over to her place now?"

"She's waiting outside," Crayne said.

Striding up to stand beside the three tempunauts, General Toad said, "You know, what made the determination go the way it did was the public reaction to how you, Doug, looked and behaved during the funeral procession. The NSC advisors came to the conclusion that the public would, like you, rather be certain it's over for all of you. That it's more of a relief to them to know you're free of your mission than to save the project and obtain a perfect reentry. I guess you really made a lasting impression on them, Doug.

That whining you did." He walked away, then, leaving the three of them standing there alone.

"Forget him," Crayne said to Addison Doug. "Forget everyone like him. We've got to do what we have to."

"Merry Lou will explain it to me," Doug said. She would know what to do, what would be right.

"I'll go get her," Crayne said, "and after that the four of us can drive somewhere, maybe to her place, and decide what to do. Okay?"

"Thank you," Addison Doug said, nodding; he glanced around for her hopefully, wondering where she was. In the next room, perhaps, somewhere close. "I appreciate that," he said.

Benz and Crayne eyed each other. He saw that, but did not know what it meant. He knew only that he needed someone, Merry Lou most of all, to help him understand what the situation was. And what to finalize on to get them out of it.

Merry Lou drove them north from Los Angeles in the superfast lane of the freeway toward Ventura, and after that inland to Ojai. The four of them said very little. Merry Lou drove well, as always; leaning against her, Addison Doug felt himself relax into a temporary sort of peace.

"There's nothing like having a chick drive you," Crayne said, after many miles had passed in silence.

"It's an aristocratic sensation," Benz murmured. "To have a woman do the driving. Like you're nobility being chauffeured."

Merry Lou said, "Until she runs into something. Some big slow object."

Addison Doug said, "When you saw me trudging up to your place . . . up the redwood round path the other day. What did you think? Tell me honestly."

"You looked," the girl said, "as if you'd done it many times. You looked worn and tired and—ready to die. At the end." She hesitated. "I'm sorry, but that's how you looked, Addi. I thought to myself, he knows the way too well."

"Like I'd done it too many times."

"Yes," she said.

"Then you vote for implosion," Addison Doug said.

"Well—"

"Be honest with me," he said.

Merry Lou said, "Look in the back seat. The box on the floor."

With a flashlight from the glove compartment the three men examined the box. Addison Doug, with fear, saw its contents. VW motor parts, rusty and worn. Still oily.

"I got them from behind a foreign-car garage near my place," Merry Lou said. "On the way to Pasadena. The first junk I saw that seemed as if it'd be heavy enough. I had heard them say on TV at launch time that anything over fifty pounds up to—"

"It'll do it," Addison Doug said. "It did do it."

"So there's no point in going to your place," Crayne said. "It's decided. We might as well head south toward the module. And initiate the procedure for getting out of ETA. And back to reentry." His voice was heavy but evenly pitched. "Thanks for your vote, Miss Hawkins."

She said, "You are all so tired."

"I'm not," Benz said. "I'm mad. Mad as hell."

"At me?" Addison Doug said.

"I don't know," Benz said. "It's just—Hell." He lapsed into brooding silence then. Hunched over, baffled and inert. Withdrawn as far as possible from the others in the car.

At the next freeway junction she turned the car south. A sense of freedom seemed now to fill her, and Addison Doug felt some of the weight, the fatigue, ebbing already.

On the wrist of each of the three men the emergency alert receiver buzzed its warning tone; they all started.

"What's that mean?" Merry Lou said, slowing the car.

"We're to contact General Toad by phone as soon as possible," Crayne said. He pointed. "There's a Standard Station over there; take the next exit, Miss Hawkins. We can phone in from there."

A few minutes later Merry Lou brought her car to a halt beside the outdoor phone booth. "I hope it's not bad news," she said.

"I'll talk first," Doug said, getting out. Bad news, he thought with labored amusement. Like what? He crunched stiffly across to the phone booth, entered, shut the door behind him, dropped in a dime, and dialed the toll-free number.

"Well, do I have news!" General Toad said when the operator had put him on the line. "It's a good thing we got hold of you. Just a minute—I'm going to let Dr. Fein tell you this himself. You're more apt to believe him than me." Several clicks, and then Dr. Fein's reedy, precise, scholarly voice, but intensified by urgency.

"What's the bad news?" Addison Doug said.

"Not bad, necessarily," Dr. Fein said. "I've had computations run since our discussion, and it would appear—by that I mean it is statistically probable but still unverified for a certainty—that you are right, Addison. You are in a closed time loop."

Addison Doug exhaled raggedly. You nowhere autocratic mother, he thought. You probably knew all along.

"However," Dr. Fein said excitedly, stammering a little, "I also calculate—we jointly do, largely through Cal Tech—that the greatest likelihood of maintaining the loop is to implode on reentry. Do you understand, Addison? If you lug all those rusty VW parts back and implode, then your statistical chance of closing the loop forever is greater than if you simply reenter and all goes well."

Addison Doug said nothing.

"In fact, Addi—and this is the severe part that I have to stress—implosion at reentry, especially a massive, calculated one of the sort we seem to see shaping up—do you grasp all this, Addi? Am I getting through to you? For Chrissake, Addi? Virtually *guarantees* the locking in of an absolutely unyielding loop such as you've got in mind. Such as we've all been worried about from the start." A pause. "Addi? Are you there?"

Addison Doug said, "I want to die."

"That's your exhaustion from the loop. God knows how many repetitions there've been already of the three of you—"

"No," he said and started to hang up.

"Let me speak with Benz and Crayne," Dr. Fein said rapidly. "Please, before you go ahead with reentry. Especially Benz; I'd like to speak with him in particular. Please, Addison. For their sake; your almost total exhaustion has—"

He hung up. Left the phone booth, step by step.

As he climbed back into the car, he heard their two alert receivers still buzzing. "General Toad said the automatic call for us would keep your two receivers doing that for a while," he said. And shut the car door after him. "Let's take off."

"Doesn't he want to talk to us?" Benz said.

Addison Doug said, "General Toad wanted to inform us that they have a little something for us. We've been voted a special Congressional Citation for valor or some damn thing like that. A special medal they never voted anyone before. To be awarded posthumously."

"Well, hell—that's about the only way it can be awarded," Crayne said.

Merry Lou, as she started up the engine, began to cry.

"It'll be a relief," Crayne said presently, as they returned bumpily to the freeway, "when it's over."

It won't be long now, Addison Doug's mind declared.

On their wrists the emergency alert receivers continued to put out their combined buzzing.

"They will nibble you to death," Addison Doug said. "The endless wearing down by various bureaucratic voices."

The others in the car turned to gaze at him inquiringly, with uneasiness mixed with perplexity.

"Yeah," Crayne said. "These automatic alerts are really a nuisance." He sounded tired. As tired as I am, Addison Doug thought. And, realizing this, he felt better. It showed how right he was.

Great drops of water struck the windshield; it had now begun to rain. That pleased him too. It reminded him of that most exalted of all experiences within the shortness of his life: the funeral procession moving slowly down Pennsylvania Avenue, the flag-draped caskets. Closing his eyes he leaned back and felt good at last. And heard, all around him once again, the sorrow-bent people. And, in his head, dreamed of the special Congressional Medal. For weariness, he thought. A medal for being tired.

He saw in his head, himself in other parades too, and in the deaths of many. But really it was one death and one parade. Slow cars moving along the street in Dallas and with Dr. King as well . . . He saw himself return again and again, in his closed cycle of life,

to the national mourning that he could not and they could not forget. He would be there; they would always be there; it would
always be, and every one of them would return together again and
again forever. To the place, the moment, they wanted to be. The
event which meant the most to all of them.

This was his gift to them, the people, his country. He had
bestowed upon the world a wonderful burden. The dreadful and
weary miracle of eternal life.

Chapter Two

from A SCANNER DARKLY

"Gentlemen of the Anaheim Lions Club," the man at the microphone said, "we have a wonderful opportunity this afternoon, for, you see, the County of Orange has provided us with the chance to hear from—and then put questions to and of—an undercover narcotics agent from the Orange County Sheriff's Department." He beamed, this man wearing his pink waffle-fiber suit and wide plastic yellow tie and blue shirt and fake leather shoes; he was an overweight man, overaged as well, overhappy even when there was little or nothing to be happy about.

Watching him, the undercover narcotics agent felt nausea.

"Now, you will notice," the Lions Club host said, "that you can barely see this individual, who is seated directly to my right, because he is wearing what is called a scramble suit, which is the exact same suit he wears—and in fact must wear—during certain parts, in fact most, of his daily activities of law enforcement. Later he will explain why."

The audience, which mirrored the qualities of the host in every possible way, regarded the individual in his scramble suit.

"This man," the host declared, "whom we will call Fred, because this is the code name under which he reports the information he gathers, once within the scramble suit, cannot be identified by voice, or by even technological voiceprint, or by appearance. He looks, does he not, like a vague blur and nothing more? Am I right?" He let loose a great smile. His audience, appreciating that this was indeed funny, did a little smiling on their own.

The scramble suit was an invention of the Bell Laboratories, conjured up by accident by an employee named S. A. Powers. He had, a few years ago, been experimenting with disinhibiting substances affecting neural tissue, and one night, having administered to himself an IV injection considered safe and mildly euphoric, had experienced a disastrous drop in the GABA fluid of his brain. Subjectively, he had then witnessed lurid phosphene activity projected on the far wall of his bedroom, a frantically progressing montage of what, at the time, he imagined to be modern-day abstract paintings.

For about six hours, entranced, S. A. Powers had watched thousands of Picasso paintings replace one another at flash-cut speed, and then he had been treated to Paul Klees, more than the painter had painted during his entire lifetime. S. A. Powers, now viewing Modigliani paintings replace themselves at furious velocity, had conjectured (one needs a theory for everything) that the Rosicrucians were telepathically beaming pictures at him, probably boosted by microrelay systems of an advanced order; but then, when Kandinsky paintings began to harass him, he recalled that the main art museum at Leningrad specialized in just such nonobjective moderns, and decided that the Soviets were attempting telepathically to contact him.

In the morning he remembered that a drastic drop in the GABA fluid of the brain normally produced such phosphene activity; nobody was trying telepathically, with or without microwave boosting, to contact him. But it did give him the idea of the scramble suit. Basically, his design consisted of a multifaced quartz lens hooked to a miniaturized computer whose memory banks held up to a million and a half physiognomic fraction-representations of various people: men and women, children, with every variant encoded and then projected outward in all directions equally onto a superthin shroudlike membrane large enough to fit around an average human.

As the computer looped through its banks, it projected every conceivable eye color, hair color, shape and type of nose, formation of teeth, configuration of facial bone structure—the entire shroudlike membrane took on whatever physical characteristics were projected at any nanosecond, and then switched to the next. Just to make his scramble suit more effective, S. A. Powers programmed the computer to randomize the sequence of characteristics within each set. And to bring the cost down (the federal people always liked that), he found the source for the material of the membrane in a by-product of a large industrial firm already doing business with Washington.

In any case, the wearer of a scramble suit was Everyman and in every combination (up to combinations of a million and a half subbits) during the course of each hour. Hence, any description of him—or her—was meaningless. Needless to say, S. A. Powers had fed his own personal physiognomic characteristics into the computer units, so that, buried in the frantic permutation of qualities, his own surfaced and combined . . . on an average, he had calculated, of once each fifty years per suit, served up and reassembled, given enough time per suit. It was his closest claim to immortality.

"Let's hear it for the vague blur!" the host said loudly, and there was mass clapping.

In his scramble suit, Fred, who was also Robert Arctor, groaned and thought: This is terrible.

Once a month an undercover narcotics agent of the county was assigned at random to speak before bubblehead gatherings such as this. Today was his turn. Looking at his audience, he realized how much he detested straights. They thought this was all great. They were smiling. They were being entertained.

Maybe at this moment the virtually countless components of his scramble suit had served up S. A. Powers.

"But to be serious for just a moment," the host said, "this man here . . ." He paused, trying to remember.

"Fred," Bob Arctor said. S. A. Fred.

"Fred, yes." The host, invigorated, resumed, booming in the direction of his audience, "You see, Fred's voice is like one of those robot computer voices down in San Diego at the bank when you drive in, perfectly toneless and artificial. It leaves in our minds no characteristics, exactly as when he reports to his superiors in the

Orange County Drug Abuse, ah, Program." He paused meaning-fully. "You see, there is a dire risk for these police officers because the forces of dope, as we know, have penetrated with amazing skill into the various law-enforcement apparatuses throughout our nation, or may well have, according to most informed experts. So for the protection of these dedicated men, this scramble suit is nec-essary."

Slight applause for the scramble suit. And then expectant gazes at Fred, lurking within its membrane.

"But in his line of work in the field," the host added finally, as he moved away from the microphone to make room for Fred, "he, of course, does not wear this. He dresses like you or I, although, of course, in the hippie garb of those of the various subculture groups within which he bores in tireless fashion."

He motioned to Fred to rise and approach the microphone. Fred, Robert Arctor, had done this six times before, and he knew what to say and what was in store for him: the assorted degrees and kinds of asshole questions and opaque stupidity. The waste of time for him out of this, plus anger on his part, and a sense of futility each time, and always more so.

"If you saw me on the street," he said into the microphone, after the applause had died out, "you'd say, 'There goes a weirdo freak doper.' And you'd feel aversion and walk away."

Silence.

"I don't look like you," he said. "I can't afford to. My life depends on it." Actually, he did not look that different from them. And anyhow, he would have worn what he wore daily anyhow, job or not, life or not. He liked what he wore. But what he was saying had, by and large, been written by others and put before him to memorize. He could depart some, but they all had a standard for-mat they used. Introduced a couple of years ago by a gung-ho divi-sion chief, it had by now become writ.

He waited while that sank in.

"I am not going to tell you first," he said, "what I am attempt-ing to do as an undercover officer engaged in tracking down deal-ers and most of all the source of their illegal drugs in the streets of our cities and corridors of our schools, here in Orange County. I am going to tell you"—he paused, as they had trained him to do in PR class at the academy—"what I am afraid of," he finished.

That gaffed them; they had become all eyes.

"What I fear," he said, "night and day, is that our children, your children and my children . . ." Again he paused. "I have two," he said. Then, extra quietly, "Little ones, very little." And then he raised his voice emphatically. "But not too little to be addicted, calculatedly addicted, for profit, by those who would destroy this society." Another pause. "We do not know as yet," he continued presently, more calmly, "specifically who these men—or rather animals—are who prey on our young, as if in a wild jungle abroad, as in some foreign country, not ours. The identity of the purveyors of the poisons concocted of brain-destructive filth shot daily, orally taken daily, smoked daily by several million men and women—or rather, that were once men and women—is gradually being unraveled. But finally we will, before God, know for sure."

A voice from the audience: "Sock it to 'em!"

Another voice, equally enthusiastic: "Get the commies!"

Applause and reprise severally.

Robert Arctor halted. Stared at them, at the straights in their fat suits, their fat ties, their fat shoes, and he thought, Substance D can't destroy their brains; they have none.

"Tell it like it is," a slightly less emphatic voice called up, a woman's voice. Searching, Arctor made out a middle-aged lady, not so fat, her hands clasped anxiously.

"Each day," Fred, Robert Arctor, whatever, said, "this disease takes its toll of us. By the end of each passing day the flow of profits—and where they go we—" He broke off. For the life of him he could not dredge up the rest of the sentence, even though he had repeated it a million times, both in class and at previous lectures.

All in the large room had fallen silent.

"Well," he said, "it isn't the profits anyhow. It's something else. What you see happen."

They didn't notice any difference, he noticed, even though he had dropped the prepared speech and was wandering on, by himself, without help from the PR boys back at the Orange County

Civic Center. What difference anyhow? he thought. So what? What, really, do they know or care? The straights, he thought, live in their fortified huge apartment complexes guarded by their guards, ready to open fire on any and every doper who scales the wall with an empty pillow-case to rip off their piano and electric clock and razor and stereo that they haven't paid for anyhow, so he can get his fix, get the shit that if he doesn't he maybe dies, out-right flatout dies, of the pain and shock of withdrawal. But, he thought, when you're living inside looking safely out, and your wall is electrified and your guard is armed, why think about that?

"If you were a diabetic," he said, "and you didn't have money for a hit of insulin, would you steal to get the money? Or just die?"

Silence.

In the headphone of his scramble suit a tinny voice said, "I think you'd better go back to the prepared text, Fred. I really do advise it."

Into his throat mike, Fred, Robert Arctor, whatever, said, "I forget it." Only his superior at Orange County GHQ, which was not Mr. F, that is to say, Hank, could hear this. This was an anonymous superior, assigned to him only for this occasion.

"Riiiight," the official tinny prompter said in his earphone. "I'll read it to you. Repeat it after me, but try to get it to sound casual." Slight hesitation, riffling of pages. "Let's see . . . 'Each day the profits flow—where they go we—' That's about where you stopped."

"I've got a block against this stuff," Arctor said.

"'—will soon determine,'" his official prompter said, unheeding, "'and then retribution will swiftly follow. And at that moment I would not for the life of me be in their shoes.'"

"Do you know why I've got a block against this stuff?" Arctor said. "Because this is what gets people on dope." He thought, This is why you lurch off and become a doper, this sort of stuff. This is why you give up and leave. In disgust.

But then he looked once more out at his audience and realized that for them this was not so. This was the only way they could be reached. He was talking to nitwits. Mental simps. It had to be put in the same way it had been put in first grade: *A* is for Apple and the Apple is Round.

"*D,*" he said aloud to his audience, "is for Substance D. Which is for Dumbness and Despair and Desertion, the desertion of your friends from you, you from them, everyone from everyone, isolation and loneliness and hating and suspecting each other. *D,*" he said then, "is finally Death. Slow Death, we——" He halted. "We, the dopers," he said, "call it." His voice rasped and faltered. "As you probably know. Slow Death. From the head on down. Well, that's it." He walked back to his chair and reseated himself. In silence.

"You blew it," his superior the prompter said. "See me in my office when you get back. Room 430."

"Yes," Arctor said. "I blew it."

They were looking at him as if he had pissed on the stage before their eyes. Although he was not sure just why.

Striding to the mike, the Lions Club host said, "Fred asked me in advance of this lecture to make it primarily a question-and-answer forum, with only a short introductory statement by him. I forgot to mention that. All right"—he raised his right hand— "who first, people?"

Arctor suddenly got to his feet again, clumsily.

"It would appear that Fred has something more to add," the host said, beckoning to him.

Going slowly back over to the microphone, Arctor said, his head down, speaking with precision, "Just this. Don't kick their asses after they're on it. The users, the addicts. Half of them, most of them, especially the girls, didn't know what they were getting on or even that they were getting on anything at all. Just try to keep them, the people, any of us, from getting on it." He looked up briefly. "See, they dissolve some reds in a glass of wine, the pushers, I mean—they give the booze to a chick, an underage little chick, with eight to ten reds in it, and she passes out, and then they inject her with a mex hit, which is half heroin and half Substance D—" He broke off. "Thank you," he said.

A man called up, "How do we stop them, sir?"

"Kill the pushers," Arctor said, and walked back to his chair.

He did not feel like returning right away to the Orange County Civic Center and Room 430, so he wandered down one of the commercial streets of Anaheim, inspecting the McDonaldburger stands and car washes and gas stations and Pizza Huts and other marvels.

Roaming aimlessly along like this on the public street with all kinds of people, he always had a strange feeling as to who he was. As he had said to the Lions types there in the hall, he looked like a doper when out of his scramble suit; he conversed like a doper; those around him now no doubt took him to be a doper and reacted accordingly. Other dopers—See there, he thought; "other," for instance—gave him a "peace, brother" look, and the straights didn't.

You put on a bishop's robe and miter, he pondered, and walk around in that, and people bow and genuflect and like that, and try to kiss your ring, if not your ass, and pretty soon you're a bishop. So to speak. What is identity? he asked himself. Where does the act end? Nobody knows.

What really fouled up his sense of who and what he was came when the Man hassled him. When harness bulls, beat cops, or cops in general, any and all, for example, came cruising up slowly to the curb near him in an intimidating manner as he walked, scrutinized him at length with an intense, keen, metallic, blank stare, and then, often as not, evidently on whim, parked and beckoned him over.

"Okay, let's see your I.D.," the cop would say, reaching out; and then, as Arctor-Fred-Whatever-Godknew fumbled in his wallet pocket, the cop would yell at him, "Ever been ARRESTED?" Or, as a variant on that, adding, "BEFORE?" As if he were about to go into the bucket right then.

"What's the beef?" he usually said, if he said anything at all. A crowd naturally gathered. Most of them assumed he'd been nailed dealing on the corner. They grinned uneasily and waited to see what happened, although some of them, usually Chicanos or blacks or obvious heads, looked angry. And those that looked angry began after a short interval to be aware that they looked angry, and they changed that swiftly to impassive. Because everybody knew that anyone looking angry or uneasy—it didn't matter which—

around cops must have something to hide. The cops especially knew that, legend had it, and they hassled such persons automatically.

This time, however, no one bothered him. Many heads were in evidence; he was only one of many.

What am I actually? he asked himself. He wished, momentarily, for his scramble suit. Then, he thought, I could go on being a vague blur and passers-by, street people in general, would applaud. Let's hear it for the vague blur, he thought, doing a short rerun. What a way to get recognition. How, for instance, could they be sure it wasn't some other vague blur and not the right one? It could be somebody other than Fred inside, or another Fred, and they'd never know, not even when Fred opened his mouth and talked. They wouldn't really know then. They'd never know. It could be Al pretending to be Fred, for example. It could be anyone in there, it could even be empty. Down at Orange County GHQ they could be piping a voice to the scramble suit, animating it from the sheriff's office. Fred could in that case be anybody who happened to be at his desk that day and happened to pick up the script and the mike, or a composite of all sorts of guys at their desks.

But I guess what I said at the end, he thought, finishes off that. That wasn't anybody back in the office. The guys back in the office want to talk to me about that, as a matter of fact.

He didn't look forward to that, so he continued to loiter and delay, going nowhere, going everywhere. In Southern California it didn't make any difference anyhow where you went; there was always the same McDonaldburger place over and over, like a circular strip that turned past you as you pretended to go somewhere. And when finally you got hungry and went to the McDonaldburger place and bought a McDonald's hamburger, it was the one they sold you last time and the time before that and so forth, back to before you were born, and in addition bad people—liars—said it was made out of turkey gizzards anyhow.

They had by now, according to their sign, sold the same original burger fifty billion times. He wondered if it was to the same person. Life in Anaheim, California, was a commercial for itself, endlessly replayed. Nothing changed; it just spread out farther and farther in the form of neon ooze. What there was always more of had been congealed into permanence long ago, as if the automatic factory that cranked out these objects had jammed in the *on* position. How the land became plastic, he thought, remembering the fairy tale "How the Sea Became Salt." Someday, he thought, it'll be mandatory that we all sell the McDonald's hamburger as well as buy it; we'll sell it back and forth to each other forever from our living rooms. That way we won't even have to go outside.

He looked at his watch. Two-thirty: time to make a buy call. According to Donna, he could score, through her, on perhaps a thousand tabs of Substance D cut with meth.

Naturally, once he got it, he would turn it over to County Drug Abuse to be analyzed and then destroyed, or whatever they did with it. Dropped it themselves, maybe, or so another legend went. Or sold it. But his purchase from her was not to bust her for dealing; he had bought many times from her and had never arrested her. That was not what it was all about, busting a small-time local dealer, a chick who considered it cool and far-out to deal dope. Half the narcotics agents in Orange County were aware that Donna dealt, and recognized her on sight. Donna dealt sometimes in the parking lot of the 7-11 store, in front of the automatic holo-scanner the police kept going there, and got away with it. In a sense, Donna could never be busted no matter what she did and in front of whom.

What his transaction with Donna, like all those before, added up to was an attempt to thread a path upward via Donna to the supplier she bought from. So his purchases from her gradually grew in quantity. Originally he had coaxed her—if that was the word— into laying ten tabs on him, as a favor: friend-to-friend stuff. Then, later on, he had wangled a bag of a hundred for recompense, then three bags. Now, if he lucked out, he could score a thousand, which was ten bags. Eventually, he would be buying in a quantity which would be beyond her economic capacity; she could not front enough bread to her supplier to secure the stuff at her end. Therefore, she would lose instead of getting a big profit. They would haggle; she would insist that he front at least part of it;

he would refuse; she couldn't front it herself to her source; time would run out—even in a deal that small a certain amount of tension would grow; everyone would be getting impatient; her supplier, whoever he was, would be holding and mad because she hadn't shown. So eventually, if it worked out right, she would give up and say to him and to her supplier, "Look, you better deal direct with each other. I know you both; you're both cool. I'll vouch for both of you. I'll set a place and a time and you two can meet. So from now on, Bob, you can start buying direct, if you're going to buy in this quantity." Because in that quantity he was for all intents and purposes a dealer; these were approaching dealer's quantities. Donna would assume he was reselling at a profit per hundred, since he was buying a thousand at a time at least. This way he could travel up the ladder and come to the next person in line, become a dealer like her, and then later on maybe get another step up and another as the quantities he bought grew.

Eventually—this was the name of the project—he would meet someone high enough to be worth busting. That meant someone who knew something, which meant someone either in contact with those who manufactured or someone who ran it in from the supplier who himself knew the source.

Unlike other drugs, Substance D had—apparently—only one source. It was synthetic, not organic; therefore, it came from a lab. It could be synthesized, and already had been in federal experiments. But the constituents were themselves derived from complex substances almost equally difficult to synthesize. Theoretically it could be manufactured by anyone who had, first, the formula and, second, the technological capacity to set up a factory. But in practice the cost was out of reach. Also, those who had invented it and were making it available sold it too cheaply for effective competition. And the wide distribution suggested that even though a sole source existed, it had a diversified layout, probably a series of labs in several key areas, perhaps one near each major urban drug-using spot in North America and Europe. Why none of these had been found was a mystery; but the implication was, both publicly and no doubt under official wraps, that the S. D. Agency—as the authorities arbitrarily termed it—had penetrated so far up into law-enforcement groups, both local and national, that those who found out anything usable about its operations soon either didn't care or didn't exist.

He had, naturally, several other leads at present besides Donna. Other dealers he pressured progressively for larger quantities. But because she was his chick—or anyhow he had hopes in that direction—she was for him the easiest. Visiting her, talking to her on the phone, taking her out or having her over—that was a personal pleasure as well. It was, in a sense, the line of least resistance. If you had to spy on and report about someone, it might as well be people you'd see anyhow; that was less suspicious and less of a drag. And if you did not see them frequently before you began surveillance, you would have to eventually anyhow; it worked out the same in the end.

Entering the phone booth, he did a phone thing.

Ring-ring-ring.

"Hello," Donna said.

Every pay phone in the world was tapped. Or if it wasn't, some crew somewhere just hadn't gotten around to it. The taps fed electronically onto storage reels at a central point, and about once every second day a printout was obtained by an officer who listened to many phones without having to leave his office. He merely rang up the storage drums and, on signal, they played back, skipping all dead tape. Most calls were harmless. The officer could identify ones that weren't fairly readily. That was his skill. That was what he got paid for. Some officers were better at it than others.

As he and Donna talked, therefore, no one was listening. The playback would come maybe the next day at the earliest. If they discussed anything strikingly illegal, and the monitoring officer caught it, then voiceprints would be made. But all he and she had to do was keep it mild. The dialogue could still be recognizable as a dope deal. A certain governmental economy came into play here—it wasn't worth going through the hassle of voiceprints and track-down for routine illegal transactions. There were too many each day of the week, over too many phones. Both Donna and he knew this.

"How you doin'?" he asked.

"Okay." Pause in her warm, husky voice.

"How's your head today?"

"Sort of in a bad space. Sort of down." Pause. "I was bum-tripped this A.M. by my boss at the shop." Donna worked behind the counter of a little perfume shop in Gateside Mall in Costa Mesa, to which she drove every morning in her MG. "You know what he said? He said this customer, this old guy, gray hair, who bilked us out of ten bucks—he said it was my fault and I've got to make it good. It's coming out of my paycheck. So I'm out ten bucks through no fucking—excuse me—fault of my own."

Arctor said, "Hey, can I get anything from you?"

She sounded sullen now. As if she didn't want to. Which was a shuck. "How—much do you want? I don't know."

"Ten of them," he said. The way they had it set up, one was a hundred; this was a request for a thousand, then.

Among fronts, if transactions had to take place over public communications, a fairly good try consisted of masking a large one by an apparently small one. They could deal and deal forever, in fact, in these quantities, without the authorities taking any interest; otherwise, the narcotics teams would be raiding apartments and houses up and down each street each hour of the day, and achieving little.

" 'Ten,' " Donna muttered, irritably.

"I'm really hurting," he said, like a user. Rather than a dealer. "I'll pay you back later, when I've scored."

"No," she said woodenly. "I'll lay them on you gratis. Ten." Now, undoubtedly, she was speculating whether he was dealing. Probably he was. "Ten. Why not? Say, three days from now?"

"No sooner?"

"These are—"

"Okay," he said.

"I'll drop over."

"What time?"

She calculated. "Say around eight in the P.M. Hey, I want to show you a book I got, somebody left it at the shop. It's cool. It has to do with wolves. You know what wolves do? The male wolf? When he defeats his foe, he doesn't snuff him—he pees on him.

Really! He stands there and pees on his defeated foe and then he splits. That's it. Territory is what they mostly fight over. And the right to screw. You know."

Arctor said, "I peed on some people a little while ago."

"No kidding? How come?"

"Metaphorically," he said.

"Not the usual way?"

"I mean," he said, "I told them—" He broke off. Talking too much; a fuckup. Jesus, he thought. "These dudes," he said, "like biker types, you dig? Around the Foster's Freeze? I was cruising by and they said something raunchy. So I turned around and said something like—" He couldn't think of anything for a moment.

"You can tell me," Donna said, "even if it's super gross. You gotta be super gross with biker types or they won't understand."

Arctor said, "I told them I'd rather ride a pig than a hog. Any time."

"I don't get it."

"Well, a pig is a chick that—"

"Oh yeah. Okay, well I get it. Barf."

"I'll see you at my place like you said," he said. "Good-bye." He started to hang up.

"Can I bring the wolf book and show you? It's by Konrad Lorenz. The back cover, where they tell, says he was the foremost authority on wolves on earth. Oh yeah, one more thing. Your roommates both came into the shop today. Ernie what's-his-name and that Barris. Looking for you, if you might have—"

"What about?" Arctor said.

"Your cephalochromoscope that cost you nine hundred dollars, that you always turn on and play when you get home—Ernie and Barris were babbling away about it. They tried to use it today and it wouldn't work. No colors and no ceph patterns, neither one. So they got Barris's tool kit and unscrewed the bottom plate."

"The hell you say!" he said, indignant.

"And they say it's been fucked over. Sabotaged. Cut wires, and like sort of weird stuff—you know, freaky things. Shorts and broken parts. Barris said he'd try to—"

"I'm going right home," Arctor said, and hung up. My primo possession, he thought bitterly. And that fool Barris tinkering with it. But I can't go home right now, he realized. I've got to go over to New-Path to check on what they're up to.

It was his assignment: mandatory.

THE LUCKY DOG PET STORE

When I look at my stories, written over three decades, I think of the Lucky Dog Pet Store. There's a good reason for that. It has to do with an aspect of not just my life but of the lives of most freelance writers. It's called poverty.

I laugh about it now, and even feel a little nostalgia, because in many ways those were the happiest goddam days of my life, especially back in the early fifties when my writing career began. But we were poor; in fact we—my wife Kleo and I—were *poor* poor. We didn't enjoy it a bit. Poverty does not build good character: that is a myth. But it does make you into a good bookkeeper; you count accurately and you count money, little money, again and again. Before you leave the house to grocery shop you know exactly what you can spend, and you know exactly what you are going to buy, because if you screw up you will not eat the next day and maybe not the day after that.

So anyhow there I am at the Lucky Dog Pet Store on San Pablo Avenue, in Berkeley, California, in the fifties, buying a pound of ground horsemeat. The reason why I'm a freelance writer and living in poverty is (and I'm admitting this for the first time) that I am terrified of Authority Figures like bosses and cops and teachers; I want to be a freelance writer so I can be my own boss. It makes sense. I had quit my job managing a record department at a music store; all night every night I was writing short stories, both science fiction and mainstream . . . and selling the science fiction. I don't really enjoy the taste or texture of horsemeat; it's too sweet . . . but I also do enjoy not having to be behind a counter at exactly nine

A.M., wearing a suit and tie and saying, "Yes ma'am, can I help you?" and so forth . . . I enjoyed being thrown out of the University of California at Berkeley because I would not take ROTC—boy, an Authority Figure in a uniform is *the* Authority Figure!—and all of a sudden, as I hand over the 35¢ to the Lucky Dog Pet Store man, I find myself once more facing my personal nemesis. Out of the blue, I am once again confronted by an Authority Figure. There is no escape from your nemesis; I had forgotten that.

The man says, "You're buying this horsemeat and you are eating it yourselves."

He now stands nine feet tall and weighs three hundred pounds. He is glaring down at me. I am, in my mind, five years old again, and I have spilled glue on the floor in kindergarten.

"Yes sir," I admit. I want to tell him, Look: I stay up all night writing science-fiction stories and I'm real poor, but I know things will get better, and I have a wife I love, and a cat named Magnificat, and a little old house I'm buying at the rate of $25 a month payments, which is all I can afford—but this man is interested in only one aspect of my desperate (but hopeful) life. I know what he is going to tell me. I have always known. The horsemeat they sell at the Lucky Dog Pet Store is only for animal consumption. But Kleo and I are eating it ourselves, and now we are before the judge; the Great Assize has come; I am caught in another Wrong Act.

I half expect the man to say, "You have a bad attitude."

That was my problem then and it's my problem now: I have a bad attitude. In a nutshell, I fear authority but at the same time I resent it—the authority *and* my own fear—so I rebel. And writing science fiction is a way to rebel. I rebelled against ROTC at U.C. Berkeley and got expelled; in fact was told never to come back. I walked off my job at the record store one day and never came back. Later on I was to oppose the Vietnam War and get my files blown open and my papers gone through and stolen, as was written about in *Rolling Stone*. Everything I do is generated by my bad attitude, from riding the bus to fighting for my country. I even have a bad attitude toward publishers; I am always behind in meeting deadlines (I'm behind in this one, for instance).

Yet, science fiction is a rebellious art form and it needs writers and readers with bad attitudes—an attitude of, "Why?" Or, "How come?" Or, "Who says?" This gets sublimated into such themes as appear in my writing as, "Is the universe real?" Or, "Are we all really human or are some of us just reflex machines?" I have a lot of anger in me. I always have had. Last week my doctor told me that my blood pressure is elevated again and there now seems to be a cardiac complication. I got mad. Death makes me mad. Human and animal suffering makes me mad; whenever one of my cats dies, I curse God and I mean it; I feel fury at him. I'd like to get him here where I could interrogate him, tell him that I think the world is screwed up, that man didn't sin and fall but was pushed—which is bad enough—but was then sold the lie that he is basically sinful, which I know he is not.

I have known all kinds of people (I'm turning fifty in a month and I'm angry about that; I've lived a long time) and those were by and large good people. I model the characters in my novels and stories on them. Now and again one of these people dies, and that makes me mad—really mad, as mad as I can get. "You took my cat," I want to say to God, "and then you took my girlfriend. What are you doing? Listen to me; listen! It's wrong what you're doing."

Basically, I am not serene. I grew up in Berkeley and inherited from it the social consciousness which spread out over this country in the sixties and got rid of Nixon and ended the Vietnam War, plus a lot of other good things, such as the whole civil rights movement. Everyone in Berkeley gets mad at the drop of a hat. I used to get mad at the FBI agents who dropped by to visit with me week after week (Mr. George Smith and Mr. George Scruggs of the Red Squad), and I got mad at friends of mine who were members of the Communist Party; I got thrown out of the only meeting of the U.S. Communist Party I ever attended because I leaped to my feet and vigorously (i.e., angrily) argued against what they were saying.

That was in the early fifties, and now here we are in the very late seventies and I am still mad. Right now I am furious because of my best friend, a girl named Doris, 24 years old. She has cancer. I am in love with someone who could die any time, and it makes fury against God and the world race through me, elevating my blood pressure and stepping up my heartbeat. And so I write. I want to write about people I love, and put them into a fictional world spun out of my own mind, not the world we actually have, because the world we actually have does not meet my standards. Okay, so I should revise my standards, I'm out of step. I should yield to reality. I have *never* yielded to reality. That's what science fiction is all about. If you wish to yield to reality, go read Philip Roth; read the New York literary establishment mainstream best-selling writers. But you are reading science fiction and I am writing it for you. I want to show you, in my writing, what I love (my friends) and what I savagely hate (what happens to them).

I have watched Doris suffer unspeakably, undergo torment in her fight against cancer to a degree that I cannot believe. One time I ran out of the apartment and up to a friend's place, literally ran. My doctor had told me that Doris wouldn't live much longer and I should say good-bye to her and tell her it was because she was dying. I tried to and couldn't, and then I panicked and ran. At my friend's house we sat around and listened to weird records (I'm into weird music in general, both in classical and in rock; it's a comfort). He is a writer, too, a young science-fiction writer named K. W. Jeter—a good one. We just sat there and then I said aloud, really just pondering aloud, "The worst part of it is I'm beginning to lose my sense of humor about cancer." Then I realized what I'd said, and he realized, and we both collapsed into laughter.

So I do get to laugh. Our situation, the human situation, is in the final analysis neither grim nor meaningful, but funny. What else can you call it? The wisest people are the clowns, like Harpo Marx, who would not speak. If I could have anything I want, I would like God to listen to what Harpo was not saying, and understand why Harpo would not talk. Remember, Harpo *could* talk; he just wouldn't. Maybe there was nothing to say; everything has been said. Or maybe, had he spoken, he would have pointed out something too terrible, something we should not be aware of. I don't know. Maybe you can tell me.

Writing is a lonely way of life. You shut yourself up in your study and work and work. For instance, I have had the same agent for twenty-seven years and I've never met him because he is in New York and I'm in California. (I saw him once on TV, on the

Tom Snyder "Tomorrow Show," and my agent is one mean dude. He really plays hardball—which an agent is supposed to do.) I've met many other science-fiction writers and become close friends with a number of them. For instance, I've known Harlan Ellison since 1954. Harlan hates my guts. When we were at the Metz Second Annual Science Fiction Festival last year, in France, Harlan tore into me; we were in the bar at the hotel, and all kinds of people, mostly French, were standing around. Harlan shredded me. It was fine; I loved it. It was sort of like a bad acid trip; you just have to kick back and enjoy; there is no alternative.

But I love that little bastard. He is a person who really exists. Likewise van Vogt and Ted Sturgeon and Roger Zelazny and, most of all, Norman Spinrad and Tom Disch, my two main men in the world. The loneliness of the writing per se is offset by the fraternity of writers. Last year a dream of mine of almost forty years was realized: I met Robert Heinlein. It was his writing, and A. E. van Vogt's, which got me interested in science fiction, and I consider Heinlein my spiritual father, even though our political ideologies are totally at variance. Several years ago, when I was ill, Heinlein offered his help, anything he could do, and we had never met; he would phone me to cheer me up and see how I was doing. He wanted to buy me an electric typewriter, God bless him—one of the few true gentlemen in this world. I don't agree with any ideas he puts forth in his writing, but that is neither here nor there. One time when I owed the IRS a lot of money and couldn't raise it, Heinlein loaned the money to me. I think a great deal of him and his wife; I dedicated a book to them in appreciation. Robert Heinlein is a fine-looking man, very impressive and very military in stance; you can tell he has a military background, even to the haircut. He knows I'm a flipped-out freak, and still he helped me and my wife when we were in trouble. That is the best in humanity, there; that is who and what I love.

My friend Doris who has cancer used to be Norman Spinrad's girlfriend. Norman and I have been close for years; we've done a lot of insane things together. Norman and I both get hysterical and start raving. Norman has the worst temper of any living mortal. He knows it. Beethoven was the same way. I now have no temper at all, which is probably why my blood pressure is so high; I can't get any of my anger out of my system. I don't really know—in the final analysis—who I'm mad at. I really envy Norman his ability to get it out of his system. He is an excellent writer and an excellent friend. This is what I get from being a science-fiction writer: not fame and fortune, but good friends. That's what makes it worth it to me. Wives come and girlfriends come and go; we science-fiction writers stay together until we literally die . . . which I may do at any time (probably to my own secret relief). Meanwhile I am writing this article, rereading stories that span a thirty-year period of writing, thinking back, remembering the Lucky Dog Pet Store, my days in Berkeley, my political involvement and how The Man got on my ass because of it . . . I still have a residual fear in me, but I do believe that the reign of police intrigue and terror is over in this country (for a time, anyhow). I now sleep okay. But there was a time when I sat up all night in fear, waiting for the knock on the door. I was finally asked to "come downtown," as they call it, and for hours the police interrogated me. I was even called in by OSI (Air Force Intelligence) and questioned by them; it had to do with terrorist activities in Marin County—not terrorist activities by the authorities this time, but by black ex-cons from San Quentin. It turned out that the house behind mine was owned by a group of them. The police thought we were in league; they kept showing me photos of black guys and asking did I know them? At that point I wouldn't have been able to answer. That was a really scary day for little Phil.

So if you thought writers live a bookish, cloistered life you are wrong, at least in my case. I was even in the street for a couple of years: the dope scene. Parts of that scene were funny and wonder-ful, and other parts were hideous. I wrote about it in *A Scanner Darkly*, so I won't write about it here. The one good thing about my being in the street was that the people didn't know I was a well-known science-fiction writer—or if they did, they didn't care. They just wanted to know what I had that they could rip off and sell. At the end of the two years everything I owned was gone—literally, including my house. I flew to Canada as Guest of Honor at the Vancouver Science Fiction Convention, lectured at the University of British Columbia, and decided to stay there. The hell with the dope scene! I had temporarily stopped writing; it was a bad time for me. I had fallen in love with several unscrupulous street girls . . . I drove an old Pontiac convertible modified with a four-barrel carburetor and wide tires, and no brakes, and we were always in trouble, always facing problems we couldn't handle. It wasn't until I left Canada and flew down here to Orange County that I got my head together and back to writing. I met a very straight girl and married her, and we had a little baby we called Christopher. He is now five. They left me a couple of years ago. Well, as Vonnegut says, so it goes. What else can you say? It's like the whole of reality: you either laugh or—I guess fold and die.

One thing I've found that I can do that I really enjoy is rereading my own writing, earlier stories and novels especially. It induces mental time travel, the same way certain songs you hear on the radio do (for instance, when I hear Don McLean sing "Vincent," I at once see a girl named Linda wearing a miniskirt and driving her yellow Camaro; we're on our way to an expensive restaurant and I am worrying if I'll be able to pay the bill and Linda is talking about how she is in love with an older science-fiction writer and I imagine—oh vain folly!—that she means me, but it turns out she means Norman Spinrad who I introduced her to); the whole thing returns, an eerie feeling which I'm sure you've experienced. People have told me that everything about me, every facet of my life, psyche, experiences, dreams and fears, is laid out explicitly in my writing, that from the corpus of my work I can be absolutely and precisely inferred. This is true. So when I read my writing, I take a trip through my own head and life, only it is my earlier head and my earlier life. I abreact, as the psychiatrists say. There's the dope theme. There's the philosophical theme, especially the vast epistemological doubts that began when I was briefly attending U.C. Berkeley. Friends who are dead are in my stories and novels. Names of streets! I even put my agent's address in one, as a character's address (Harlan once put his own phone number in a story, which he was to regret later). And of course, in my writing, there is the constant theme of music, love of, preoccupation with, music. Music is the single thread making my life into a coherency.

You see, had I not become a writer I'd be somewhere in the music industry now, almost certainly the record industry. I remember back in the mid-sixties when I first heard Linda Ronstadt; she was a guest on Glen Campbell's TV show, and no one had ever heard of her. I went nuts listening to her and looking at her. I had been a buyer in retail records and it had been my job to spot new talent that was hot property, and seeing and hearing Ronstadt, I knew I was hearing one of the great people in the business; I could see down the pipe of time into the future. Later, when she'd recorded a few records, none of them hits, all of which I faithfully bought, I calculated to the exact *month* when she'd make it big. I even wrote Capitol Records and told them; I said the next record Ronstadt cuts will be the beginning of a career unparalleled in the record industry. Her next record was "Heart Like a Wheel." Capitol didn't answer my letter, but what the hell; I was right, and happy to be right. And that's what I'd be into now, had I not gone into writing science fiction. My fantasy number which I run in my head is that I discover Linda Ronstadt, and am remembered as the scout for Capitol who signed her. I would have wanted that on my gravestone:

HE DISCOVERED LINDA RONSTADT
AND SIGNED HER UP!

My friends are caustically and disdainfully amused by my fantasy life about discovering Ronstadt and Grace Slick and Streisand and so forth. I have a good stereo system (at least my cartridge and speakers are good) and I own a huge record collection, and every night from eleven P.M. to five A.M. I write while wearing my Stax electrostatic top-of-the-line headphones. It's my job and my vice mixed together. You can't hope for better than that: having your job and your sin commingled. There I am, writing away, and into my ears is pouring Bonnie Koloc and no one can hear it but me. The joke is, though, that there's no one but me here anyhow, all the wives and girlfriends having long since left. That's another of the ills of writing; because it is such a solitary occupation, and requires such long-term concentrated attention, it tends to drive your wife or girlfriend away, whoever you're living with. It's probably the most painful price the writer pays. All I have to keep me company are two cats. Like my doper friends (ex-doper friends, since most of them are dead now) my cats don't know I'm a well-known writer, and, as with my doper friends, I prefer it that way.

When I was in France, I had the interesting experience of being famous. I am the best-liked science-fiction writer there, best of all in the entire whole complete world! (I tell you that for what it's worth.) I was Guest of Honor at the Metz Festival, which I mentioned, and I delivered a speech which, typically, made no sense whatever. Even the French couldn't understand it, despite a translation. Something goes haywire in my brain when I write speeches; I think I imagine I'm a reincarnation of Zoroaster bringing news of God. So I try to make as few speeches as possible. Call me up, offer me a lot of money to deliver a speech, and I'll give a tacky pretext to get out of doing it; I'll say anything palpably a lie. But it was fantastic (in the sense of not real) to be in France and see all my books in beautiful, expensive editions instead of little paperbacks with what Spinrad calls "peeled eyeball" covers. Owners of bookstores came to shake my hand. The Metz City Council had a dinner and a reception for us writers. Harlan was there, as I mentioned; so was Roger Zelazny and John Brunner and Harry Harrison and Robert Sheckley. I had never met Sheckley before; he is a gentle man. Brunner, like me, has gotten stout. We all had endless meals together; Brunner made sure everyone knew he spoke French. Harry Harrison sang the Fascist national anthem in Italian in a loud voice, which showed what he thought of prestige (Harry is the iconoclast of the known universe). Editors and publishers skulked everywhere, as well as the media. I got interviewed from eight in the morning until three-thirty the next morning; and, as always, I said things which will come back to haunt me. It was the best week of my life. I think that there at Metz I was really happy for the first time—not because I was famous but because there was so much excitement in those people. The French get wildly excited about ordering from a menu; it's like the old political discussions we used to have back in Berkeley, only it's simply food that's involved. Deciding which street to walk up involves ten French people gesticulating and yelling, and then running off in different directions. The French, like myself and Spinrad, see the most improbable possibility in every situation, which is certainly why I am popular there. Take a number of possibilities, and the French and I will select the wildest. So I had come home at last. I could get hysterical among people acculturated to hysteria, people never able to make decisions or execute actions because of the drama in the very process of choosing. That's me: paralyzed by imagination. For me a flat tire on my car is (*a*) The End of the World; and (*b*) An Indication of Monsters (although I forget why).

This is why I love science fiction. I love to read it; I love to write it. The science-fiction writer sees not just possibilities but *wild* possibilities. It's not just "What if—." It's "My God; what if—." In frenzy and hysteria. The Martians are always coming. Mr. Spock is the only one calm. This is why Spock has become a cult god to us; he calms our normal hysteria. He balances the proclivity of science-fiction people to imagine the impossible.

KIRK (*frantically*): Spock, the *Enterprise* is about to blow up!
SPOCK (*calmly*): Negative, Captain; it's merely a faulty fuse.

Spock is always right, even when he's wrong. It's the tone of voice, the supernatural reasonability; this is not a man like us; this is a god. God talks this way; every one of us senses it instinctively. That's why they have Leonard Nimoy narrating pseudo-science TV programs. Nimoy can make anything sound plausible. They can be in search of a lost button or the elephants' graveyard, and Nimoy will calm our doubts and fears. I would like him as a psychotherapist; I would rush in frantically, filled with my usual hysterical fears, and he would banish them.

PHIL (*hysterically*): Leonard, the sky is falling!
NIMOY (*calmly*): Negative, Phil; it's merely a faulty fuse.

And I'd feel okay and my blood pressure would drop and I could resume work on the novel I'm three years behind on vis-à-vis my deadline.

In reading my stories, you should bear in mind that most were written when science fiction was so looked down upon that it virtually was not there, in the eyes of all America. This was not funny, the derision felt towards science-fiction writers. It made our lives wretched. Even in Berkeley—or especially in Berkeley—people would say, "But are you writing anything serious?" We made no money; few publishers published science fiction (Ace Books was the only regular book publisher of it); and really cruel abuse was inflicted on us. To select science-fiction writing as a career was an act of self-destruction; in fact, most *writers*, let alone other people, could not even conceive of someone considering it. The only non-science-fiction writer who ever treated me with courtesy was Herbert Gold, whom I met at a literary party in San Francisco. He autographed a file card to me this way: "To a colleague, Philip K. Dick." I kept the card until the ink faded and was gone, and I still feel grateful to him for his charity. (Yes, that was what it was, then, to treat a science-fiction writer with courtesy.) To get hold of a copy of my first published novel, *Solar Lottery*, I had to special-order it from the City Lights Bookshop in San Francisco, which specialized in the outré. So in my head I have to collate the experience in 1977 of the mayor of Metz shaking hands with me at an official city function, and the ordeal of the fifties when Kleo and I lived on ninety dollars a month, when we could not even pay the fine on an overdue library book and when I wanted to read a magazine I had to go to the library because I could not afford to buy it, when we were literally living on dog food. But I think you should know this—specifically, in case you are, say, in your twenties and rather poor and perhaps becoming filled with despair, whether you are a science-fiction writer or not, whatever you want to make of your life. There can be a lot of fear, and often it is justified fear. People do starve in America. My financial ordeal did not end in the fifties; as late as the mid-seventies I still could not pay my rent, nor afford to take Christopher to the doctor, nor own a car, nor have a phone. In the month that Christopher and his mother left me I earned nine dollars, and that was just three years ago. Only the kindness of my agent, Scott Meredith, in loaning me money when

I was broke got me through. In 1971 I actually had to beg friends for food. Now look; I don't want sympathy; what I am trying to do is tell you that your crisis, your ordeal, assuming you have one, is not something that is going to be endless, and I want you to know that you will probably survive it through your courage and wits and sheer drive to live. I have seen uneducated street girls survive horrors that beggar description. I have seen the faces of men whose brains had been burned out by drugs, men who still could think enough to be able to realize what happened to them; I watched their clumsy attempts to weather that which cannot be weathered. As in Heine's poem "Atlas," this line: "I carry that which can't be carried." And the next line is, "And in my body my heart would like to break!" But this is not the sole constituent of life, and it is not the sole theme in fiction, mine or anyone else's, except perhaps for the nihilist French existentialists. Kabir, the sixteenth-century Sufi poet, wrote, "If you have not lived through something, it is not true." So live through it; I mean, go all the way to the end. Only then can it be understood, not along the way.

If I had to come forth with an analysis of the anger that lies inside me, which expresses itself in so many sublimations, I would guess that probably what arouses my indignation is seeing the meaningless. That which is disorder, the force of entropy—there is no redemptive value of something that can't be understood, as far as I am concerned. My writing, in toto, is an attempt on my part to take my life and everything I've seen and done, and fashion it into a work which makes sense. I'm not sure I've been successful. First, I cannot falsify what I have seen. I see disorder and sorrow, and so I have to write about it; but I've seen bravery and humor, and so I put that in, too. But what does it all add up to? What is the vast overview which is going to impart sense into the entirety?

What helps for me—if help comes at all—is to find the mustard seed of the funny at the core of the horrible and futile. I've been researching ponderous and solemn theological matters for five years now, for my novel-in-progress, and much of the Wisdom of the World has passed from the printed page and into my brain, there to be processed and secreted in the form of more words: words in, words out, and a brain in the middle wearily trying to determine the meaning of it all. Anyhow, the other night I started on the article on Indian Philosophy in the *Encyclopedia of Philosophy*, an eight-volume learned reference set which I esteem. The time was four A.M.; I was exhausted—I have been working endlessly like this on this novel, doing this kind of research. And there, at the heart of this solemn article, was this:

> The Buddhist idealists used various arguments to show that perception does not yield knowledge of external objects distinct from the percipient . . . The external world supposedly consists of a number of different objects, but they can be known as different only because there are different sorts of experiences "of" them. Yet if the experiences are thus distinguishable, there is no need to hold the superfluous hypothesis of external objects.

In other words, by applying Ockham's razor to the basic epistemological question of "What is reality?" the Buddhist idealists reach the conclusion that belief in an external world is a "superfluous hypothesis"—i.e., it violates the Principle of Parsimony—which is the principle underlying all Western science. Thus the external world is abolished, and we can go about more important business—whatever that might be.

That night I went to bed laughing. I laughed for an hour. I am still laughing. Push philosophy and theology to their ultimate (and Buddhist idealism probably is the ultimate of both) and what do you wind up with? Nothing. Nothing exists (they also proved that the self doesn't exist, either). As I said earlier, there is only one way out: seeing it all as ultimately funny. Kabir, whom I quoted, saw dancing and joy and love as ways out, too; and he wrote about the sound of "the anklets on the feet of an insect as it walks." I would like to hear that sound; perhaps if I could, my anger and fear, and my high blood pressure, would go away.

I HOPE I SHALL ARRIVE SOON

After takeoff the ship routinely monitored the condition of the sixty people sleeping in its cryonic tanks. One malfunction showed, that of person nine. His EEG revealed brain activity.

Shit, the ship said to itself.

Complex homeostatic devices locked into circuit feed, and the ship contacted person nine.

"You are slightly awake," the ship said, utilizing the psychotronic route; there was no point in rousing person nine to full consciousness—after all, the flight would last a decade.

Virtually unconscious, but unfortunately still able to think, person nine thought, Someone is addressing me. He said, "Where am I located? I don't see anything."

"You're in faulty cryonic suspension."

He said, "Then I shouldn't be able to hear you."

"'Faulty,' I said. That's the point; you can hear me. Do you know your name?"

"Victor Kemmings. Bring me out of this."

"We are in flight."

"Then put me under."

"Just a moment." The ship examined the cryonic mechanisms; it scanned and surveyed and then it said, "I will try."

Time passed. Victor Kemmings, unable to see anything, unaware of his body, found himself still conscious. "Lower my temperature," he said. He could not hear his voice; perhaps he only imagined he spoke. Colors floated toward him and then rushed at him. He liked the colors; they reminded him of a child's paint box, the semianimated kind, an artificial life form. He had used them in school, two hundred years ago.

"I can't put you under," the voice of the ship sounded inside Kemmings's head. "The malfunction is too elaborate; I can't correct it and I can't repair it. You will be conscious for ten years."

The semianimated colors rushed toward him, but now they possessed a sinister quality, supplied to them by his own fear. "Oh my God," he said. Ten years! The colors darkened.

As Victor Kemmings lay paralyzed, surrounded by dismal flickerings of light, the ship explained to him its strategy. This strategy did not represent a decision on its part; the ship had been programmed to seek this solution in case of a malfunction of this sort.

"What I will do," the voice of the ship came to him, "is feed you sensory stimulation. The peril to you is sensory deprivation. If you are conscious for ten years without sensory data, your mind will deteriorate. When we reach the LR4 System, you will be a vegetable."

"Well, what do you intend to feed me?" Kemmings said in panic. "What do you have in your information storage banks? All the video soap operas of the last century? Wake me up and I'll walk around."

"There is no air in me," the ship said. "Nothing for you to eat. No one to talk to, since everyone else is under."

Kemmings said, "I can talk to you. We can play chess."

"Not for ten years. Listen to me; I say, I have no food and no air. You must remain as you are . . . a bad compromise, but one forced on us. You are talking to me now. I have no particular information stored. Here is policy in these situations: I will feed you your own buried memories, emphasizing the pleasant ones. You possess two hundred and six years of memories and most of them have sunk down into your unconscious. This is a splendid source of sensory data for you to receive. Be of good cheer. This situation, which you are in, is not unique. It has never happened within my domain before, but I am programmed to deal with it. Relax and trust me. I will see that you are provided with a world."

"They should have warned me," Kemmings said, "before I agreed to emigrate."

"Relax," the ship said.

He relaxed, but he was terribly frightened. Theoretically, he should have gone under, into the successful cryonic suspension, then awakened a moment later at his star of destination; or rather the planet, the colony planet, of that star. Everyone else aboard the ship lay in an unknowing state—he was the exception, as if bad karma had attacked him for obscure reasons. Worst of all, he had to depend totally on the goodwill of the ship. Suppose it elected to feed him monsters? The ship could terrorize him for ten years— ten objective years and undoubtedly more from a subjective stand-point. He was, in effect, totally in the ship's power. Did interstellar ships enjoy such a situation? He knew little about interstellar ships; his field was microbiology. Let me think, he said to himself. My first wife, Martine; the lovely little French girl who wore jeans and a red shirt open at the waist and cooked delicious crepes.

"I hear," the ship said. "So be it."

The rushing colors resolved themselves into coherent, stable shapes. A building: a little old yellow wooden house that he had owned when he was nineteen years old, in Wyoming. "Wait," he said in panic. "The foundation was bad; it was on a mud sill. And the roof leaked." But he saw the kitchen, with the table that he had built himself. And he felt glad.

"You will not know, after a little while," the ship said, "that I am feeding you your own buried memories."

"I haven't thought of that house in a century," he said wonder-ingly; entranced, he made out his old electric drip coffeepot with the box of paper filters beside it. This is the house where Martine and I lived, he realized. "Martine!" he said aloud.

"I'm on the phone," Martine said from the living room.

The ship said, "I will cut in only when there is an emergency. I will be monitoring you, however, to be sure you are in a satisfactory state. Don't be afraid."

"Turn down the rear right burner on the stove," Martine called. He could hear her and yet not see her. He made his way from the kitchen through the dining room and into the living room. At the VF, Martine stood in rapt conversation with her brother; she wore shorts and she was barefoot. Through the front windows of the living room he could see the street; a commercial vehicle was trying to park, without success.

It's a warm day, he thought. I should turn on the air conditioner.

He seated himself on the old sofa as Martine continued her VF conversation, and he found himself gazing at his most cherished possession, a framed poster on the wall above Martine: Gilbert Shelton's "Fat Freddy Says" drawing in which Freddy Freak sits with his cat on his lap, and Fat Freddy is trying to say "Speed kills," but he is so wired on speed—he holds in his hand every kind of amphetamine tablet, pill, spansule, and capsule that exists—that he can't say it, and the cat is gritting his teeth and wincing in a mixture of dismay and disgust. The poster is signed by Gilbert Shelton himself; Kemmings's best friend Ray Torrance gave it to him and Martine as a wedding present. It is worth thousands. It was signed by the artist back in the 1980s. Long before either Victor Kemmings or Martine lived.

If we ever run out of money, Kemmings thought to himself, we could sell the poster. It was not *a* poster; it was *the* poster. Martine adored it. The Fabulous Furry Freak Brothers—from the golden age of a long-ago society. No wonder he loved Martine so; she herself loved back, loved the beauties of the world, and treasured and cherished them as she treasured and cherished him; it was a protective love that nourished but did not stifle. It had been her idea to frame the poster; he would have tacked it up on the wall, so stupid was he.

"Hi," Martine said, off the VF now. "What are you thinking?"

"Just that you keep alive what you love," he said.

"I think that's what you're supposed to do," Martine said. "Are you ready for dinner? Open some red wine, a cabernet."

"Will an '07 do?" he said, standing up; he felt, then, like taking hold of his wife and hugging her.

"Either an '07 or a '12." She trotted past him, through the dining room and into the kitchen.

Going down into the cellar, he began to search among the bottles, which, of course, lay flat. Musty air and dampness; he liked the smell of the cellar, but then he noticed the redwood planks lying half-buried in the dirt and he thought, I know I've got to get a concrete slab poured. He forgot about the wine and went over to the far corner, where the dirt was piled highest; bending down, he poked a board . . . he poked with a trowel and then he thought, Where did I get this trowel? I didn't have it a minute ago. The board crumbled against the trowel. This whole house is collapsing, he realized. Christ sake. I better tell Martine.

Going back upstairs, the wine forgotten, he started to say to her that the foundations of the house were dangerously decayed, but Martine was nowhere in sight. And nothing cooked on the stove—no pots, no pans. Amazed, he put his hands on the stove and found it cold. Wasn't she just cooking? he asked himself.

"Martine!" he said loudly.

No response. Except for himself, the house was empty. Empty, he thought, and collapsing. Oh my God. He seated himself at the kitchen table and felt the chair give slightly under him; it did not give much, but he felt it; he felt the sagging.

I'm afraid, he thought. Where did she go?

He returned to the living room. Maybe she went next door to borrow some spices or butter or something, he reasoned. Nonetheless, panic now filled him.

He looked at the poster. It was unframed. And the edges had been torn.

I know she framed it, he thought; he ran across the room to it, to examine it closely. Faded . . . the artist's signature had faded; he could scarcely make it out. She insisted on framing it and under glare-free, reflection-free glass. But it isn't framed and it's torn! The most precious thing we own!

Suddenly he found himself crying. It amazed him, his tears. Martine is gone; the poster is deteriorated; the house is crumbling away; nothing is cooking on the stove. This is terrible, he thought. And I don't understand it.

The ship understood it. The ship had been carefully monitoring Victor Kemmings's brain wave patterns, and the ship knew that something had gone wrong. The wave-forms showed agitation and pain. I must get him out of this feed-circuit or I will kill him, the ship decided. Where does the flaw lie? it asked itself. Worry dormant in the man; underlying anxieties. Perhaps if I intensify the signal. I will use the same source, but amp up the charge. What has happened is that massive subliminal insecurities have taken possession of him; the fault is not mine, but lies, instead, in his psychological makeup.

I will try an earlier period in his life, the ship decided. Before the neurotic anxieties got laid down.

In the backyard, Victor scrutinized a bee that had gotten itself trapped in a spider's web. The spider wound up the bee with great care. That's wrong, Victor thought. I'll let the bee loose. Reaching up, he took hold of the encapsulated bee, drew it from the web, and, scrutinizing it carefully, began to unwrap it.

The bee stung him; it felt like a little patch of flame.

Why did it sting me? he wondered. I was letting it go.

He went indoors to his mother and told her, but she did not listen; she was watching television. His finger hurt where the bee had stung it, but, more important, he did not understand why the bee would attack its rescuer. I won't do that again, he said to himself.

"Put some Bactine on it," his mother said at last, roused from watching the TV.

He had begun to cry. It was unfair. It made no sense. He was perplexed and dismayed and he felt a hatred toward small living things, because they were dumb. They didn't have any sense.

He left the house, played for a time on his swings, his slide, in his sandbox, and then he went into the garage because he heard a strange flapping, whirring sound, like a kind of fan. Inside the gloomy garage, he found that a bird was fluttering against the cob-webbed rear window, trying to get out. Below it, the cat, Dorky, leaped and leaped, trying to reach the bird.

He picked up the cat; the cat extended its body and its front legs; it extended its jaws and bit into the bird. At once the cat scrambled down and ran off with the still-fluttering bird.

Victor ran into the house. "Dorky caught a bird!" he told his mother.

"That goddam cat." His mother took the broom from the closet in the kitchen and ran outside, trying to find Dorky. The cat had concealed itself under the bramble bushes; she could not reach it with the broom. "I'm going to get rid of that cat," his mother said.

Victor did not tell her that he had arranged for the cat to catch the bird; he watched in silence as his mother tried and tried to pry Dorky out from her hiding place; Dorky was crunching up the bird; he could hear the sound of breaking bones, small bones. He felt a strange feeling, as if he should tell his mother what he had done, and yet if he told her she would punish him. I won't do that again, he said to himself. His face, he realized, had turned red. What if his mother figured it out? What if she had some secret way of knowing? Dorky couldn't tell her and the bird was dead. No one would ever know. He was safe.

But he felt bad. That night he could not eat his dinner. Both his parents noticed. They thought he was sick; they took his temperature. He said nothing about what he had done. His mother told his father about Dorky and they decided to get rid of Dorky. Seated at the table, listening, Victor began to cry.

"All right," his father said gently. "We won't get rid of her. It's natural for a cat to catch a bird."

The next day he sat playing in his sandbox. Some plants grew up through the sand. He broke them off. Later his mother told him that had been a wrong thing to do.

Alone in the backyard, in his sandbox, he sat with a pail of water, forming a small mound of wet sand. The sky, which had been blue and clear, became by degrees overcast. A shadow passed over him and he looked up. He sensed a presence around him, something vast that could think.

You are responsible for the death of the bird, the presence thought; he could understand its thoughts.

"I know," he said. He wished, then, that he could die. That he could replace the bird and die for it, leaving it as it had been, fluttering against the cobwebbed window of the garage.

The bird wanted to fly and eat and live, the presence thought.

"Yes," he said miserably.

"You must never do that again," the presence told him.

"I'm sorry," he said, and wept.

This is a very neurotic person, the ship realized. I am having an awful lot of trouble finding happy memories. There is too much fear in him and too much guilt. He has buried it all, and yet it is still there, worrying him like a dog worrying a rag. Where can I go in his memories to find him solace? I must come up with ten years of memories, or his mind will be lost.

Perhaps, the ship thought, the error that I am making is in the area of choice on my part; I should allow him to select his own memories. However, the ship realized, this will allow an element of fantasy to enter. And that is not usually good. Still—

I will try the segment dealing with his first marriage once again, the ship decided. He really loved Martine. Perhaps this time if I keep the intensity of the memories at a greater level the entropic factor can be abolished. What happened was a subtle vitiation of the remembered world, a decay of structure. I will try to compensate for that. So be it.

"Do you suppose Gilbert Shelton really signed this?" Martine said pensively; she stood before the poster, her arms folded; she rocked back and forth slightly, as if seeking a better perspective on the brightly colored drawing hanging on their living room wall. "I mean, it could have been forged. By a dealer somewhere along the line. During Shelton's lifetime or after."

"The letter of authentication," Victor Kemmings reminded her.

"Oh, that's right!" She smiled her warm smile. "Ray gave us the letter that goes with it. But suppose the letter is a forgery? What we

need is another letter certifying that the first letter is authentic."
Laughing, she walked away from the poster.

"Ultimately," Kemmings said, "we would have to have Gilbert
Shelton here to personally testify that he signed it."

"Maybe he wouldn't know. There's that story about the man
bringing the Picasso picture to Picasso and asking him if it was
authentic, and Picasso immediately signed it and said, 'Now it's
authentic.'" She put her arm around Kemmings and, standing on
tiptoe, kissed him on the cheek. "It's genuine. Ray wouldn't have
given us a forgery. He's the leading expert on counterculture art of
the twentieth century. Do you know that he owns an actual lid of
dope? It's preserved under—"

"Ray is dead," Victor said.

"What?" She gazed at him in amazement. "Do you mean something happened to him since we last—"

"He's been dead two years," Kemmings said. "I was responsible.
I was driving the buzzcar. I wasn't cited by the police, but it was my
fault."

"Ray is living on Mars!" She stared at him.

"I know I was responsible. I never told you. I never told anyone.
I'm sorry. I didn't mean to do it. I saw it flapping against the win-
dow, and Dorky was trying to reach it, and I lifted Dorky up, and
I don't know why but Dorky grabbed it—"

"Sit down, Victor." Martine led him to the overstuffed chair and
made him seat himself. "Something's wrong," she said.

"I know," he said. "Something terrible is wrong. I'm responsible
for the taking of a life, a precious life that can never be replaced.
I'm sorry. I wish I could make it okay, but I can't."

After a pause, Martine said, "Call Ray."

"The cat—" he said.

"What cat?"

"There." He pointed. "In the poster. On Fat Freddy's lap. That's
Dorky. Dorky killed Ray."

Silence.

"The presence told me," Kemmings said. "It was God. I didn't
realize it at the time, but God saw me commit the crime. The mur-
der. And he will never forgive me."

His wife stared at him numbly.

"God sees everything you do," Kemmings said. "He sees even the falling sparrow. Only in this case it didn't fall; it was grabbed. Grabbed out of the air and torn down. God is tearing this house down which is my body, to pay me back for what I've done. We should have had a building contractor look this house over before we bought it. It's just falling goddam to pieces. In a year there won't be anything left of it. Don't you believe me?"

Martine faltered, "I—"

"Watch." Kemmings reached up his arms toward the ceiling; he stood; he reached; he could not touch the ceiling. He walked to the wall and then, after a pause, put his hand through the wall.

Martine screamed.

The ship aborted the memory retrieval instantly. But the harm had been done.

He has integrated his early fears and guilts into one interwoven grid, the ship said to itself. There is no way I can serve up a pleasant memory to him because he instantly contaminates it. However pleasant the original experience in itself was. This is a serious situation, the ship decided. The man is already showing signs of psychosis. And we are hardly into the trip; years lie ahead of him.

After allowing itself time to think the situation through, the ship decided to contact Victor Kemmings once more.

"Mr. Kemmings," the ship said.

"I'm sorry," Kemmings said. "I didn't mean to foul up those retrievals. You did a good job, but I—"

"Just a moment," the ship said. "I'm not equipped to do psychiatric reconstruction of you; I am a simple mechanism, that's all. What is it you want? Where do you want to be and what do you want to be doing?"

"I want to arrive at our destination," Kemmings said. "I want this trip to be over."

Ah, the ship thought. That is the solution.

One by one the cryonic systems shut down. One by one the people returned to life, among them Victor Kemmings. What amazed

him was the lack of a sense of the passage of time. He had entered
the chamber, lain down, had felt the membrane cover him and the
temperature begin to drop—

And now he stood on the ship's external platform, the unloading platform, gazing down at a verdant planetary landscape. This,
he realized, is LR4–6, the colony world to which I have come in
order to begin a new life.

"Looks good," a heavyset woman beside him said.

"Yes," he said, and felt the newness of the landscape rush up at him,
its promise of a beginning. Something better than he had known the
past two hundred years. I am a fresh person in a fresh world, he
thought. And he felt glad.

Colors raced at him, like those of a child's semianimate kit. Saint
Elmo's fire, he realized. That's right; there is a great deal of ioniza-
tion in this planet's atmosphere. A free light show, such as they had
back in the twentieth century.

"Mr. Kemmings," a voice said. An elderly man had come up
beside him, to speak to him. "Did you dream?"

"During the suspension?" Kemmings said. "No, not that I can
remember."

"I think I dreamed," the elderly man said. "Would you take my
arm on the descent ramp? I feel unsteady. The air seems thin. Do
you find it thin?"

"Don't be afraid," Kemmings said to him. He took the elderly
man's arm. "I'll help you down the ramp. Look; there's a guide
coming this way. He'll arrange our processing for us; it's part of the
package. We'll be taken to a resort hotel and given first-class accommodations. Read your brochure." He smiled at the uneasy older
man to reassure him.

"You'd think our muscles would be nothing but flab after ten
years in suspension," the elderly man said.

"It's just like freezing peas," Kemmings said. Holding on to the
timid older man, he descended the ramp to the ground. "You can
store them forever if you get them cold enough."

"My name's Shelton," the elderly man said.

"What?" Kemmings said, halting. A strange feeling moved
through him.

"Don Shelton." The elderly man extended his hand; reflexively, Kemmings accepted it and they shook. "What's the matter, Mr. Kemmings? Are you all right?"

"Sure," he said. "I'm fine. But hungry. I'd like to get something to eat. I'd like to get to our hotel, where I can take a shower and change my clothes." He wondered where their baggage could be found. Probably it would take the ship an hour to unload it. The ship was not particularly intelligent.

In an intimate, confidential tone, elderly Mr. Shelton said, "You know what I brought with me? A bottle of Wild Turkey bourbon. The finest bourbon on Earth. I'll bring it over to our hotel room and we'll share it." He nudged Kemmings.

"I don't drink," Kemmings said. "Only wine." He wondered if there were any good wines here on this distant colony world. Not distant now, he reflected. It is Earth that's distant. I should have done like Mr. Shelton and brought a few bottles with me.

Shelton. What did the name remind him of? Something in his far past, in his early years. Something precious, along with good wine and a pretty, gentle young woman making crepes in an old-fashioned kitchen. Aching memories; memories that hurt.

Presently he stood by the bed in his hotel room, his suitcase open; he had begun to hang up his clothes. In the corner of the room, a TV hologram showed a newscaster; he ignored it, but, liking the sound of a human voice, he kept it on.

Did I have any dreams? he asked himself. During these past ten years?

His hand hurt. Gazing down, he saw a red welt, as if he had been stung. A bee stung me, he realized. But when? How? While I lay in cryonic suspension? Impossible. Yet he could see the welt and he could feel the pain. I better get something to put on it, he realized. There's undoubtedly a robot doctor in the hotel; it's a first-rate hotel.

When the robot doctor had arrived and was treating the bee sting, Kemmings said, "I got this as punishment for killing the bird."

"Really?" the robot doctor said.

"Everything that ever meant anything to me has been taken away from me," Kemmings said. "Martine, the poster—my little old house with the wine cellar. We had everything and now it's gone. Martine left me because of the bird."

"The bird you killed," the robot doctor said.

"God punished me. He took away all that was precious to me because of my sin. It wasn't Dorky's sin; it was my sin."

"But you were just a little boy," the robot doctor said.

"How did you know that?" Kemmings said. He pulled his hand away from the robot doctor's grasp. "Something's wrong. You shouldn't have known that."

"Your mother told me," the robot doctor said.

"My mother didn't know!"

The robot doctor said, "She figured it out. There was no way the cat could have reached the bird without your help."

"So all the time that I was growing up she knew. But she never said anything."

"You can forget about it," the robot doctor said.

Kemmings said, "I don't think you exist. There is no possible way that you could know these things. I'm still in cryonic suspension and the ship is still feeding me my own buried memories. So I won't become psychotic from sensory deprivation."

"You could hardly have a memory of completing the trip."

"Wish fulfillment, then. It's the same thing. I'll prove it to you. Do you have a screwdriver?"

"Why?"

Kemmings said, "I'll remove the back of the TV set and you'll see; there's nothing inside it; no components, no parts, no chassis— nothing."

"I don't have a screwdriver."

"A small knife, then. I can see one in your surgical supply bag." Bending, Kemmings lifted up a small scalpel. "This will do. If I show you, will you believe me?"

"If there's nothing inside the TV cabinet—"

Squatting down, Kemmings removed the screws holding the back panel of the TV set in place. The panel came loose and he set it down on the floor.

There was nothing inside the TV cabinet. And yet the color

hologram continued to fill a quarter of the hotel room, and the voice of the newscaster issued forth from his three-dimensional image.

"Admit you're the ship," Kemmings said to the robot doctor.

"Oh dear," the robot doctor said.

Oh dear, the ship said to itself. And I've got almost ten years of this lying ahead of me. He is hopelessly contaminating his experiences with childhood guilt; he imagines that his wife left him because, when he was four years old, he helped a cat catch a bird. The only solution would be for Martine to return to him, but how am I going to arrange that? She may not still be alive. On the other hand, the ship reflected, maybe she is alive. Maybe she could be induced to do something to save her former husband's sanity. People by and large have very positive traits. And ten years from now it will take a lot to save—or rather restore—his sanity; it will take something drastic, something I myself cannot do alone.

Meanwhile, there was nothing to be done but recycle the wish fulfillment arrival of the ship at its destination. I will run him through the arrival, the ship decided, then wipe his conscious memory clean and run him through it again. The only positive aspect of this, it reflected, is that it will give me something to do, which may help preserve *my* sanity.

Lying in cryonic suspension—faulty cryonic suspension—Victor Kemmings imagined, once again, that the ship was touching down and he was being brought back to consciousness.

"Did you dream?" a heavyset woman asked him as the group of passengers gathered on the outer platform. "I have the impression that I dreamed. Early scenes from my life . . . over a century ago."

"None that I can remember," Kemmings said. He was eager to reach his hotel; a shower and a change of clothes would do wonders for his morale. He felt slightly depressed and wondered why.

"There's our guide," an elderly lady said. "They're going to escort us to our accommodations."

"It's in the package," Kemmings said. His depression remained.

The others seemed so spirited, so full of life, but over him only a weariness lay, a weighing-down sensation, as if the gravity of this colony planet were too much for him. Maybe that's it, he said to himself. But, according to the brochure, the gravity here matched Earth's; that was one of the attractions.

Puzzled, he made his way slowly down the ramp, step by step, holding on to the rail. I don't really deserve a new chance at life anyhow, he realized. I'm just going through the motions . . . I am not like these other people. There is something wrong with me; I cannot remember what it is, but nonetheless it is there. In me. A bitter sense of pain. Of lack of worth.

An insect landed on the back of Kemmings's right hand, an old insect, weary with flight. He halted, watched it crawl across his knuckles. I could crush it, he thought. It's so obviously infirm; it won't live much longer anyhow.

He crushed it—and felt great inner horror. What have I done? he asked himself. My first moment here and I have wiped out a little life. Is this my new beginning?

Turning, he gazed back up at the ship. Maybe I ought to go back, he thought. Have them freeze me forever. I am a man of guilt, a man who destroys. Tears filled his eyes.

And, within its sentient works, the interstellar ship moaned.

During the ten long years remaining in the trip to the LR4 System, the ship had plenty of time to track down Martine Kemmings. It explained the situation to her. She had emigrated to a vast orbiting dome in the Sirius System, found her situation unsatisfactory, and was en route back to Earth. Roused from her own cryonic suspension, she listened intently and then agreed to be at the colony world LR4-6 when her ex-husband arrived—if it was at all possible.

Fortunately, it was possible.

"I don't think he'll recognize me," Martine said to the ship. "I've allowed myself to age. I don't really approve of entirely halting the aging process."

He'll be lucky if he recognizes anything, the ship thought.

At the intersystem spaceport on the colony world of LR4–6, Martine stood waiting for the people aboard the ship to appear on the outer platform. She wondered if she would recognize her former husband. She was a little afraid, but she was glad that she had gotten to LR4–6 in time. It had been close. Another week and his ship would have arrived before hers. Luck is on my side, she said to herself, and scrutinized the newly landed interstellar ship.

People appeared on the platform. She saw him. Victor had changed very little.

As he came down the ramp, holding on to the railing as if weary and hesitant, she came up to him, her hands thrust deep in the pockets of her coat; she felt shy and when she spoke she could hardly hear her own voice.

"Hi, Victor," she managed to say.

He halted, gazed at her. "I know you," he said.

"It's Martine," she said.

Holding out his hand, he said, smiling, "You heard about the trouble on the ship?"

"The ship contacted me." She took his hand and held it. "What an ordeal."

"Yeah," he said. "Recirculating memories forever. Did I ever tell you about a bee that I was trying to extricate from a spider's web when I was four years old? The idiotic bee stung me." He bent down and kissed her. "It's good to see you," he said.

"Did the ship—"

"It said it would try to have you here. But it wasn't sure if you could make it."

As they walked toward the terminal building, Martine said, "I was lucky; I managed to get a transfer to a military vehicle, a high-velocity-drive ship that just shot along like a mad thing. A new propulsion system entirely."

Victor Kemmings said, "I have spent more time in my own unconscious mind than any other human in history. Worse than early-twentieth-century psychoanalysis. And the same material over and over again. Did you know I was scared of my mother?"

"*I* was scared of your mother," Martine said. They stood at the baggage depot, waiting for his luggage to appear. "This looks like a really nice little planet. Much better than where I was . . . I haven't been happy at all."

"So maybe there's a cosmic plan," he said grinning. "You look great."

"I'm old."

"Medical science—"

"It was my decision. I like older people." She surveyed him. He has been hurt a lot by the cryonic malfunction, she said to herself. I can see it in his eyes. They look broken. Broken eyes. Torn down into pieces by fatigue and—defeat. As if his buried early memories swam up and destroyed him. But it's over, she thought. And I did get here in time.

At the bar in the terminal building, they sat having a drink.

"This old man got me to try Wild Turkey bourbon," Victor said. "It's amazing bourbon. He says it's the best on Earth. He brought a bottle with him from . . ." His voice died into silence.

"One of your fellow passengers," Martine finished.

"I guess so," he said.

"Well, you can stop thinking of the birds and the bees," Martine said.

"Sex?" he said, and laughed.

"Being stung by a bee, helping a cat catch a bird. That's all past."

"That cat," Victor said, "has been dead one hundred and eighty-two years. I figured it out while they were bringing us out of suspension. Probably just as well. Dorky. Dorky, the killer cat. Nothing like Fat Freddy's cat."

"I had to sell the poster," Martine said. "Finally."

He frowned.

"Remember?" she said. "You let me have it when we split up. Which I always thought was really good of you."

"How much did you get for it?"

"A lot. I should pay you something like—" She calculated. "Taking inflation into account, I should pay you about two million dollars."

"Would you consider," he said, "instead of the money, my share of the sale of the poster, spending some time with me? Until I get used to this planet?"

"Yes," she said. And she meant it. Very much.

They finished their drinks and then, with his luggage transported by robot spacecap, made their way to his hotel room.

"This is a nice room," Martine said, perched on the edge of the bed. "And it has a hologram TV. Turn it on."

"There's no use turning it on," Victor Kemmings said. He stood by the open closet, hanging up his shirts.

"Why not?"

Kemmings said, "There's nothing on it."

Going over to the TV set, Martine turned it on. A hockey game materialized, projected out into the room, in full color, and the sound of the game assailed her ears.

"It works fine," she said.

"I know," he said. "I can prove it to you. If you have a nail file or something, I'll unscrew the back plate and show you."

"But I can—"

"Look at this." He paused in his work of hanging up his clothes. "Watch me put my hand through the wall." He placed the palm of his right hand against the wall. "See?"

His hand did not go through the wall because hands do not go through walls; his hand remained pressed against the wall, unmoving.

"And the foundation," he said, "is rotting away."

"Come and sit down by me," Martine said.

"I've lived this often enough now," he said. "I've lived this over and over again. I come out of suspension; I walk down the ramp; I get my luggage; sometimes I have a drink at the bar and sometimes I come directly to my room. Usually I turn on the TV and then—" He came over and held his hand toward her. "See where the bee stung me?"

She saw no mark on his hand; she took his hand and held it.

"There is no bee sting," she said.

"And when the robot doctor comes, I borrow a tool from him and take off the back plate of the TV set. To prove to him that it has no chassis, no components in it. And then the ship starts me over again."

"Victor," she said. "Look at your hand."

"This is the first time you've been here, though," he said.

"Sit down," she said.

"Okay." He seated himself on the bed, beside her, but not too close to her.

"Won't you sit closer to me?" she said.

"It makes me too sad," he said. "Remembering you. I really loved you. I wish this was real."

Martine said, "I will sit with you until it is real for you."

"I'm going to try reliving the part with the cat," he said, "and this time *not* pick up the cat and *not* let it get the bird. If I do that, maybe my life will change so that it turns into something happy. Something that is real. My real mistake was separating from you. Here; I'll put my hand through you." He placed his hand against her arm. The pressure of his muscles was vigorous; she felt the weight, the physical presence of him, against her. "See?" he said. "It goes right through you."

"And all this," she said, "because you killed a bird when you were a little boy."

"No," he said. "All this because of a failure in the temperature-regulating assembly aboard the ship. I'm not down to the proper temperature. There's just enough warmth left in my brain cells to permit cerebral activity." He stood up then, stretched, smiled at her. "Shall we go get some dinner?" he asked.

She said, "I'm sorry. I'm not hungry."

"I am. I'm going to have some of the local seafood. The brochure says it's terrific. Come along anyhow; maybe when you see the food and smell it you'll change your mind."

Gathering up her coat and purse, she came with him.

"This is a beautiful little planet," he said. "I've explored it dozens of times. I know it thoroughly. We should stop downstairs at the pharmacy for some Bactine, though. For my hand. It's beginning to swell and it hurts like hell." He showed her his hand. "It hurts more this time than ever before."

"Do you want me to come back to you?" Martine said.

"Are you serious?"

"Yes," she said. "I'll stay with you as long as you want. I agree; we should never have been separated."

Victor Kemmings said, "The poster is torn."

"What?" she said.

"We should have framed it," he said. "We didn't have sense enough to take care of it. Now it's torn. And the artist is dead."

THE ZEBRA PAPERS

February 11, 1977

[TO MARK HURST, *VALIS* editor]
Dear Mark,

Having told you that I am preparing a major new theme for VALIS I called Sydney [*Weinberg, Bantam Books*] and told her, too. She asked what the new theme was and I told her. I'd like now to outline it for you.

Ten years ago (by way of preamble) John Brunner sent me a French scientific book called THE MASKS OF MEDUSA, which studied the phenomenon of insect mimicry. The author's main conclusion was that no theory existed by which such mimicry could be explained; a spinoff conclusion was that if high-order mimicry existed (e.g. at a level to fool humans, not just birds and other insects) we would probably not be aware of it, any more than the birds are aware of the insect mimicry at their level. John thought I'd be interested because of my preoccupation with the question, What is reality? and secondarily, Are some of us not really human but merely appear human?

For years I reread the book, annotating the margins throughout, but no idea for a novel came out of it and finally I gave the book away. However, I had virtually memorized it. Well, Mark, about a month and a half ago, while reworking VALIS, the idea—not an idea but THE IDEA—suddenly popped fullblown into my mind, having germinated subconsciously over the years. What I call it is the Zebra Principle. It is (to me anyhow) terribly exciting and fantastic, and I have literally hundreds of pages of notes on it now. I talked to Jack Scovil at SMLA and he thought it'd make an entire complete novel on its own, and that I should hold it for that, not using it in VALIS. But in my opinion it would go perfectly into VALIS. In point of fact it was produced by my mind *for* VALIS. Viz.

Houston Paige is employed by the Fremont Administration as a top-ranking scientist probing possible enemies of the state. In conjunction with police computers Paige has developed the Zebra Principle: that it is possible, even likely, that high-order mimicry exists, undetected. (1) The mimicking organism is undoubtedly benign; (2) There is no reason to suppose that it mimics humans but rather that it mimics inanimate objects. Houston Paige supposes that there must be tests which can be arranged which will smoke Zebra out (Zebra being their code word for the mimicking organisms). Science-fiction writers are especially suspected of knowing of—of having contact with—Zebra, who, in the minds of the government, has become just one more enemy of the state. Because of this, Houston Paige approaches s-f author Philip K. Dick with a commission, through a government-owned publishing house, to write a novel about Zebra. Phil Dick accepts the advance but never gets anything actually written. This makes Paige very suspicious.

Paige is an interesting person, being a total fuckup and a lush as well. He never, even at the end of VALIS, even gets near to detecting Zebra. But Zebra does in fact exist.

Zebra is enormous in physical size, which is one reason why Paige never manages to detect it. Zebra, in fact, spans thousands, possibly even millions of miles of our space, having grown very large over the past three thousand years. Paige can't detect Zebra because he is inside Zebra every day of his life. In fact a portion of Zebra has assimilated the police computers which predicted the theoretical existence of Zebra. When Paige drinks an Old Fashioned, Zebra is the bottle of bourbon, the ice, the slice of orange, the bitters, the glass. When Paige takes notes on the probable characteristics of Zebra, Zebra is the ballpoint pen, clipboard and paper.

The relationship of this Zebra plot to the main plot of VALIS is not visible offhand; I will have my customary twin threads which eventually I weave together. In point of fact, Zebra is the Aramchek satellite—as well as the police computers. It allows itself to be blown up (i.e., the satellite portion of it) by the Russians. This overcomes a great weakness of the present plot: the fact that the Russians so easily shoot the satellite down. Another, much smaller weak point is that Phil Dick the character in VALIS is not working on anything. The Zebra theme overcomes both.

The new, final version of VALIS will be much longer. As it stands, the ending is weak. The new ending will consist of a manifestation by Zebra of itself to one of the characters in the novel, probably to me (in the slave labor camp). The satellite is gone, but Zebra remains. Its body is plasmatic and invisible. It is always there, no matter what happens. It made use of a portion of itself to become what seemed to be a communications, teaching satellite. There is no way that the tyranny can perceive Zebra, much less blow it up.

By means of this superimposed theme I can edit out much of the merely Christian material and bias (as well as explanation at the end of the novel), which I would like to do. Zebra, if it can be said to resemble the contents of any religion, resembles the Hindu concept of Brahman:

> "They reckon ill who leave me out,
> When me they fly I am the wings.
> I am the doubter and the doubt,
> And I the hymn the Brahman sings."

The Zebra theme will also enable me to add the elements of black humor which are presently missing from VALIS. We will have a lot of fun with Houston Paige as he constantly encounters Zebra, never realizing it and always drunkenly theorizing as to the nature and location of Zebra. Paige who seeks to apprehend Zebra is denied that very vision, and Phil Dick (in the novel) who has ripped off the tyranny and doesn't care a shit about Zebra—he just needs the money—gets finally to see it.

One ability which Zebra has that Paige doesn't suspect is its capacity to restructure human memory. Every time Paige sets up a test to detect Zebra and obtains positive results, Zebra lays down a false memory template in Paige's head so that he is deluded into thinking the results are negative. This ability to delude is a major aspect of Zebra. It does not assimilate humans but it can and does tamper—not just with their percept systems—but their memories as well. Zebra creates what the Hindu religions call Maya; it lays a veil over the world so that its enormous plasmatic body cannot be distinguished. "Zebra" is indeed the right term for it . . . which is natural, inasmuch as Zebra itself programmed the computer's findings.

Zebra is in fact a non-terrestrial life form which came here to live and grow, but being as benign as it is it aids all life as much as it can. Every now and then the characters get a glimpse of a dreadful "alternate world" which is just a cruel, crushing prison (represented in the novel already by the visionary encounter with A.D. 70 Rome); this is our world as it would be without Zebra; it allows the characters a glimpse of this non-Zebra world with the purpose of eventually disclosing not only itself to man but what it has achieved for man. Zebra regards the biological and historic forces on this planet as malign, and seeks to ameliorate them. It is finally revealed to one of the characters—probably Phil Dick—what this black iron prison world actually is (or would have been).

Part of Zebra's ability to disguise itself grows out of its ability to move along a fourth orthogonal spatial axis unknown to us, in fact denied to us; thus Zebra can appear and disappear at will, without our understanding how. To our eyes, any object moving along this fourth axis is simply invisible. From our standpoint, then, Zebra is capable of transcending time, which permits it also to move retrograde in time, or to leave the temporal world, be "not there" and then to reenter wherever (to us, whenever) it wishes. Thus Zebra spans three thousand years of an extended present; to it both past and future are now. Like the vast life form which took over Palmer Eldritch and could extend itself between star systems, over millions of miles, Zebra extends itself in the fourth axis world, and thus, to us, is godlike (but in fact it is limited; it is merely superior by one whole spatial dimension to us, giving the impression of infinite power and knowledge—but it is an impression only).

Through the manifesting of Zebra into visibility, Phil Dick in the novel realizes that what has always been called "god" by mankind is in fact merely a superior life form.

However, Zebra is so superior that it might as well be god. But it is timid and retiring (like Lord Running Clam in CLANS OF THE ALPHANE MOON), and can be destroyed—although not by us. If it could not be destroyed it would not need to hide itself continually. The character Phil Dick understands that on its lofty level Zebra has enemies which could destroy it; hence the religious myths about Satan. Phil Dick conjectures that there may exist in the universe life forms even *superior* to Zebra, since Zebra has come here and hidden itself from sight as best it can. There may well be hostile life forms which can better distinguish Zebra, Phil Dick realizes. Part of Zebra's sympathy for man derives from its own vulnerability.

However, I will not treat this theme with the continual seriousness which it would seem to entail. For instance, one of the characters (Phil Dick, Nicholas Brady or Houston Paige) finds himself able to obtain answers from Zebra by means of bowls of alphabet soup. The letters swim to the surface and form words (which is of course a parody on the I CHING, but also something like the way Glimmung speaks to them in GALACTIC POT-HEALER and the way Runciter communicates in UBIK; this should be a lot of fun—and I no doubt will be able to find other "trash in the gutter" ways by which great Zebra communes with man). (As you know, Mark, this is a favorite theme of mine: the sentient universe speaking to us in these trite ways. Each time I use this theme I find new ways to do it, and new explanations—such as Zebra—to account for the phenomenon. It all goes back to the early sixties when I was trying to find an explanation for how the I CHING works.)

(For example, Paige deliberately sets up 26 bowling pins with a different letter on each and then rolls bowling balls at them; the pattern of remaining pins—he hopes—will spell out words; but all he gets is:

AQW PVC XSLLR

And the like—which, once again, seems to indicate that Zebra does not exist. But Zebra has deliberately caused the pins to form a non-pattern.)

(Also, for example, Paige, with all the funds and laboratory and research facilities of the tyranny available to him, could construct a vast device operating on the principle of randomness, which continually constructs arrangements of letters, in order to see if they eventually form words. I can envision them forming nothing for days, even weeks, and finally this message is arrived at by mere randomness:

THER IS NO ZE

Which Paige construes to mean, "There is no Zebra," which, he realizes, is a paradox.)

Using huge, expensive computers and a large staff of trained technicians he employs a variety of antique methods of divination: from apantomancy to xylomancy (with the possible exception of sciomancy). The only method which gives him any results is oneiromancy; he keeps dreaming of a great zebra which smiles at him. But this may mean nothing. However, as Paige deliberately employs all these means to no avail, Phil or Nicholas is puzzling over a bowl of alphabet soup which spells out such things as:

WARNING YOU MUST BE CAUTIOUS ALL DAY

The fact of the matter is that Paige with his Zebra hypothesis and Nicholas Brady with his weird experiences between them have both halves of the puzzle. Brady, on his own, without the part which Paige has, cannot account for what has been happening to him all his life; Paige, with his giant computers and highly skilled work-staff, cannot get a manifestation or revelation of Zebra no matter what. It is the reader who, possessing both halves in the twin themes of the novel, can perhaps put it all together. In other words, when Paige approaches Phil Dick with his Zebra plot idea, he is bringing the missing clues into focus for the astute reader. The ele-

ment of suspense, then, is greatly enhanced in VALIS by introducing this new material.

In essence: what I have written in the rough draft is only one side
of the coin . . . the Zebra material will add the other. The novel will
open with twin, opposed plot-lines (which I love to do and am
good at), but will end with a dovetailed single plot outline. Brady is
having the experiences with Zebra but has no theory to explain it;
Paige, whom we encounter through Phil Dick, not through Brady,
has the theory but can't get specific experiences. Brady has the concrete examples, Paige the abstract reasoning. In the character Phil
Dick, who knows both men, it all comes together, for the edifica-
tion and amusement of the reader.

This way, Mark, we can get rid of the Christian, theological
explanation at the end; we will have just that one phase of Brady's
theorizing; the *true* explanation is quite different (i.e., a superior
but limited life form which has taken refuge here to escape its own
enemies, and who helps us, but only in a limited fashion—the best
it can do). As VALIS stands now I am forced to fall back onto
stereotyped explanations for the assistance, for the satellite, and this
is not good, as you pointed out. In fact, it was you who gave me
the insight that much more was needed in VALIS by way of explanation.

There will even be a scene in which Paige gets loaded on good
hash (or Angel's Dust) and hallucinates clowns from a circus wearing zebra suits and jeering at him; as the epitome of this ersatz
vision, the Chief Clown removes his zebra head and tells Paige that
the ultimate manifestation of Zebra is Mortimer Snerd. Paige then
has a dope-inspired vision of Mortimer Snerd as Brahman, saying
in his Snerd voice:

"Sometimes Mortimer sleeps and sometimes Mortimer dances."

Which are the two phases of the Brahman's cycle. In this vision
(which I will try to make funny) it is revealed to Paige that Zebra
is only a mask which Mortimer Snerd wears to delude mankind,
that in reality we are all carved from trees. For a whole week Paige
keeps seeing people as pine trees—a parody of my own "android as
human" theme. When he tries to ball his chick he suffers the annoy-
ing delusion that her sexual organ is a knothole in a felled tree on

its way down Kalamath [*sic, Klamath*] River in Oregon. Instead of
an orgasm he hallucinates a huge buzzsaw.

Thus I offset Brady's genuine visions with Paige's phony (and
absurd) ones.

Paige kills himself, and as he lies dying he receives a final vision:
Edgar Bergan [*sic, Bergen*] is gazing down at him from heaven and
there is a whole host of Mortimer Snerds, all of whom are singing.
At Bergan's right hand sits Charley McCarthy. Charley's wooden
mouth moves and he says,

"Welcome to the next world. You will become one with your
maker."

Paige has been metamorphosed into a ventriloquist's dummy.

Anyhow, Mark, I do feel that it would be better to use the Zebra
material in VALIS since, as I say, I feel it is the other half of the
coin, the theoretical analog to Brady's experiences (for which I
wasn't able to come up with a completely satisfactory explanation;
the satellite is fine but not fine enough, so to say). I asked Sydny for
permission to at least try superimposing Zebra onto VALIS, and
she said to talk with you, which I am herewith doing. If I start
reconstructing the novel and it doesn't work, well, then I will finish VALIS more or less as it stands. But this superimpositionary
method is how I wrote some of my best novels, and as the author
not only of them but of the rough draft of VALIS, I feel it would
work here.

Please let me know.

> *With warm personal regards to both you and Jodie,*
> *Phil Dick*

March 6, 1977

[TO MARK HURST]
Dear Mark,

I am now working until *five* A.M. on the VALIS/Zebra Project,
rather than just until three. A lot of what I'm doing consists of scientific or quasi-scientific research, and into the most varied areas.
Mark, this Zebra concept leads to fascinating speculative possibilities, which I hadn't been able to see originally. For instance, I've

been reading about Hegel's idea of an "Absolute Spirit" at work in human history which evolves us upward through a dialectic process toward greater and greater human freedom—this is exactly what VALIS does, is it not? Only I've set VALIS up in the sky, not on the ground, so to speak. As Zebra, VALIS so to speak superimposes itself downward onto mankind, as if arriving from above—like a vast invisible ship descending. Although as I conceive it, Zebra/VALIS was minute at the start, and only now is becoming planet-size and truly capable of significantly affecting historic events. It's as if VALIS has been trying to affect these events in the past, but its efforts were not that successful until the Ferris Fremont situation (i.e., VALIS is literally growing, like any organism which is viable & healthy). Then, too, there is Spinoza's fascinating heretical "atheistic" idea that the world is somehow the literal, physical body of God (which can't be "god" in any sense that we normally understand it, but rather the ancient Greek idea of the universe is a living body or creature or organism). This view (panpsychism) believes that everything without exception is alive; it's just a question of degree. We're inside a huge living creature, they thought . . . and can you see how this fits with my conception of Zebra? We're not aware of it because (1) it is everywhere; and (2) it has to some extent always been there . . . and then I add, in contrast to the Greeks, that there is a not-organism, a not-Zebra, into which Zebra has inserted itself in such a way as to look like a further extension of the not-Zebra which came *before* Zebra. From a strictly paranoid standpoint—that which the Government thinkers would have—Zebra is an ETI taking over the world. In a sense this is true; Zebra certainly is taking it over— literally, as if consuming it, as if devouring it and replacing it with itself. The Government thinkers compare this to cancer—alien cells replacing "natural" cells, although what they can't see is that these invading "cells" are benign. From their standpoint, however, Zebra is not benign—and here again they are right. I want to have the Government view clearly delineated as being subjectively correct: an alien, hostile entity is slowly and invisibly spreading throughout the world, and it is getting ready to do in the "legitimate" (sic) authorities and take complete control. Well, Zebra is not God;

Zebra (VALIS) is not all-powerful. What it can do is make a decisive intrusion into the historical process, but it is not the historical process as such, any more than when I turn on a light switch I am the switch, the wires, the electricity and the bulb; all I do is so to speak intervene. But to the paranoid Government thinkers, Zebra is everywhere. And since Zebra can't be seen, well, who knows . . . perhaps he is; he could be (or it could be). Houston Paige is forever watchful, in true paranoid style. When the ice cubes from his drink creep across the counter and slide to the floor and crawl under the refrigerator—imagine his reaction:

It seemed to him that he was either going crazy or else was already crazy, and in the most terrible way. This fear, as a furious onrush of insight, paralyzed him with its intensity, and the near-absolute quality of it—not as emotion or mood—but as a glimpse of reality. And yet, he realized, this was precisely what he was supposed to be looking for, this life-like mobility of the mere inanimate. Was this not how Zebra would give itself away, a lapse of this kind? So, in his head, two utterly opposing theories conflicted, now, one good, the other dreadful: he had seen Zebra, and he was crazy; both views, perhaps—and this was the most threatening insight of all—were correct. To perceive Zebra, he realized, you must be insane. This is what classical schizophrenia is: the paranormal perceptual ability to distinguish as set-ground the real and actual Presence of this great invading and alien being, inserting itself into the normal world; to this process the "sane" man was oblivious—and this was exactly what Zebra wanted. This was how its deception functioned! Sanity, then, in the strict clinical sense, was playing into Zebra's clutches. Zebra had a vested interest in human sanity—for *its* advantage. Where Zebra failed was when some so-called "schizophrenic," jeered at by his human peers, saw around the corner of the world too suddenly or too unexpectedly for Zebra to scuttle off . . . this unfortunate human, then, had glimpsed what indeed truly was. And his reward? Given twice-daily injections of Thorazine and shut away. It could happen to me, Houston said to himself grimly; my reward for uncovering Zebra could be imprisonment in the ultimate dungeon of the modern world: the up-to-date psy-

chiatric hospital. This is what our society has become like: you go
to jail for seeing what others can't see. And you go to jail especially
if you raise a warning, a warning of invasion. (etc.)

I've run the text somewhat together, Mark, because I am trying
to give a general impression of the Government viewpoint, not the
strict presentation I'm doing of this, but I think you'll be able to
pick it up as it will be in finished form. Notice how Houston's
brain, by the end of the paragraph, has cleverly weeded out his own
insight that he may be crazy; he winds up with a new definition of
crazy which is it's not something you are; it's something they say you
are. But the real irony, of course, is that Zebra does exist and Houston Paige is (as he realizes) NOT crazy. The reader knows this—
despite the internal evidence of classic schizophrenic paranoia on
Houston's part—because of the experiences which Nicholas Brady
and Phil Dick are also having. If there is group validation, it is not
hallucination. Naturally, Houston Paige is highly motivated in this
novel to get this consensual validation and he astutely thinks he
could get it from a noted s-f writer, if he could get it anywhere.

Of course Houston Paige has a deeper plan vis-à-vis Phil Dick
which he is craftily unfolding. If the Zebra Concept gets written
up in a work of *fiction*, and published and widely read, then perhaps
the other people who've encountered Zebra—and, like Houston,
had to suffer the imaginary fear that they're psychotic—maybe
these people will contact Phil Dick and describe how their own
secret experiences have been along the lines put forth in Phil's
novel. Because as it stands, Houston must put forth his idea as fact,
in a report or article, and he dreads the inevitable consequences:
"The author of this article," they'll say, "is a paranoid psychotic."

Houston's projected titled article stands as:

THE COOPERATION OF DISCRETE OBJECTS: A CLUE TO POSSIBLE HIGH-ORDER MIMICRY

If discrete objects can be observed functioning in a cooperative
way, so that distinct results occur which deviate meaningfully
from the statistically probable outcome, is it possible or even
likely that we have been witnessing high order sentient mim-

icry? No other hypothesis seems to account for such occurrences, assuming they do exist.

This is how he'd have it appear in, say, *Scientific American*. He has mingled hopes for fame & immortality—versus being sent off to the hospital forever; it could go both ways—he could be considered psychotic now but—ah! how pleasing this thought!—history will some day show he was right (unconsciously Houston has a martyr complex, and without realizing it is being drawn, through his T.A. inner script, to seek this outcome: hospitalization and stigma now, but historic vindication later on, *after* Zebra has destroyed half the world . . . and aren't they all sorry they laughed at Houston Paige now?).

So, Mark, you can see I'm creating a very complex character in Houston Paige, who is working toward goals he himself has no conscious conception of. Phil Dick, though, through whom Houston is seen, gets a clear view of all these fucked up conflicting motivations. For instance, although consciously Houston would like Phil to write up Zebra in a novel, Houston is simultaneously incredibly jealous and hateful toward Phil for "stealing all the glory" of being the first to write about Zebra. In his fantasy world—which Phil glimpses—Houston is motivated to rub out Phil for "stealing" Houston's ideas.

Well, enough progress report to date for right now, Mark, and back to VALIS itself. But you can see how menacing I am making Houston vis-à-vis Phil, and how really schizophrenic he is . . . although ironically not because he believes in Zebra.

Love,
Phil Dick

Chapter One

from VALIS

Horselover Fat's nervous breakdown began the day he got the phone call from Gloria asking if he had any Nembutals. He asked her why she wanted them and she said that she intended to kill herself. She was calling everyone she knew. By now she had fifty of them, but she needed thirty or forty more to be on the safe side.

At once Horselover Fat leaped to the conclusion that this was her way of asking for help. It had been Fat's delusion for years that he could help people. His psychiatrist once told him that to get well he would have to do two things; get off dope (which he hadn't done) and to stop trying to help people (he still tried to help people).

As a matter of fact, he had no Nembutals. He had no sleeping pills of any sort. He never did sleeping pills. He did uppers. So giving Gloria sleeping pills by which she could kill herself was beyond his power. Anyhow, he wouldn't have done it if he could.

"I have ten," he said. Because if he told her the truth she would hang up.

"Then I'll drive up to your place," Gloria said in a rational, calm voice, the same tone in which she had asked for the pills.

He realized then that she was not asking for help. She was trying to die. She was completely crazy. If she were sane she would realize that it was necessary to veil her purpose, because this way she made him guilty of complicity. For him to agree, he would need to want her dead. No motive existed for him—or anyone—to want that. Gloria was gentle and civilized, but she dropped a lot of acid.

It was obvious that the acid, since he had last heard from her six months ago, had wrecked her mind.

"What've you been doing?" Fat asked.

"I've been in Mount Zion Hospital in San Francisco. I tried suicide and my mother committed me. They discharged me last week."

"Are you cured?" he said.

"Yes," she said.

That's when Fat began to go nuts. At the time he didn't know it, but he had been drawn into an unspeakable psychological game. There was no way out. Gloria Knudson had wrecked him, her friend, along with her own brain. Probably she had wrecked six or seven other people, all friends who loved her, along the way, with similar phone conversations. She had undoubtedly destroyed her mother and father as well. Fat heard in her rational tone the harp of nihilism, the twang of the void. He was not dealing with a person; he had a reflex-arc thing at the other end of the phone line.

What he did not know then is that it is sometimes an appropriate response to reality to go insane. To listen to Gloria rationally ask to die was to inhale the contagion. It was a Chinese finger trap, where the harder you pull to get out, the tighter the trap gets.

"Where are you now?" he asked.

"Modesto. At my parents' home."

Since he lived in Marin County, she was several hours' drive away. Few inducements would have gotten him to make such a drive. This was another serving-up of lunacy: three hours' drive each way for ten Nembutals. Why not just total the car? Gloria was not even committing her irrational act rationally. Thank you, Tim Leary, Fat thought. You and your promotion of the joy of expanded consciousness through dope.

He did not know his own life was on the line. This was 1971. In 1972 he would be up north in Vancouver, British Columbia, involved in trying to kill himself, alone, poor and scared, in a foreign city. Right now he was spared that knowledge. All he wanted to do was coax Gloria up to Marin County so he could help her. One of God's greatest mercies is that he keeps us perpetually occluded. In 1976, totally crazy with grief, Horselover Fat would slit his wrist (the Vancouver suicide attempt having failed), take forty-nine tablets of high-grade digitalis, and sit in a closed garage with his car motor running—and fail there, too. Well, the body has powers unknown to the mind, Gloria's mind had total control over her body; she was *rationally* insane.

Most insanity can be identified with the bizarre and the theatrical. You put a pan on your head and a towel around your waist, paint yourself purple and go outdoors. Gloria was as calm as she had ever been; polite and civilized. If she had lived in ancient Rome or Japan, she would have gone unnoticed. Her driving skills probably remained unimpaired. She would stop at every red light and not exceed the speed limit—on her trip to pick up the ten Nembutals.

I am Horselover Fat, and I am writing this in the third person to gain much-needed objectivity. I did not love Gloria Knudson, but I liked her. In Berkeley, she and her husband had given elegant parties, and my wife and I always got invited. Gloria spent hours fixing little sandwiches and served different wines, and she dressed up and looked lovely, with her sandy-colored short-cut curly hair.

Anyhow, Horselover Fat had no Nembutal to give her, and a week later Gloria threw herself out of a tenth floor window of the Synanon Building in Oakland, California, and smashed herself to bits on the pavement along MacArthur Boulevard, and Horselover Fat continued his insidious, long decline into misery and illness, the sort of chaos that astrophysicists say is the fate in store for the whole universe. Fat was ahead of his time, ahead of the universe. Eventually he forgot what event had started off his decline into entropy; God mercifully occludes us to the past as well as the future. For two months, after he learned of Gloria's suicide, he cried and watched TV and took more dope—his brain was going too, but he didn't know it. Infinite are the mercies of God.

As a matter of fact, Fat had lost his own wife, the year before, to mental illness. It was like a plague. No one could discern how much was due to drugs. This time in America—1960 to 1970— and this place, the Bay Area of Northern California, was totally fucked. I'm sorry to tell you this, but that's the truth. Fancy terms and ornate theories cannot cover this fact up. The authorities became as psychotic as those they hunted. They wanted to put all persons who were not clones of the establishment away. The authorities were filled with hate. Fat had seen police glower at him with the ferocity of dogs. The day they moved Angela Davis, the black Marxist, out of the Marin County jail, the authorities dismantled the whole civic center. This was to baffle radicals who might intend trouble. The elevators got unwired; doors got relabeled with spurious information; the district attorney hid. Fat saw all this. He had gone to the civic center that day to return a library book. At the electronic hoop at the civic center entrance, two cops had ripped open the book and papers that Fat carried. He was perplexed. The whole day perplexed him. In the cafeteria, an armed cop watched everyone eat. Fat returned home by cab, afraid of his own car and wondering if he was nuts. He was, but so was everyone else.

I am by profession, a science-fiction writer. I deal in fantasies. My life is a fantasy. Nonetheless, Gloria Knudson lies in a box in Modesto, California. There's a photo of her funeral wreaths in my photo album. It's a color photo so you can see how lovely the wreaths are. In the background a VW is parked. I can be seen crawling into the VW, in the midst of the service. I am not able to take any more.

After the graveside service Gloria's former husband Bob and I and some tearful friend of his—and hers—had a late lunch at a fancy restaurant in Modesto near the cemetery. The waitress seated us in the rear because the three of us looked like hippies even though we had suits and ties on. We didn't give a shit. I don't remember what we talked about. The night before, Bob and I— I mean, Bob and Horselover Fat—drove to Oakland to see the movie *Patton*. Just before the graveside service Fat met Gloria's parents for the first time. Like their deceased daughter, they treated him with utmost civility. A number of Gloria's friends stood around the corny California ranch-style living room recalling the person who linked them together. Naturally, Mrs. Knudson wore too much makeup; women always put on too much makeup when someone dies. Fat petted the dead girl's cat, Chairman Mao. He remembered the few days Gloria had spent with him upon her futile trip to his house for the Nembutal which he did not have. She greeted the disclosure of his lie with aplomb, even a neutrality. When you are going to die you do not care about small things.

"I took them," Fat had told her, lie upon lie.

They decided to drive to the beach, the great ocean beach of the Point Reyes Peninsula. In Gloria's VW, with Gloria driving (it never entered his mind that she might, on impulse, wipe out him, herself and the car) and, an hour later, sat together on the sand smoking dope.

What Fat wanted to know most of all was why she intended to kill herself.

Gloria had on many-times-washed-jeans and a T-shirt with Mick Jagger's leering face across the front of it. Because the sand felt nice she took off her shoes. Fat noticed that she had pink-painted toe-nails and that they were perfectly pedicured. To himself he thought, she died as she lived.

"They stole my bank account," Gloria said.

After a time he realized, from her measured, lucidly stated narration, that no "they" existed. Gloria unfolded a panorama of total and relentless madness, lapidary in construction. She had filled in all the details with tools as precise as dental tools. No vacuum existed anywhere in her account. He could find no error, except of course for the premise, which was that everyone hated her, was out to get her, and she was worthless in every respect. As she talked she began to disappear. He watched her go; it was amazing. Gloria, in her measured way, talked herself out of existence word by word. It was rationality at the service of—well, he thought, at the service of nonbeing. Her mind had become one great, expert eraser. All that really remained now was her husk; which is to say, her uninhabited corpse.

She is dead now, he realized that day on the beach.

After they had smoked up all their dope, they walked along and commented on seaweed and the height of waves. Seagulls croaked by overhead, sailing themselves like Frisbees. A few people sat or walked here and there, but mostly the beach was deserted. Signs warned of undertow. Fat, for the life of him, could not figure out why Gloria didn't simply walk out into the surf. He simply could not get into her head. All she could think of was the Nembutal she still needed, or imagined she needed.

"My favorite Dead album is *Workingman's Dead*," Gloria said at one point. "But I don't think they should advocate taking cocaine. A lot of kids listen to rock."

"They don't advocate it. The song's just about someone taking it. And it killed him, indirectly; he smashed up his train."

"But that's why I started on drugs," Gloria said.

"Because of the Grateful Dead?"

"Because," Gloria said, "everyone wanted me to do it. I'm tired of doing what other people want me to do."

"Don't kill yourself," Fat said. "Move in with me. I'm all alone. I really like you. Try it for a while, at least. We'll move your stuff up, me and my friends. There's lots of things we can do, like go places, like to the beach today. Isn't it nice here?"

To that, Gloria said nothing.

"It would really make me feel terrible," Fat said. "For the rest of my life, if you did away with yourself." Thereby, as he later realized, he presented her with all the wrong reasons for living. She would be doing it as a favor to others. He could not have found a worse reason to give had he looked for years. Better to back the VW over her. This is why suicide hotlines are not manned by nitwits; Fat learned this later in Vancouver, when, suicidal himself, he phoned the British Columbia Crisis Center and got expert advice. There was no correlation between this and what he told Gloria on the beach that day.

Pausing to rub a small stone loose from her foot, Gloria said, "I'd like to stay overnight at your place tonight."

Hearing this, Fat experienced involuntary visions of sex.

"Far out," he said, which was the way he talked in those days. The counterculture possessed a whole book of phrases which bordered on meaning nothing. Fat used to string a bunch of them together. He did so now, deluded by his own carnality into imagining that he had saved his friend's life. His judgment, which wasn't worth much anyhow, dropped to a new nadir of acuity. The existence of a good person hung in the balance, hung in a balance which Fat held, and all he could think of now was the prospect of scoring. "I can dig it," he prattled away as they walked. "Out of sight."

A few days later she was dead. They spent that night together, sleeping fully dressed; they did not make love; the next afternoon Gloria drove off, ostensibly to get her stuff from her parents' house in Modesto. He never saw her again. For several days he waited for her to show up and then one night the phone rang and it was her ex-husband Bob.

"Where are you right now?" Bob asked.

The question bewildered him; he was at home, where his phone was, in the kitchen. Bob sounded calm. "I'm here," Fat said.

"Gloria killed herself today," Bob said.

I have a photo of Gloria holding Chairman Mao in her arms; Gloria is kneeling and smiling and her eyes shine. Chairman Mao is trying to get down. To their left, part of a Christmas tree can be seen. On the back, Mrs. Knudson has written in tidy letters:

How we made her feel gratitude for our love.

I've never been able to fathom whether Mrs. Knudson wrote that after Gloria's death or before. The Knudsons mailed me the photo a month—mailed Horselover Fat the photo a month—after Gloria's funeral. Fat had written asking for a photo of her. Initially he had asked Bob, who replied in a savage tone, "What do you want a picture of Gloria for?" To which Fat could give no answer. When Fat got me started writing this, he asked me why I thought Bob Langley got so mad at this request. I don't know. I don't care. Maybe Bob knew that Gloria and Fat had spent a night together and he was jealous. Fat used to say Bob Langley was a schizoid; he claimed that Bob himself told him that. A schizoid lacks proper affect to go with his thinking; he's got what's called "flattening of affect." A schizoid would see no reason not to tell you that about himself. On the other hand, Bob bent down after the graveside service and put a rose on Gloria's coffin. That was about when Fat had gone crawling off to the VW. Which reaction is more appropriate? Fat weeping in the parked car by himself, or the ex-husband bending down with the rose, saying nothing, showing nothing, but doing something . . . Fat contributed nothing to the funeral except a bundle of flowers which he had belatedly bought on the trip down to Modesto. He had given them to Mrs. Knudson, who remarked that they were lovely. Bob had picked them out.

After the funeral, at the fancy restaurant where the waitress had moved the three of them out of view, Fat asked Bob what Gloria had been doing at Synanon, since she was supposed to be getting her possessions together and driving back up to Marin County to live with him—he had thought.

"Carmina talked her into going to Synanon," Bob said. That was Mrs. Knudson. "Because of her history of drug involvement."

Timothy, the friend Fat didn't know, said, "They sure didn't help her very much."

What had happened was that Gloria walked in the front door of Synanon and they had gamed her right off. Someone, on purpose, had walked past her as she sat waiting to be interviewed and had remarked on how ugly she was. The next person to parade past her informed her that her hair looked like something a rat slept in. Gloria had always been sensitive about her curly hair. She wished it was long like all the other hair in the world. What the third Synanon member would have said was moot, because by then Gloria had gone upstairs to the tenth floor.

"Is that how Synanon works?" Fat asked.

Bob said, "It's a technique to break down the personality. It's a fascist therapy that makes the person totally outer-directed and dependent on the group. Then they can build up a new personality that isn't drug-oriented."

"Didn't they realize she was suicidal?" Timothy asked.

"Of course," Bob said. "She phoned in and talked to them; they knew her name and why she was there."

"Did you talk to them after her death?" Fat asked.

Bob said, "I phoned them up and asked to talk to someone high up and told him they had killed my wife, and the man said that they wanted me to come down there and teach them how to handle suicidal people. He was super upset. I felt sorry for him."

At that, hearing that, Fat decided that Bob himself was not right in the head. Bob felt sorry for Synanon. Bob was all fucked up. Everyone was fucked up, including Carmina Knudson. There wasn't a sane person left in Northern California. It was time to move somewhere else. He sat eating his salad and wondering where he could go. Out of the country. Flee to Canada, like the draft protesters. He personally knew ten guys who had slipped across into Canada rather than fight in Vietnam. Probably in Vancouver he would run into half a dozen people he knew. Vancouver was supposed to be one of the most beautiful cities in the world. Like San Francisco, it was a major port. He could start life all over and forget the past.

It entered his head as he sat fooling with his salad that when Bob phoned he hadn't said, "Gloria killed herself" but rather, "Gloria killed herself today," as if it had been inevitable that she would do it one day or another. Perhaps this had done it, this assumption. Gloria had been timed, as if she were taking a math test. Who really was the insane one? Gloria or himself (probably himself) or her ex-husband or all of them, the Bay Area, not insane in the loose sense of the term but in the strict technical sense? Let it be said that one of the first symptoms of psychosis is that the person feels perhaps he is becoming psychotic. It is another Chinese finger trap. You cannot think about it without becoming part of it. By thinking about madness, Horselover Fat slipped by degrees into madness.

I wish I could have helped him.

Chapter Two

from VALIS

Although there was nothing I could do to help Horselover Fat, he did escape death. The first thing that came along to save him took the form of an eighteen-year-old high school girl living down the street from him and the second was God. Of the two of them the girl did better.

I'm not sure God did anything at all for him; in fact in some ways God made him sicker. This was a subject on which Fat and I could not agree. Fat was certain that God had healed him completely. That is not possible. There is a line in the *I Ching* reading, "Always ill but never dies." That fits my friend.

Stephanie entered Fat's life as a dope dealer. After Gloria's death he did so much dope that he had to buy from every source available to him. Buying dope from high school kids is not a smart move. It has nothing to do with dope itself but with the law and morality. Once you begin to buy dope from kids you are a marked man. I'm sure it's obvious why. But the thing I knew—which the authorities did not—is this: Horselover Fat really wasn't interested in the dope that Stephanie had for sale. She dealt hash and grass but never uppers. She did not approve of uppers. Stephanie never sold anything she did not approve of. She never sold psychedelics no matter what pressure was put on her. Now and then she sold cocaine. Nobody could quite figure out her reasoning, but it was a form of reasoning. In the normal sense, Stephanie did not think at all. But she did arrive at decisions, and once she arrived at them no one could budge her. Fat liked her.

There lay the gist of it; he liked her and not the dope, but to maintain a relationship with her he had to be a buyer, which meant he had to do hash. For Stephanie, hash was the beginning and end of life—life worth living, anyhow.

If God came in a poor second, at least he wasn't doing anything illegal, as Stephanie was. Fat was convinced that Stephanie would wind up in jail; he expected her to be arrested any day. All Fat's friends expected him to be arrested any day. We worried about that and about his slow decline into depression and psychosis and isolation. Fat worried about Stephanie. Stephanie worried about the price of hash. More so, she worried about the price of cocaine. We used to imagine her suddenly sitting bolt upright in the middle of the night and exclaiming, "Coke has gone up to a hundred dollars a gram!" She worried about the price of dope the way normal women worry about the price of coffee.

We used to argue that Stephanie could not have existed before the sixties. Dope had brought her into being, summoned her out of the very ground. She was a coefficient of dope, part of an equation. And yet it was through her that Fat made his way eventually to God. Not through her dope; it has nothing to do with dope. There is no door to God through dope; that is a lie peddled by the unscrupulous. The means by which Stephanie brought Horselover Fat to God was by means of a little clay pot which she threw on her kickwheel, a kickwheel which Fat had helped pay for, as a present on her eighteenth birthday. When he fled to Canada he took the pot with him, wrapped up in shorts, socks and shirts, in his single suitcase.

It looked like an ordinary pot: squat and light brown, with a small amount of blue glaze as trim. Stephanie was not an expert potter. This pot was one of the first she threw, at least outside of her ceramics class in high school. Naturally, one of her first pots would go to Fat. She and he had a close relationship. When he'd get upset, Stephanie would quiet him down by supercharging him with her hashpipe. The pot was unusual in one way, however. In it slumbered God. He slumbered in the pot for a long time, for almost too long. There is a theory among some religions that God intervenes at the eleventh hour. Maybe that is so; I couldn't say. In

Horselover Fat's case God waited until three minutes before twelve, and even then what he did was barely enough: barely enough and virtually too late. You can't hold Stephanie responsible for that; she threw the pot, glazed it and fired it as soon as she had the kickwheel. She did her best to help her friend Fat, who, like Gloria before him, was beginning to die. She helped her friend the way Fat had tried to help his friend, only Stephanie did a better job. But that was the difference between her and Fat. In a crisis she knew what to do. Fat did not. Therefore Fat is alive today and Gloria is not. Fat had a better friend than Gloria had had. Perhaps he would have wanted it the other way around but the option was not his. We do not serve up people to ourselves; the universe does. The universe makes certain decisions and on the basis of these decisions some people live and some people die. This is a harsh law. But every creature yields to it out of necessity. Fat got God, and Gloria Knudson got death. It is unfair and Fat would be the first person to say so. Give him credit for that.

After he had encountered God, Fat developed a love for him which was not normal. It is not what is usually meant in saying that someone "loves God." With Fat it was an actual hunger. And stranger still, he explained to us that God had injured him and still he yearned for him, like a drunk yearns for booze. God, he told us, had fired a beam of pink light directly at him, at his head, his eyes; Fat had been temporarily blinded and his head had ached for days. It was easy, he said, to describe the beam of pink light; it's exactly what you get as a phosphene after-image when a flashbulb has gone off in your face. Fat was spiritually haunted by that color. Sometimes it showed up on a TV screen. He lived for that light, that one particular color.

However, he could never really find it again. Nothing could generate that color for light but God. In other words, normal light did not contain that color. One time Fat studied a color chart, a chart of the visible spectrum. The color was absent. He had seen a color which no one can see; it lay off the end.

What comes after light in terms of frequency? Heat? Radio waves? I should know but I don't. Fat told me (I don't know how true this is) that in the solar spectrum what he saw was above seven hundred millimicrons; in terms of Fraunhofer Lines, past B in the direction of A. Make of that what you will. I deem it a symptom of Fat's breakdown. People suffering nervous breakdowns often do a lot of research, to find explanations for what they are undergoing. The research, of course, fails.

It fails as far as we are concerned, but the unhappy fact is that it sometimes provides a spurious rationalization to the disintegrating mind—like Gloria's "they." I looked up the Fraunhofer Lines one time, and there is no "A." The earliest letter-indication that I could find is B. It goes from G to B, from ultraviolet to infrared. That's it. There is no more. What Fat saw, or thought he saw, was not light.

After he returned from Canada—after he got God—Fat and I spent a lot of time together, and in the course of our going out at night, a regular event with us, cruising for action, seeing what was happening, we one time were in the process of parking my car when all at once a spot of pink light showed up on my left arm. I knew what it was, although I had never seen such a thing before; someone had turned a laser beam on us.

"That's a laser," I said to Fat, who had seen it, too, since the spot was moving all around, onto telephone poles and the cement wall of the garage.

Two teenagers stood at the far end of the street holding a square object between them.

"They built the goddam thing," I said.

The kids walked up to us, grinning. They had built it, they told us, from a kit. We told them how impressed we were, and they walked off to spook someone else.

"That color pink?" I asked Fat.

He said nothing. But I had the impression that he was not being up front with me. I had the feeling that I had seen his color. Why he would not say so, if such it was, I do not know. Maybe the notion spoiled a more elegant theory. The mentally disturbed do not employ the Principle of Scientific Parsimony: the most simple theory to explain a given set of facts. They shoot for the baroque.

The cardinal point which Fat had made to us regarding his experience with the pink beam which had injured and blinded him was this: he claimed that instantly—as soon as the beam struck him—he knew things he had never known. He knew, specifically, that his five-year-old son had an undiagnosed birth defect and he knew what that birth defect consisted of, down to the anatomical details. Down, in fact, to the medical specifics to relate to the doctor.

I wanted to see how he told it to the doctor. How he explained knowing the medical details. His brain had trapped all the information the beam of pink light had nailed him with, but how would he account for it?

Fat later developed a theory that the universe is made out of information. He started keeping a journal—had been, in fact, secretly doing so for some time: the furtive act of a deranged person. His encounter with God was all there on the pages in his—Fat's, not God's—handwriting.

The term "journal" is mine, not Fat's. His term was "exegesis," a theological term meaning a piece of writing that explains or interprets a portion of scripture. Fat believed that the information fired at him and progressively crammed into his head in successive waves had a holy origin and hence should be regarded as a form of scripture, even if it just applied to his son's undiagnosed right inguinal hernia which had popped the hydrocele and gone down into the scrotal sack. This was the news Fat had for the doctor. The news turned out to be correct, as was confirmed when Fat's ex-wife took Christopher in to be examined. Surgery was scheduled for the next day, which is to say as soon as possible. The surgeon cheerfully informed Fat and his ex-wife that Christopher's life had been in danger for years. He could have died during the night from a strangulated piece of his own gut. It was fortunate, the surgeon said, that they had found out about it. Thus again Gloria's "they," except that in this instance the "they" actually existed.

The surgery came off a success, and Christopher stopped being such a complaining child. He had been in pain since birth. After that, Fat and his ex-wife took their son to another GP, one who had eyes.

One of the paragraphs in Fat's journal impressed me enough to copy it out and include it here. It does not deal with right inguinal hernias but is more general in nature, expressing Fat's growing opinion that the nature of the universe is information. He had

begun to believe this because for him the universe—his universe—
was indeed fast turning into information. Once God started talking
to him he never seemed to stop. I don't think they report that in
the Bible.

**Journal entry 37. Thoughts of the Brain are experienced by us
as arrangements and rearrangements—change—in a physical
universe; but in fact it is really information and information-
processing which we substantialize. We do not merely see its
thoughts as objects, but rather as the movement, or, more precisely, the placement of objects: how they become linked to one
another. But we cannot read the patterns of arrangement; we
cannot extract the information in it—i.e., it as information,
which is what it is. The linking and relinking of objects by the
Brain is actually a language, but not a language like ours (since it
is addressing itself and not someone or something outside itself).**

Fat kept working this particular theme over and over again, both
in this journal and in his oral discourse to his friends. He felt sure
the universe had begun to talk to him. Another entry in his journal reads:

**36. We should be able to hear this information, or rather nar-
rative, as a neutral voice inside us. But something has gone wrong.
All creation is a language and nothing but a language, which for
some inexplicable reason we can't read outside and can't hear
inside. So I say, we have become idiots. Something has happened
to our intelligence. My reasoning is this: arrangement of parts of
the Brain is a language. We are parts of the Brain; therefore we
are language. Why, then, do we not know this? We do not even
know what we are, let alone what the outer reality is of which we
are parts. The origin of the word "idiot" is the word "private."
Each of us has become private, and no longer shares the common thought of the Brain, except at a subliminal level. Thus our
real life and purpose are conducted below our threshold of consciousness.**

To which I personally am tempted to say, Speak for yourself, Fat.

Over a long period of time (or "Deserts of vast Eternity," as he would have put it) Fat developed a lot of unusual theories to account for his contact with God, and the information derived therefrom. One in particular struck me as interesting, being different from the others. It amounted to a kind of mental capitulation by Fat to what he was undergoing. This theory held that in actuality he wasn't experiencing anything at all. Sites of his brain were being selectively stimulated by tight energy beams emanating from far off, perhaps millions of miles away. These selective brain-site stimulations generated in his head the *impression*—for him—that he was in fact seeing and hearing words, pictures, figures of people, printed pages, in short God and God's Message, or, as Fat liked to call it, the Logos. But (this particular theory held) he really only imagined he experienced these things. They resembled holograms. What struck me was the oddity of a lunatic discounting his hallucinations in this sophisticated manner; Fat had intellectually dealt himself out of the game of madness while still enjoying its sights and sounds. In effect, he no longer claimed that what he experienced was actually there. Did this indicate he had begun to get better? Hardly. Now he held the view that "they" or God or someone owned a long-range very tight information-rich beam of energy focused on Fat's head. In this I saw no improvement, but it did represent a change. Fat could now honestly discount his hallucinations, which meant he recognized them as such. But, like Gloria, he now had a "they." It seemed to me a Pyrrhic victory. Fat's life struck me as a litany of exactly that, as, for example, the way he had rescued Gloria.

The exegesis Fat labored on month after month struck me as a Pyrrhic victory if there ever was one—in this case an attempt by a beleaguered mind to make sense out of the inscrutable. Perhaps this is the bottom line to mental illness: incomprehensible events occur; your life becomes a bin for hoax-like fluctuations of what used to be reality. And not only that—as if that weren't enough—but you, like Fat, ponder forever over these fluctuations in an effort to order them into a coherency, when in fact the only sense they make is the

sense you impose on them, out of the necessity to restore everything into shapes and processes you can recognize. The first thing to
depart in mental illness is the familiar. And what takes its place is bad
news because not only can you not understand it, you also cannot
communicate it to other people. The madman experiences something, but what it is or where it comes from he does not know.

In the midst of his shattered landscape, which one can trace
back to Gloria Knudson's death, Fat imagined God had cured him.
Once you notice Pyrrhic victories they seem to abound.

It reminds me of a girl I once knew who was dying of cancer. I
visited her in the hospital and did not recognize her; sitting up in her
bed she looked like a little old hairless man. From the chemotherapy
she had swollen up like a great grape. From the cancer and the therapy she had become virtually blind, nearly deaf, underwent constant
seizures, and when I bent close to her to ask her how she felt she
answered, when she could understand my question, "I feel that God
is healing me." She had been religiously inclined and had planned to
go into a religious order. On the metal stand beside her bed she had,
or someone had, laid out her rosary. In my opinion a FUCK YOU,
GOD sign would have been appropriate; the rosary was not.

Yet in all fairness, I have to admit that God—or someone calling
himself God, a distinction of mere semantics—had fired precious
information at Horselover Fat's head by which their son Christopher's life had been saved. Some people God cures and some he
slays. Fat denies that God slays anyone. Fat says, God never harms
anyone. Illness, pain and undeserved suffering arise not from God
but from elsewhere, to which I say, How did this elsewhere arise?
Are there two gods? Or is part of the universe out from under
God's control? Fat used to quote Plato. In Plato's cosmology, *noös*
or Mind is persuading *ananke* or blind necessity—or blind chance,
according to some experts—into submission. *Noös* happened to
come along and to its surprise discovered blind chance: chaos, in
other words, onto which *noös* imposes order (although how this
"persuading" is done Plato nowhere says). According to Fat, my
friend's cancer consisted of disorder not yet persuaded into sentient
shape. *Noös* or God had not yet gotten around to her, to which I
said, "Well, when he did get around to her it was too late." Fat had

no answer for that, at least in terms of oral rebuttal. Probably he sneaked off and wrote about it in his journal. He stayed up to four A.M. every night scratching away in his journal. I suppose all the secrets of the universe lay in it somewhere amid the rubble.

We enjoyed baiting Fat into theological disputation because he always got angry, taking the point of view that what we said on the topic mattered—that the topic itself mattered. By now he had become totally whacked out. We enjoyed introducing the discussion by way of some careless comment: "Well, God gave me a ticket on the freeway today" or something like that. Ensnared, Fat would leap into action. We whiled away the time pleasantly in this fashion, torturing Fat in a benign way. After we left his place we had the added satisfaction of knowing he was writing it all down in the journal. Of course, in the journal his view always prevailed.

No need existed to bait Fat with idle questions, such as, "If God can do anything can he create a ditch so wide he can't jump over it?" We had plenty of real questions that Fat couldn't field. Our friend Kevin always began his attack one way. "What about my dead cat?" Kevin would ask. Several years ago, Kevin had been out walking his cat in the early evening. Kevin, the fool, had not put the cat on a leash, and the cat had dashed into the street and right into the front wheel of a passing car. When he picked up the remains of the cat it was still alive, breathing in bloody foam and staring at him in horror. Kevin liked to say, "On judgment day when I'm brought up before the great judge I'm going to say, 'Hold on a second,' and then I'm going to whip out my dead cat from inside my coat. 'How do you explain *this*?' I'm going to ask." By then, Kevin used to say, the cat would be as stiff as a frying pan; he would hold out the cat by its handle, its tail, and wait for a satisfactory answer.

Fat said, "No answer would satisfy you."

"No answer you could give," Kevin sneered. "Okay, so God saved your son's life; why didn't he have my cat run out into the street five seconds later? *Three* seconds later? Would that have been too much trouble? Of course, I suppose a cat doesn't matter."

"You know, Kevin," I pointed out one time, "you could have put the cat on a leash."

"No," Fat said. "He has a point. It's been bothering me. For him the cat is a symbol of everything about the universe he doesn't understand."

"I understand fine," Kevin said bitterly. "I just think it's fucked. God is either powerless, stupid or he doesn't give a shit. Or all three. He's evil, dumb and weak. I think I'll start my own exegesis."

"But God doesn't talk to you," I said.

"You know who talks to Horse?" Kevin said. "Who really talks to Horse in the middle of the night? People from the planet Stupid. Horse, what's the wisdom of God called again? Saint what?"

"Hagia Sophia," Horse said cautiously.

Kevin said, "How do you say Hagia Stupid? St. Stupid?"

"Hagia Moron," Horse said. He always defended himself by giving in. "Moron is a Greek word like Hagia. I came across it when I was looking up the spelling of oxymoron."

"Except that the -*on* suffix is the neuter ending," I said.

That gives you an idea of where our theological arguments tended to wind up. Three malinformed people disagreeing with one another. We also had David our Roman Catholic friend and the girl who had been dying of cancer, Sherri. She had gone into remission and the hospital had discharged her. To some extent her hearing and vision were permanently impaired, but otherwise, she seemed to be fine.

Fat, of course, used this as an argument for God and God's healing love, as did David and of course Sherri herself. Kevin saw her remission as a miracle of radiation therapy and chemotherapy and luck. Also, he confided to us, the remission was temporary. At any time, Sherri could get sick again. Kevin hinted darkly that the next time she got sick there wouldn't be a remission. We sometimes thought that he hoped so, since it would confirm his view of the universe.

It was a mainstay of Kevin's bag of verbal tricks that the universe consisted of misery and hostility and would get you in the end. He looked at the universe the way most people regard an unpaid bill; eventually they will force payment. The universe reeled you out, let you flop and thrash and then reeled you in. Kevin waited constantly for this to begin with him, with me, with David and especially with Sherri. As to Horselover Fat, Kevin believed that the line hadn't been payed out in years; Fat had long been in the part of the cycle where they reel you back in. He considered Fat not just potentially doomed but doomed in fact.

Fat had the good sense not to discuss Gloria Knudson and her death in front of Kevin. Had he done so, Kevin would add her to his dead cat. He would be talking about whipping her out from under his coat on judgment day, along with the cat.

Being a Catholic, David always traced everything wrong back to man's free will. This used to annoy even me. I once asked him if Sherri getting cancer consisted of an instance of free will, knowing as I did that David kept up with all the latest news in the field of psychology and would make the mistake of claiming that Sherri had subconsciously wanted to get cancer and so had shut down her immune system, a view floating around in advanced psychological circles at that time. Sure enough, David fell for it and said so.

"Then why did she get well?" I asked. "Did she subconsciously want to get well?"

David looked perplexed. If he consigned her illness to her own mind he was stuck with having to consign her remission to mundane and not supernatural causes. God had nothing to do with it.

"What C. S. Lewis would say," David began, which at once angered Fat, who was present. It maddened him when David turned to C. S. Lewis to bolster his straight-down-the-pipe orthodoxy.

"Maybe Sherri overrode God," I said. "God wanted her sick and she fought to get well." The thrust of David's impending argument would of course be that Sherri had neurotically gotten cancer due to being fucked up, but God had stepped in and saved her; I had turned it around in anticipation.

"No," Fat said. "It's the other way around. Like when he cured me."

Fortunately, Kevin was not present. He did not consider Fat cured (nor did anyone else) and anyway God didn't do it. That is a logic which Freud attacks, by the way, the two-proposition self-canceling structure. Freud considered this structure a revelation of rationalization. Someone is accused of stealing a horse, to which he replies, "I don't steal horses and anyhow you have a crummy horse."

If you ponder the reasoning in this you can see the actual thought-process behind it. The second statement does not reinforce the first. It only looks like it does. In terms of our perpetual theological disputations—brought on by Fat's supposed encounter with the divine—the two-proposition self-canceling structure would appear like this:

1) God does not exist.
2) And anyhow he's stupid.

A careful study of Kevin's cynical rantings reveals this structure at every turn. David continually quoted C. S. Lewis; Kevin contradicted himself logically in his zeal to defame God; Fat made obscure references to information fired into his head by a beam of pink light; Sherri, who had suffered dreadfully, wheezed out pious mummeries: I switched my position according to who I was talking to at the time. None of us had a grip on the situation, but we did have a lot of free time to waste in this fashion. By now the epoch of drug-taking had ended, and everyone had begun casting about for a new obsession. For us the new obsession, thanks to Fat, was theology.

A favorite antique quotation of Fat's goes:

> *"And can I think the great Jehovah sleeps,*
> *Like Shemosh, and such fabled deities?*
> *Ah! no; heav'n heard my thoughts, and wrote them down—*
> *It must be so."*

Fat doesn't like to quote the rest of it.

> *" 'Tis this that racks my brain,*
> *And pours into my breast a thousand pangs,*
> *That lash me into madness . . ."*

It's from an aria by Handel. Fat and I used to listen to my Seraphim LP of Richard Lewis singing it. *Deeper, and deeper still.*

Once I told Fat that another aria on the record described his mind perfectly.

"Which aria?" Fat said guardedly.

"Total eclipse," I answered.

> *"Total eclipse! no sun, no moon,*
> *All dark amidst the blaze of noon!*
> *Oh, glorious light! no cheering ray*
> *To glad my eyes with welcome day!*
> *Why thus deprived Thy prime decree?*
> *Sun, moon and stars are dark to me!"*

To which Fat said, "The opposite is true in my case. I am illuminated by holy light fired at me from another world. I see what no other man sees."

He had a point there.

Clans of the Alphane Moon
When CIA agent Chuck Rittersdorf and his psychiatrist wife, Mary, file for divorce, they have no idea that in a few weeks they'll be shooting it out on Alpha III M2, the distant moon ruled by various psychotics liberated from a mental ward.
Science Fiction/0-375-71928-8

Confessions of a Crap Artist
Jack Isidore is a crap artist—a collector of crackpot ideas and worthless objects, a man so grossly unequipped for real life that his sister and brother-in-law feel compelled to rescue him from it. But seen through Jack's murderously innocent gaze, Charlie and Judy Hume prove to be just as sealed off from reality.
Science Fiction/0-679-74114-3

The Cosmic Puppets
Yielding to a compulsion he can't explain, Ted Barton interrupts his vacation in order to visit the town of his birth, Millgate, Virginia. But upon entering the sleepy, isolated little hamlet, Ted is distraught to find that the place bears no resemblance to the one he left behind—and never did.
Science Fiction/1-4000-3005-6

Counter-Clock World
In *Counter-Clock World*, the world has entered the Hobart Phase—a vast sidereal process in which time moves in reverse. As a result, libraries are busy eradicating books, copulation signifies the end of pregnancy, people greet with, "Good-bye," and part with, "Hello,"

and underneath the world's tombstones, the dead are coming back to life.
Science Fiction/0-375-71933-4

The Crack in Space
A repairman discovers that a hole in a faulty Jifi-scuttler leads to a parallel world. Jim Briskin, campaigning to be the first black president of the United States, thinks alter-Earth is the solution to the chronic overpopulation that has seventy million people cryogenically frozen. But when the other Earth turns out to be inhabited, everything changes.
Science Fiction/1-4000-3006-4

Deus Irae
With Roger Zelazny
In the years following World War III, a new and powerful faith has arisen from a scorched and poisoned Earth, a faith that embraces the architect of worldwide devastation. The Servants of Wrath have deified Carlton Lufteufel and rechristened him the Deus Irae.
Science Fiction/1-4000-3007-2

The Divine Invasion
In *The Divine Invasion*, Philip K. Dick asks: What if God—or a being called Yah—were alive and in exile on a distant planet? How could a second coming succeed against the high technology and finely tuned rationalized evil of the modern police state?
Science Fiction/0-679-73445-7

Dr. Bloodmoney
Dr. Bloodmoney is a post–nuclear holocaust masterpiece filled with a host of memorable characters: Hoppy Harrington, a deformed mutant with telekinetic powers; Walt Dangerfield, a selfless disc jockey stranded in a satellite circling the globe; and Stuart McConchie and Bonny Keller, two unremarkable people bent on the survival of goodness in a world devastated by evil.
Science Fiction/0-375-71929-6

Dr. Futurity
Jim Parsons is a talented doctor, dedicated to saving lives. But after a bizarre road accident leaves him hundreds of years in the future, Parsons is horrified to discover an incredibly advanced civilization that zealously embraces death. Now he is caught between his own instincts and a society where it is illegal to save lives.
Science Fiction/1-4000-3009-9

Eye in the Sky
While sightseeing at the Belmont Bevatron, Jack Hamilton, along with seven others, is caught in a lab accident. When he regains consciousness, he is in a fantasy world of Old Testament morality gone awry—a place of instant plagues, immediate damnations, and death to all perceived infidels.
Science Fiction/1-4000-3010-2

Flow My Tears, the Policeman Said
On October 11 the television star Jason Taverner is so famous that thirty million viewers eagerly watch his prime-time show. On October 12 Jason Taverner is not a has-been but a never-was—a man who has lost not only his audience but all proof of his existence.
Science Fiction/0-679-74066-X

Galactic Pot-Healer
What could an omnipresent and seemingly omnipotent entity want with a humble pot-healer? Or with the dozens of other odd creatures it has lured to Plowman's Planet? Combining quixotic adventure, spine-chilling horror, and deliriously paranoid theology, *Galactic Pot-Healer* is a uniquely Dickian voyage to alternate worlds of the imagination.
Science Fiction/0-679-75297-8

The Game-Players of Titan
Poor Pete Garden has just lost Berkeley. He's also lost his wife, but he'll get a new one as soon as he rolls a three. It's all part of the rules of Bluff, the game that's become a blinding obsession for the last inhabitants of planet Earth. But the rules are about to change—

drastically and terminally—because Pete Garden will be playing his next game against an opponent who isn't even human.
Science Fiction/0-679-74065-1

Lies, Inc.
A masterwork by Philip K. Dick, this is the final, expanded version of the novella *The Unteleported Man*, which Dick worked on shortly before his death. In *Lies, Inc.*, fans of the science-fiction legend will immediately recognize his hallmark themes of life in a security state, conspiracy, and the blurring of reality and illusion.
Science Fiction/1-4000-3008-0

The Man in the High Castle
It's America in 1962. Slavery is legal once again. The few Jews who still survive hide under assumed names. In San Francisco the *I Ching* is as common as the Yellow Pages. All because some twenty years earlier the United States lost a war—and is now occupied jointly by Nazi Germany and Japan.
Science Fiction/0-679-74067-8

The Man Who Japed
A mesmerizing and terrifying tale of a society so eager for order that it will sacrifice anything, including its freedom. Newer York is a post-holocaust city governed by the laws of an oppressively rigid morality. Highly mobile and miniature robots monitor the behavior of every citizen, and the slightest transgression can spell personal doom.
Science Fiction/0-375-71935-0

Martian Time-Slip
On the arid colony of Mars the only thing more precious than water may be a ten-year-old schizophrenic boy named Manfred Steiner. For although the UN has slated "anomalous" children for deportation and destruction, other people—especially Supreme Goodmember Arnie Kott of the Water Workers' Union—suspect that Manfred's disorder may be a window into the future.
Science Fiction/0-679-76167-5

A Maze of Death

Fourteen strangers came to Delmak-O. Thirteen of them were transferred by the usual authorities. One got there by praying. But once they arrived on that planet whose very atmosphere seemed to induce paranoia and psychosis, the newcomers found that even prayer was useless. For on Delmak-O, God is either absent or intent on destroying His creations.
Science Fiction/0-679-75298-6

Now Wait for Last Year

Dr. Eric Sweetscent has problems. His planet is enmeshed in an unwinnable war. His wife is lethally addicted to a drug that whips its users helplessly back and forth across time—and is hell-bent on making Eric suffer along with her. And Sweetscent's newest patient is not only the most important man on the embattled planet Earth but quite possibly the sickest.
Science Fiction/0-679-74220-4

Our Friends from Frolix 8

Nick Appleton is a menial laborer. Willis Gram is the despotic oligarch of a planet ruled by big-brained elites. When they both fall in love with Charlotte, Nick seems destined for doom. But everything takes a decidedly unpredictable turn when the revolution's leader returns from ten years of intergalactic hiding with a ninety-ton protoplasmic slime that is bent on creating a new world order.
Science Fiction/0-375-71934-2

The Penultimate Truth

The Penultimate Truth imagines a future in which Americans have been shipped underground, where they toil in crowded industrial anthills and receive a steady diet of inspiring speeches from a president who never seems to age. Nick St. James, like the rest of the masses, believed in the words of his leaders. But that all changes when he travels to the surface.
Science Fiction/1-4000-3011-0

Radio Free Albemuth

In his last novel, Philip K. Dick morphed and recombined themes that had informed his fiction from *A Scanner Darkly* to *VALIS* and produced a wild, impassioned work that reads like a visionary alternate history of the United States. Agonizingly suspenseful, darkly hilarious, and filled with enough conspiracy theories to thrill the most hardened paranoid.

Science Fiction/0-679-78137-4

A Scanner Darkly

Bob Arctor is a dealer of the lethally addictive drug Substance D. Fred is the police agent assigned to tail and eventually bust him. To do so, Fred takes on the identity of a drug dealer named Bob Arctor. And since Substance D—which Arctor takes in massive doses—gradually splits the user's brain into two distinct, combative entities, Fred doesn't realize he is narcing on himself.

Science Fiction/0-679-73665-4

The Shifting Realities of Philip K. Dick
Selected Literary and Philosophical Writings

Written by Philip K. Dick
Edited by Lawrence Sutin

As Philip K. Dick wrote about androids and virtual reality, schizophrenic prophets and amnesiac gods, Dick was also posing fundamental questions: What is reality? What is sanity? And what is human?

Science Fiction/Literary Criticism & Collections/Essays/0-679-74787-7

The Simulacra

Set in the middle of the twenty-first century, *The Simulacra* is the story of an America where the whole government is a fraud and the president is an android. Against this backdrop Dr. Superb, the sole remaining psychotherapist, is struggling to practice in a world full of the maladjusted. In classic fashion, Dick shows there is always another layer of conspiracy beneath the one we see.

Science Fiction/0-375-71926-1

Solar Lottery

The year is 2203, and the ruler of the Universe is chosen according to the random laws of a strange game under the control of Quizmaster Verrick. But when Ted Bentley, a research technician recently dismissed from his job, signs on to work for Verrick, he has no idea that Leon Cartwright is about to become the new Quizmaster.

Science Fiction/1-4000-3013-7

The Three Stigmata of Palmer Eldritch

In this wildly disorienting funhouse of a novel, populated by God-like—or perhaps Satanic—takeover artists and corporate psychics, Philip K. Dick explores mysteries that were once the property of St. Paul and Aquinas.

Science Fiction/0-679-73666-2

Time Out of Joint

The year is 1998, although Ragle Gumm doesn't know that. He thinks it's 1959. He also thinks that he served in World War II, that he lives in a quiet little community, and that he really is the world's long-standing champion of newspaper puzzle contests. It is only after a series of troubling hallucinations that he begins to suspect otherwise.

Science Fiction/0-375-71927-X

The Transmigration of Timothy Archer

The Transmigration of Timothy Archer, the final novel in the trilogy that also includes *VALIS* and *The Divine Invasion*, is the story of Timothy Archer, an urbane Episcopal bishop haunted by the suicides of his son and mistress—and driven by them into a bizarre quest for the identity of Christ.

Science Fiction/0-679-73444-9

Ubik

Philip K. Dick's searing metaphysical comedy of death and salvation is a tour de force of paranoiac menace and unfettered slapstick,

in which the departed give business advice, shop for their next incarnation, and run the continual risk of dying yet again.
Science Fiction/0-679-73664-6

VALIS

VALIS is the first book in Philip K. Dick's incomparable final trio of novels (the others are *The Divine Invasion* and *The Transmigration of Timothy Archer*). This disorienting and bleakly funny work is about a schizophrenic hero named Horselover Fat; the hidden mysteries of Gnostic Christianity; and reality as revealed through a pink laser.
Science Fiction/0-679-73446-5

Vulcan's Hammer

Objective, unbiased, and hyperrational, the Vulcan 3 should have been the perfect ruler. The omnipotent computer dictates policy that is in the best interests of all citizens—or at least, that is the idea. But when the machine begins to lose control of the "Healer" movement of religious fanatics and the mysterious force behind their rebellion, all hell breaks loose.
Science Fiction/1-4000-3012-9

We Can Build You

Louis Rosen and his partners sell people—ingeniously designed, historically authentic simulacra of personages such as Edwin M. Stanton and Abraham Lincoln. The problem is that the only prospective buyer is a rapacious billionaire whose plans for the simulacra could land Louis in jail. Then there's the added complication that someone—or something—may not want to be sold.
Science Fiction/0-679-75296-X

The World Jones Made

Floyd Jones is sullen, ungainly, and quite possibly mad, but in a very short time he will rise from telling fortunes at a mutant carnival to convulsing an entire planet. For although Jones has the power to see the future—a power that makes his life a torment—his real

gift lies elsewhere: in his ability to make people dream again in a world where dreaming has been made illegal.
Science Fiction/0-679-74219-0

The Zap Gun

Lars Powderdry and Lilo Topchev are counterpart weapons fashion designers for a world divided into two factions—Wes-bloc and Peep-East. Their job is to invent elaborate weapons that only seem massively lethal. But when alien satellites hostile to both sides appear in the sky, the two are brought together in the dire hope that they can create a weapon to save the world.
Science Fiction/0-375-71936-9

VINTAGE **READERS**

Authors available in this series

Martin Amis

Nicholson Baker

James Baldwin

A. S. Byatt

Willa Cather

John Cheever

Sandra Cisneros

Philip K. Dick

Joan Didion

Richard Ford

Dashiell Hammett

Langston Hughes

Barry Lopez

Alice Munro

Haruki Murakami

Vladimir Nabokov

V. S. Naipaul

Michael Ondaatje

Oliver Sacks

Representing a wide spectrum of some of our most significant modern authors, the Vintage Readers offer an attractive, accessible selection of writing that matters.